THE CONFESSIONS OF MAX TIVOLI

THE CONFESSIONS OF

MAX TIVOLI

ANDREW SEAN GREER

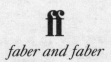

faber and faber

First published in the United States in 2004
by Farrar, Straus and Giroux
19 Union Square West, New York 10003

First published in Great Britain in 2004
by Faber and Faber Limited
3 Queen Square, London, WC1N 3AU
This paperback edition published in 2005

Printed and bound in Great Britain by
Bookmarque Limited, Croydon

Designed by Debbie Glasserman

A CIP record for this book is available from the British Library

ISBN 0–571–22022–3

1 3 5 7 9 10 8 6 4 2

For Bill Clegg

Love . . . , ever unsatisfied, lives always in the moment that is about to come.

—MARCEL PROUST

I

We are each the love of someone's life.

I wanted to put that down in case I am discovered and unable to complete these pages, in case you become so disturbed by the facts of my confession that you throw it into the fire before I get to tell you of great love and murder. I would not blame you. So many things stand in the way of anyone ever hearing my story. There is a dead body to explain. A woman three times loved. A friend betrayed. And a boy long sought for. So I will get to the end first and tell you we are each the love of someone's life.

I sit here on a lovely April day. It keeps changing all around me; the sun alternates between throwing deep shadows behind the children and trees and then sweeping them back up again the moment a cloud crosses the sky. The grass fills with gold, then falls to nothing. The whole school yard is being inked with sun and blotted, glowing and reaching a point of great beauty, and I am breathless to be in the audience. No one else notices. The little girls sit in a circle, dresses crackling with starch and conspiracy, and the boys are on the baseball field or in the trees, hanging upside down. Above, an airplane astounds me with its roar and schoolmarm line of chalk. An airplane; it's not the sky I once knew.

And I sit in a sandbox, a man of almost sixty. The chill air has made the sand a bit too tough for the smaller kids to dig; besides, the field's changing sunlight is too tempting, so everyone else is out there charging at shadows, and I'm left to myself.

We begin with apologies:

For the soft notebook pages you hold in your hands, a sad reliquary for my story and apt to rip, but the best I could steal. For stealing, both the notebooks and the beautiful lever-fed pen I'm writing with, which I have admired for so many months on my teacher's desk and simply had to take. For the sand stuck between the pages, something I could not avoid. There are more serious sins, of course, a lost family, a betrayal, and all the lies that have brought me to this sandbox, but I ask you to forgive me one last thing: my childish handwriting.

We all hate what we become. I'm not the only one; I have seen women staring at themselves in restaurant mirrors while their husbands are away, women under their own spell as they see someone they do not recognize. I have seen men back from war, squinting at themselves in shopwindows as they feel their skull beneath their skin. They thought they would shed the worst of youth and gain the best of age, but time drifted over them, sand-burying their old hopes. Mine is a very different story, but it all turns out the same.

One of the reasons I sit here in the sand, hating what I've become, is the boy. Such a long time, such a long search, lying to clerks and parish priests to get the names of children living in the town and suburbs, making up ridiculous aliases, then crying in a motel room and wondering if I would ever find you. You were so well hidden. The way the young prince in fairy tales is hidden from the ogre: in a trunk, in a thorny grove, in a dull place of meager enchantment. Little hidden Sammy. But the ogre always finds the child, doesn't he? For here you are.

If you are reading this, dear Sammy, don't despise me. I am a poor old man; I never meant you any harm. Don't remember me just as a childhood demon, though I have been that. I have lain in your room at night and heard your breathing roughen the air. I have whispered in your ear when you were dreaming. I am what my father always said I was—I am a freak, a monster—and even as I write this (forgive me) I am watching you.

You are the one playing baseball with your friends as the sunlight comes and goes through your golden hair. The sunburned one, clearly the boss, the one the other boys resent but love; it's good to see how much they love you. You are up to bat but hold out your hand because something has annoyed you; an itch, perhaps, as just now your hand scratches wildly at the base of your blond skull, and after this sudden dervish, you shout and return to the game. Boys, you don't mean to be wonders, but you are.

You haven't noticed me. Why would you? To you I am just the friend in the sandbox, scribbling away. Let's try an experiment: I'll wave my hand to you. There, see, you just put down your bat to wave back at me, a smile cocked across your freckled face, arrogant but innocent of everything around you. All the years and trouble it took for me to be here. You know nothing, fear nothing. When you look at me, you see another little boy like you.

A boy, yes, that's me. I have so much to explain, but first you must believe:

Inside this wretched body, I grow old. But outside—in every part of me but my mind and soul—I grow young.

There is no name for what I am. Doctors do not understand me; my very cells wriggle the wrong way in the slides, divide and echo back their ignorance. But I think of myself as having an ancient curse. The one that Hamlet put upon Polonius before he punctured the old man like a balloon:

That, like a crab, I go backwards.

For even now as I write, I look to be a boy of twelve. At nearly sixty, there is sand in my knickers and mud across the brim of my cap. I have a smile like the core of an apple. Yet once I seemed a handsome man of twenty-two with a gun and a gas mask. And before that, a man in his thirties, trying to find his lover in an earthquake. And a hardworking forty, and a terrified fifty, and older and older as we approach my birth.

"Anyone can grow old," my father always said through the bouquet of his cigar smoke. But I burst into the world as if from the other end of life, and the days since then have been ones of physical reversion, of erasing the wrinkles around my eyes, darkening the white and then the gray in my hair, bringing younger muscle to my arms and dew to my skin, growing tall and then shrinking into the hairless, harmless boy who scrawls this pale confession.

A mooncalf, a changeling; a thing so out of joint with the human race that I have stood in the street and hated every man in love, every widow in her long weeds, every child dragged along by a loving dog. Drunk on gin, I have sworn and spat at passing strangers who took me for the opposite of what I was inside—an adult when I was a child, a boy now that I am an old man. I have learned compassion since then, and pity passersby a little, as I, more than anyone, know what they have yet to live through.

I was born in San Francisco in September 1871. My mother was from a wealthy Carolina family, raised in the genteel area of South Park, originally planned for Southern gentry, but, with the loss of the war, open to anyone with enough wealth to throw an oyster supper. By then, the distinction among people in my city was no longer money—the blue silver clay of the Comstock had made too many beggars into fat, rich men—so society became divided into two classes: the chivalry and the shovelry. My mother was of the first, my father of the wretched second.

No surprise that when they met in the swimming pool of the Del Monte hotel, staring at each other through the fine net that separated the sexes, they fell in love. They met again that very night, on the balcony, away from her chaperones, and I am told my mother wore the latest Paris fashion: a live beetle, iridescently winged, attached to her dress with a golden chain. "I'll kiss you," my father whispered to her, shivering with love. The beetle, green and metal, scampered on her bare shoulder, then tried to take flight. "I'll do it, I'll kiss you this moment," he insisted, but did nothing, so she took him by the handles of his muttonchops and brought his lips to hers. The beetle tugged at its leash and landed in her hair. Her heart exploded.

Throughout the autumn of 1870, the Dane and the debutante met on the sly, finding secluded spots in the new Golden Gate Park to kiss and grope, the nearby bison grumbling in their corrals. But like a clambering vine, lust must lead somewhere or wither, and so it led to this: the detonation of Blossom Rock. It was a city celebration, and Mother somehow slipped away from Grandmother and South Park to meet her Danish lover, her Asgar, and watch the great event. It was to be the greatest explosion yet in the city's history—the dynamiting of Blossom Rock, a shoal in the Golden Gate that had been shattering hulls for a century—and while optimistic fishermen prepared for what they assumed would be the best catch of the century, pessimistic scientists warned of a great "earth wave" that would roll across the continent, wreaking havoc on every standing structure; the populace should flee. Did they flee? Only to the highest hills, for the best view of the end of the world.

So my parents found themselves among the thousands on Telegraph Hill, and afraid of being recognized, they rushed inside

the old heliograph station for privacy. I imagine my mother sitting
in her pink silk dress in the old operator's chair, pressing her finger against the window and clearing an oval from the window's
dust. There, she saw the crowds in their black wool looking out
to sea. Even as she felt my father's fingers upon her lace she saw
the young boys chucking oyster shells at the tallest of the stovepipe
hats. "My love," her lover whispered, undoing her rows of buttons. She did not turn to take his kisses but shivered at the sensation of her skin. She had rarely been naked since the day she was
born, not even in the bath, having always worn a long white
nightgown into the warm water. As my father-to-be shucked her
like a rare oyster, she wriggled like one, too, chilled and weeping
now not just with love—"*mine dyr, mine dyr,*" he whispered—but
with relief at what she was about to lose.

At 1:28 a warning shot came from Alcatraz and that is the exact moment that my mother's technical girlhood ended. A little
gasp in the cold air, a glare from the heliographic plates across the
room, and my father was shuddering into her ear, whispering
things he could not possibly mean and that no one but an angry
parent would ever hold him to. Mother was calm, watching the
cheering boys outside the grimed window. The crowd was restless
but excited. And Mother—who knows what mothers feel when
fathers first possess them?

And then—at 2:05 exactly (well endured, my young and eager
father)—her lover cried out in ecstasy as a great rumbling seized
the air. To her right, through the window, she witnessed the most
extraordinary sight of her lost girlhood: a column of water two
hundred feet in diameter, black as jet, rising into the crisp air of
the Golden Gate. At the top floated great hunks of the dissipated
Blossom Rock, and it looked for all the world like the conquering
fist of a Titan punching at the clouds. So huge, so menacing. The
world around her shouted so loudly she could barely hear her
young man's cries. Steamers whistled; guns fired by the hundreds

into the skies. The dark column fell back into the water and then, to her gasping surprise, another column heaved into the air—just as her lover's moans were rising once again—and fell back in boiling blackness into great circular wells of bay water that lashed at every fishing boat at sea.

The young man calmed at last, mumbled something foreign and ecstatic into her collarbone. "Yes, my love," she replied, and for the first time looked back upon her lover. He mewled like a child on her breast. She touched the hot gold of his hair and he whimpered, his strong hands moving spastically in the froth of her ripped lacework. Like the shining beetle on the night of their first kiss, he lay chained and happy on her shoulder. In that moment, she panicked a little, remembering the girls who had made mistakes in her neighborhood and had disappeared. She could hear in her lover's sighs how little he was thinking of the future.

And somewhere in the postcoital pawing and fussing, somewhere in the softening swells of the blackened Golden Gate, as bits of rock fell through the sooty waters to rest forever on the deep bottom, somewhere in the weeping sorrow of the glaziers and fishermen who found none of the booty they had hoped for, somewhere in the cheers and gun salutes and steam-whistling of the hysterical hat-tossing crowds, somewhere in that chivaree, I came into being.

But the question is: Was the crazed explosion of Blossom Rock enough to jolt my cells into a backwards growth? Was my mother so shocked by the sound, or so saddened by herself, that she distorted what little existed of me? It seems ludicrous, but my mother fretted until her death over the price she paid for love.

❦

On the morning I was born, according to my mother, the midwife handed me down in my flannel wrap and whispered, *You should probably let him go, the doctor says he's a little wrong.* I was not much to look at. Wrinkled, palsied, opening my blind, clouded eyes as I wailed into the room, I'm sure my mother was horrified. I believe she might even have screamed. But in the corner stood my father; arms crossed, smoking his ever-present Sweet Caporals, he looked at me and expressed no horror. Father came close, squinting through his pince-nez, and saw a mythical creature from his Danish boyhood:

"Aha!" he cried aloud, laughing, smoking again as my terrified mother looked on, as the midwife held me away. "He is a *Nisse*!"

"Asgar . . ."

"He is a *Nisse*! He is lucky, darling." He leaned down to kiss her forehead and then my own, which was falsely lined with decades of worry. He smiled at his wife and then spoke sternly to the midwife: "He is ours, we will not let him go."

It was untrue; I was not lucky. But what he meant was that I looked like those little old men who lived beneath the Danish countryside. I looked like a gnome. A monster. And aren't I?

I didn't smell like a baby. My mother said she noticed this as I suckled at her breast, and though she could never be brought to speak unkindly of me and always bathed my liver-spotted arms as if they were the tenderest baby's skin, she admitted that my scent was wonderful but not like any infant she'd ever held. Something more like a book, musty and lovely but wrong. And my proportions were unusual: skinny torso and small head, long arms and legs, and a surprisingly sharp nose that must have been the cause of at least one chloroformed cry from the birthing room. Babies have no noses—anybody will tell you this—but I had one. And a chin. And a face reupholstered in elephant's skin, buttoned with the clouded, sad blue eyes of the blind.

"What's wrong with him, suh?" Grandmother whispered in her Carolina accent. She was dressed in the black bombazine and veils that encrust her in my memory.

The doctor tested me with everything in his bag—a leather tube to hear my heart, doses of castor, jalap, and calomel, plasters across my body—but came away shaking his head. "It isn't clear yet, Leona," he said.

"The royal curse?" she whispered, meaning Mongolism.

He pushed the idea away with a jab of his hand. "He's rhinocer-ine," he said, a word I'm convinced he made up that very moment, but Grandmother accepted it as at least something to whisper to God in her prayers.

Later on, I was able to pass myself off (in a gaslit room) as a man in his early fifties while being a terrified seventeen, but during my first few years it was not at all obvious what I was, or what I might become. So can you blame my poor maid, Mary, for whispering her Irish prayers, dropping her tears onto my head as she bathed me—thrice daily—in cream, soaking me over and over like a strip of salt cod? Can you blame my mother and grandmother for their careful preparations on calling days—the second and fourth Fridays of the month—when, fearing a prominent lady visitor, they delicately daubed my mother's breast with laudanum and fed me so gently and intoxicatingly that I stayed in drugged slumber upstairs, unwailing, while they sat on the settees in long striped skirts? I take it as the best compliment I can: that I was unlike anything they had ever seen among the elms, the rich stone houses, the lacy parasols of their Christian Confederate world.

As the years passed, I changed as startlingly as a normal child, but my condition made it seem as if my body aged in reverse, grew younger, as it were. Born a wizened creature of seemingly great age, I soon became an infant with the thick white hair of a man in his sixties, curls of which my mother cut to place in her hair album. But I was not an old man; I was a child. I aged backwards only in what I seemed. I looked like a creature out of myth, but underneath I was the same as any boy—just as now I look like a boy in knickers and a cap, though inside I'm the same as any regretful old man.

Doctors may read this; I should be more precise. In physical appearance, I have aged exactly opposite the world. Strangely, my real age and the age I appear to be always add up to seventy. So when I was twenty years old, I met fifty-year-old women who flirted with me as if I were their contemporary; when I was fifty at last, young women on streets were snapping their gum at me. Aged when I was young, and youthful now that I am old. I offer no explanations; that is for you, dear doctors of the future. I offer merely my life.

I am a rare thing. I have gone through centuries of medical history and found only a few like me in all the world, and even those, sadly, not like enough.

The first time-altered creatures in the literature are the Frabbonière twins, born in 1250 in a small village in the viscounty of Béarn. Named Aveline and Fleur, they were born with the ill-fortuned physical appearance of old women. As babies, they were brought to the kings of England and France, as well as to the pope, for they were judged to be not demonic children but signs from God that Christ was to come again. Pilgrims came to touch the children and listen to their babbling, hoping somewhere in there was a prophecy of the coming end. Their appearance, unlike my own, stayed the same while they aged, and as soon as they grew convincingly tall, they were treated as old peasant women and forgotten. Only doctors and the religious wanted to pay them visits. As soon as Aveline and Fleur reached the age they appeared to be, they both lay down in their common bed, holding hands, and died. There is a grotesque woodcut of this scene. It used to hang above my own bed.

Another set of twins, Ling and Ho, famous through a series of eighteenth-century antisyphilis pamphlets, led lives that more closely resembled my own. Actually, only one of them did: poor, cursed Ho. They were born the children of a Shanghai prostitute (so the pamphlet read), and while Ling was an ordinary, drooling, pink baby, Ho was born much as I was: from the other end of life. So while Ling grew to crawl and giggle, Ho began to reverse. Our mutual disease, however, had crippled Ho from birth. He was always a kind of mummy in his bed. Even when he appeared to be more youthful, more ordinary, he still lay stiff and stupid, able to drink only beef tea, while seething at his brother's good fortune. Eventually, nearing thirty, the brothers approached the same visual age. It was then that Ho was able, at last, to thaw the life that had been frozen in him for so long. Ling left his village, wife, and children to meet his brother on their birthday. When he came into his brother's room and leaned over the bed to kiss him, Ho brought down the knife he had been hiding and, after letting his twin fall to the floor, turned it on himself. Lying in their sticky blood, the twins had at last become identical, and as no one could tell them apart, they were buried in a common tomb with the inscription that one man was blessed and the other a devil, but which was which could not be told.

The last I have found is a more recent man: Edgar Hauer. It's a curious case that even my grandmother remembered. Son of a Viennese merchant, Edgar lived until the age of thirty before any of his symptoms manifested. It was only then that his appearance began to reverse, as mine has, and he led the rest of his life seeming to become younger and younger. I read his case carefully, hoping for a clue to his death (a major preoccupation for me now that the end is so near), but fortunately for him, he died of influenza before his fiftieth birthday, and his wife was left weeping on the bed, holding what appeared to be the body of a ten-year-old boy in her arms.

And that is all. These are not lucky stories.

I should explain this disguise of mine. It's no excuse to say that I pretend to be a boy of twelve simply because I look like one, but the fact is that I do. I am small and freckled and lonely; I have patches on my knickers and frogs in every pocket. Only a careful observer would notice that I have too many faded scars for a child of twelve, too mean a squint, and that I sometimes stroke my soft chin as if I'd worn a beard. But no one looks that closely. I know it seems hard to believe, but the world is wholly convinced that I am what I claim to be, and not merely because I'm so good an imitator after all these awful years. It's because nobody notices little ill-dressed boys. We simply disappear into the dirt.

As far as anybody in this town knows, I am an orphan. According to the local gossip, I lost my father nearly two months ago, lost him in the spring lake-mist, and I was left here absolutely on my own. I was staying at the house of a boy in town and I fell upon the mercy of his mother to take me in. That boy was you, Sammy, my unwitting accomplice. That mother was your mother, Mrs. Ramsey, a local artist. I have lived here ever since.

Ah, now you recognize me, don't you, Sammy? The sad blond orphan forced to share the bedroom of your boyhood. The odd child in the bunk below whose snore, I'm sure, you've memorized by now. If you are reading this, you are older yourself, and perhaps you will forgive me.

To play out this disguise, however, I have to walk to school each day and sit in idiotic classes. Today, for instance, was the Geography of America, during which we were told all manner of lies, including the fact that California (my native state) contains every possible kind of terrain. I had to bite my best Ticonderoga to keep from speaking. *Volcano? Steppe? Tundra?* But twelve-year-olds would never know these words, and I must keep my cover above all else.

But why pretend to be a boy? Why not just enter the town, like any malformed midget, on the back of a circus elephant? Why not wear the crumpled hat and coat of the old man I really am? There are two reasons. The first, which I will get to shortly, is the Rule. The second, dear Sammy, is you. I have had time enough to consider how to find you, how to make my way into your life, how to slip into the bunk below yours and listen to the dog-yelps of your dreams.

I am told that the first person to realize my condition was not a doctor at all but our maid Mary. Much fun had been made of Mary in our household—Grandmother liked to tell visitors that, having been used to descending farm ladders, the poor young woman still walked backwards down the stairs—but the truth of it was she was a fragile and neurotic girl, given to fits of jealousy and tears, and to giggles at any flattery or praise, a ripe thing for any clever man's picking. And just as in any Irish ballad, she went astray. I was still a baby when Mary was sent away—and sent away she was, because the unnamed lover left poor Mary with only a stillborn baby, a thistle pendant, and a broken promise. She was replaced with a girl remarkably similar—red-haired and simple Maggie—and was never mentioned again except by Father, enjoying a cigar with the men, and then as a different kind of joke. And so Mary was erased from the books at 90 South Park Avenue.

But she returned several years later, got in through the back door and reached the upstairs hall before Grandmother spotted her.

"Mary!" the old woman exclaimed, clutching her jet brooch.

"Mrs. Arnold, I—"

"How did you get in here?"

She no longer looked the part of a young woman. Her face was still attractive, but with the hardness of unripe fruit, and her eyes, which used to puppy-leap about the room, had been leashed and trained by the necessity of the streets. Her clothes were good, if a little flashy, but a closer look revealed how faded they were, as if she wore and washed them daily. Her hands were lined with the soot of the city, the ash that snowed from factories. Back then, all good women wore gloves, and why? Because the world was filth. But Mary had no gloves and here she was, fighting against the filth but no longer a maid; that was clear. Mary had fallen.

She smiled as she never would have when she lived here. "John let me in," meaning John Chinaman, our name for the cook. "It's a little thing, just a—"

"I am sorry, Mary," Grandmother answered furiously, "but you have made your bed . . ." She launched into her usual speech about linens and destiny, but just then my nurse was bringing me from my mother's room on my morning visit. Though I was nearly three, Nurse was still carrying me in her arms. Judging from the few photos taken of me then, I was in my most hideous stage, and all alather in lace when I caught sight of Mary. Permanently in purdah, it wasn't often I saw anyone but my grandmother, mother, and nurse. I must have squealed in delight.

"Ah, look at him!" Mary exclaimed to Grandmother's horror. The old lady cast an arm into the hallway to stop her, but Mary walked towards me and touched my raisin's face. "Why," she said, astounded, facing Grandmother squarely. "He looks like me pa, and he's lost his white hair!"

Grandmother became stern. "Mary, I must ask that you turn out your pockets."

"Mum, he's growing younger."

Both Nurse and Grandmother looked. It took a pair of eyes

that had been away from me that could compare my gnarled baby self to this new, smoother form. The addled Irish girl was quickly whisked out of the house (what had her purpose been: to steal, to beg, to haunt?) but no one could deny her effect on the household. What legions of doctors had failed to notice, a scarlet woman saw in an instant.

"I'm afraid," the doctor told Grandmother when she called for him with the offer of old brandy, "that she's right." He sat in the upstairs parlor, sipping the brandy and looking about the room as if he planned to inherit it. "For what he is, he's healthy as a pig."

It was Grandmother who raised me. She directed my feeding and care, opened the windows to let in the chill city fog she hoped would cure me. My mother later told me that the old woman barred her from the nursery because she was sure I would be a source of grief, just a little headstone in a month or so, as with most children, but I like to think Grandmother kept me to herself in that high, bare room because she was lonely, and she hoped to love me a little: one last old man for her life.

Grandmother was an odd woman, and is only a faint memory for me, but I loved her. I loved peering at her rubbery nose and the roman candle of vessels that spread outwards from it across her cheeks; I loved the weird lace Regina bonnet she wore, and how its tight ribbon cut into her slack jowls, forming long pink welts when she removed it. I loved her because she was my only companion and because we grow to love the ones beside us.

I bet you've done the arithmetic. A boy born in 1871, seeming to be seventy, how long would he expect to live? Seventy years, of course. And if, like my grandmother, you sat above my cradle and worked at your pearl necklace like an abacus, you would take this expected age and arrive at the next obvious conclusion: the year of my death. This is what Grandmother did, standing at the open window in her furs and studying my cooing form overflowing from my cradle with the warm, wrinkled skin of a pudding.

When Grandmother had calculated the date, she brought my mother in and commanded her to run an errand of such extravagance that poor Mama gasped with the bit of her still left to breathe above her corset. You would think it was an errand run for a prince in a fairy tale; you would almost think the old woman loved me above all else, and gathered these numbers like blankets to tuck around me in my fragile youth. But it was God she loved. Like the Fox sisters in their drafty mansion, she listened for the rappings of His spirit on my body's wooden hull. So the gold pendant she had shaped and hammered at great expense was not for me; it was for Him, to show, as it hung around my hideous neck, that she had not been blind; she had seen Him at last.

I wept the day she was buried. I was not allowed to attend the funeral, but I remember very clearly a carriage pulling up in front of the house and my family standing at the front door, utterly veiled, wreathed, and enshrouded in black. Mother leaned down to explain that I was not to come and handed me, in consolation, her black-bordered handkerchief, dampened by her tears. Father waved to me and took her by the shoulder as they left, and I slipped from Nurse's grip to climb the box ottoman and press my face against the window. I wiped Mother's handkerchief against the glass, cleaning it of fireplace soot, and watched, weeping, as they rode away. The horses were plumed; the carriages were lacquered and plate-glass. The procession turned slowly around the elms of South Park and vanished behind the window's filmy panes as it went on, as everything always did, without me.

I keep the pendant still. I have lost all the things I've loved—they have been sold or taken or burned—but this glittering collar, which I have hated all my life, has never left. Angels desert you; devils are constant fiends. Here, on this page, I have made a rubbing. Remembering the date at the top of this diary, you may see for yourself the fate Grandmother gilt for me:

I have told you of my birth, and of my certain death. It's time at last for my life.

My writing was interrupted by a boy. It was you, Sammy.

You came over in your usual flurry of action, as if you were ten boys all running together, and stopped short of me in the sad dust of this school yard. In the trees, birds or girls were twittering. Your usual newsboy cap was jettisoned in some bush where you would later be sent, petulant, by the yard-nag to find it, but now your hair blasted freely into the wind, twisting and glinting like a bright idea; your knickers were unbuckled and rolled high; your stockings' elastics had snapped and were rolled low; your vest, your pants, your shirt, everything about you was smeared in dust as a roll is smeared in butter, and you arrived before me more alive than I, surely, have ever been.

"Wanna play ball?"

"Can I be second base?" I asked. I was asking for a high honor.

"We need right field."

"Oh."

"Can you play?" you asked, impatient now.

"No," I said. "I'm writing. Here, write something," I added, ripping a sheet from the notebook, "something for your mom." To which you laughed girlishly and flew off because you are a monkey, Sammy, you are a monkey that approaches on all fours and screams and screams, but when anybody reaches to you, you leap into the branches, howling. When I reach to you. For I am a sham boy, a counterfeit, and like a foraging animal you can smell the truth, born with blood that shivers at a stinking beast no matter how boy-shaped he may be, so today you ran away from me towards a group of wrestling boys, who now lay spent and dazzled in a cloud of dust, lifting their heads eagerly as you shouted to them: true boys.

Let it rest. The recess hag has appeared at the door, piping furiously away. I have to stash these pages for another day; the times tables await me.

My life's story really begins with Alice, when my deformity is at its worst, but in order to understand Alice, and why I needed so badly to fall in love, you must hear about Woodward's Gardens, and Hughie. But, first, you must understand the Rule.

It happened one winter evening, not long after Grandmother's death. I awoke to the *piff* of the gaslight in my room and saw, as its fluttering magic brightened, my parents sitting near my bed in their opera clothes, rustling with silk and starch. I don't know what had happened to them that evening, what tragedy they had witnessed or which famous hypnotist they had confessed their case to, but they had the expressions of repentant murderers who have called their victim up in a séance, and as Father turned the key of the lamp to fill my room with rosy light and a bitter smell, Mother kneeled close to my tired face and told me the Rule. She offered no explanation, but simply repeated it so that I would know this was a lesson we were learning, and no dream; this was a spell she was casting, and if I was a dutiful son I would let her weave her charmed circle. My father stood by the lamp, his eyes closed in holy dread. And then I fell asleep and remember nothing else. The Rule has dictated my actions throughout most of my life. It has allowed me to relax all great decisions before its simplicity, and has therefore taken me further than I ever would have gone, all the way from my home city to the cold sandbox that now immerses my naked toes.

"*Be what they think you are*," my mother whispered to me that evening, a tear at the corner of each eye. "*Be what they think you are. Be what they think you are.*"

I have tried, Mother. It has brought me heartache, but it has also brought me here.

In those days after Grandmother's death, everything began to change for me. We moved to a smaller but more stylish house high on the new Nob Hill. South Park had "gone down," as mother ruefully acknowledged; the newer houses around the park were being built of wood rather than stone, divided into flats, and merchants and newly married couples began to replace the rich old Virginians who used to promenade with their black sunshades and ribboned bonnets. We turned the old house into flats and rented the upper floor to a married couple, the lower to a Jewish widow and her little daughter. Then we left, with the rest of the rich, for Nob Hill's promise of a view, which was nearly always wrapped in thick ermine fog.

And I was freed. I had gone outside a few times with Mother, to the market or the park. Mostly, though, my adventures were confined to the narrow view I had from the nursery—a crowd of geese with goslings, an open carriage with a picnic party inside, the milkman passing with a wetted carpet thrown over his cans to keep them cool on hot autumn days, and any dog or cat that passed and sniffed and looked up gave me the same thrill an as-

tronomer might have seeing the creatures on the moon turn to
smile at him.

So it was something like an annunciation when Mother told
me, one morning at her vanity, that I was being taken to Woodward's Gardens. I was six years old, slightly larger than a child
but looking nothing like one. She sat holding a hairpin over a candle, heating it to curl her lashes, and I was engaged in pulling the
hair from her brush and feeding it to the ceramic hair receiver. I
loved the way the thick and wondrous dead stuff knotted and
clumped so evilly; I loved feeling the long strands of her hair, so
fine and airy as I plucked them from the brush and fed them to
the receiver, so dark and twisted in those porcelain guts. Mother
used to take the hair and weave it. She made a bracelet from Grandfather's hair that Grandmother still wears in her grave, and, later,
another with my father's hair and a green ribbon. It hung on
Mother's wrist, with a small enamel portrait of him, long after he
was gone.

"What's Woodward's Gardens?" I asked, pressed beside her.

She smiled sadly and took my hand. "It's a park. Outside."

"Oh."

"I should warn you, there will be children there."

Not "other children," just "children."

"Oh."

"Little bear," she said softly; I was always her "little bear." I fed
the last of her hair into the little hole and looked at her nervously.
She was so young then, with the shimmering beauty of a sky after
a rain.

"Don't you want to go?" she asked me in that young, sweet
voice.

Sammy, more than anything in the world.

WOODWARD'S GARDENS
THE EDEN OF THE WEST!
Unequaled and Unrivaled on the American Continent
NATURE, ART AND SCIENCE ILLUSTRATED
Education, Recreation and Amusement the Aim
Admission, 25 cts. Children, 10 cts.
Performance Free
SKATING EVERY DAY.

There are still people alive who remember Woodward's Gardens, and the May Days when Woodward, rich from the famous What Cheer House down at Meigg's Wharf, would pay for all the children, hordes and hordes of the city's youth, to come to his backyard and play:

The rows of small and furry dromedaries, dried brown tears streaking from their eyes, bearing children and teenage men in derbies; a lake with an Oriental bridge and pavilion; a racetrack; a maypole; pools full of bellowing sea lions; a Rotary Boat shaped like a doughnut within its little pool, which kids could row endlessly; fantastic inventions of all sorts including the zoographicon, orchestrion, and Edison's talking machine; an aviary where young couples hid among the ferns and spooned beneath a cloud of birds; herds of emus, ostriches, cassowaries; a "Happy Family House" where the monkeys would sit and mimic the humans by hugging and kissing each other; but what I remember most from that day were two events marvelous to behold, one by looking down, the other by looking up. Those and, of course, meeting Hughie.

As our neat two-in-hand drew closer to the great hedgework wall on Thirteenth and Mission, I could barely breathe. "There's seals," Father told me through his whiskers, which, like cupped hands, gave his words the hush and excitement of a secret, "and parrots and cockatoos." Of course he loved the gardens; hadn't he changed his own name in memory of a playland like this? On his voyage from Denmark, Asgar Van Daler had remembered a place long ago where the swans cried out like Loreleis from the lily ponds and, believing his own name unsuitable for this new land of Smiths and Blacks and Joneses, christened himself after that old candle-glittering park—his Tivoli.

"Swans!" he shouted to me, grinning. "A famous performing bear!"

"Like me? A bear like me?"

"Like you!"

And before I knew it, we were already inside. I had been so distracted by his descriptions, so entranced also by the schools of children lined up behind their schoolmistresses, the prams and crowds and stuffed ibises and flamingos posed before me in the bushes, I did not even notice a small and sad detail. At the very moment that I began to run through the grass, Father was pocketing three red ticket stubs. He had paid for three adults.

I was not even a very convincing old man in those days, of course—beardless, too short for an adult, too large for a boy—but people stared only briefly before letting me pass by. There was so much else to see. As I was trying to take in the wonders around me, a bell rang and a man announced that Splitnose Jim was to perform in the bear pit. I looked at my parents, pleading with my eyes, and Mother, tightening the veil beneath her chin, nodded approval. Within minutes we were sitting on a pine board in an amphitheater full of children and well-dressed couples, smelling the never-changing popcorn-and-dust odor of childhood. A man appeared in the ring below and announced the arrival of "a terrifying bear who used to dance for an Italian on the streets of our city, but who one day, in rage, tore the ring from his nose and lunged at his master! Too dangerous for the sidewalks, Mr. Woodward brought him here for your enjoyment." And out he shambled, Splitnose Jim.

An old bear is not too exciting for those of you who met lions and hyenas at the circus as a child, but I had never seen such an enormous creature in my life. I screamed twice, once in fear, then again in delight, to see old Jim lean back on his haunches and sniff the air, nodding repeatedly at us like a gentleman entering a restaurant where he is known.

He did a few miserable tricks for a peanut, and climbed up poles to rest dolefully on the platforms high above us. Each time, as the trainer shouted out how dangerous Jim had been wandering through the parklands of Yellowstone, how he was captured, and what marvelous thing he would do for us now, we applauded. As we clapped, Jim sat back against a rail, the peanut balanced on the tip of that dusty split nose, and daydreamed like any workman until the boss snapped his whip and it was time to earn the wage again. I loved old Jim, and I pitied him a little. I understood full well that he lived in a cage, lonely, confused, with just his keepers as his friends. Children, however, can sustain pity only so long. It burns; it itches; and we imagine a quick cure to the oppressed: ourselves. And so in my slippery boyhood mind I saved old Jim by bringing him home with me, making him live again within the fortress of Nob Hill, hide in the staircase ferns, crawl into the dumbwaiter and thereby sneak into the cellar where we kept the potatoes and old wines, watch over me with those tired eyes as I slept, and in general imbue my life with the very terror and adventure they had caged him for. I would save Jim and he, grateful and loving, licking my forehead with his tongue as black and big as a boot, would save me.

After the bear pit, my father wanted us all to go roller-skating, but Mother thought this was too risqué. Instead, we followed the signs to the aerial ascension, something even Mother, dabbing beads of perspiration from her hairline, could not resist.

The balloon drew sighs and a big smile from my father, who stood arms akimbo, staring up at its great silvery magnificence.

He loved invention and technology, especially anything electrical, and our house would have been one of the first with a telephone had my mother not pointed out that, besides its being extraordinarily expensive, there would only be three thousand other people in the country to call, and that all of them, family histories unknown, could call us. He was forbidden to indulge his technological urges, but I remember one night years after Woodward's Gardens when—driven by either his love for my mother or his love of the new—he presented her with an electrical jewel fitted into a scarf pin. He inserted the tiny battery and clipped it to her lapel, where it shone with an eerie beauty. She smiled while Father explained its principles, telling us it was the newest fashion. Then Mother turned to him with a look of pity and said, "Asgar, thank you, but I can't," informing him that, as with French dresses, one always lets others try the newest fashion.

That was the last of Father's transgressions, but not the first. By the time of my outing he had already been relegated to concealing his beloved wonders—such as the clear, pointed filament bulbs I discovered hidden in his study's hollow globe one day, resting on a bed of cotton like the newly deposited eggs of a glass lizard—or resigning himself to public marvels like the one before us.

"Look at that, old man," my father said to me in his odd accent. "Look at that!"

High above the grounds, above the wooden corral of onlookers, dwarfing even the great striped Arabian tent of the aviary beside it, rose the shimmering quilted silver of Professor Martin's balloon. Enormous and swaying silently in the breeze, as a barker announced its wonders to the crowds below and the professor prepared for his ascension, the balloon seemed to exist in some opposite dimension, hanging from the earth in a huge reversed raindrop that trembled towards the sky.

"Man alive!" I heard beside me in a chirping voice. This wasn't something my parents would have said; it was a phrase I'd only heard from Nurse. "Man alive, what is it?"

That was exactly what I was asking myself. In all the excitement of the gardens, I had not paid any attention to the crowds. And there, standing beside me, was the most extraordinary exhibit of them all: an ordinary boy.

I knew I was different. Father had sat me down in his dark parlor and explained, through the forest of his cigar smoke, that my doctor's frequent visits were unusual, but it was only because I was, as he put it, "somewhat enchanted." Mother, whose terms of endearment included "old man" and "little bear," explained one morning as she applied her magnolia balm that I was unlike anyone else in the world, not like any boy, or even my father as a boy, not like the servants or the cook or anyone. But all children are told these things; we are great, we are special, we are rare. I only knew I was truly different because servants whisper too much and once, as I lay hidden in the root cellar, crammed against the boards, eavesdropping, I heard Maggie telling Nurse how sorry she felt for me that I was born "so sweet but so wrong."

But here, squinting amiably through the dust, was the thing I was not. It was a little copper-headed boy dressed, as was the fashion, like a little man in a tiny-brimmed black soft hat and suit which must have come off during the day because it was done up all wrong, like a crooked smile, with burrs and woolly fluff caught in the nap of the velvet. He glared with fresh blue eyes and wrinkled his strawberry nose, a souvenir of yesterday's too-tempting sun. What he thought of me I cannot say. But I thought him the strangest thing I had ever seen. I knew that other little boys looked like this—I saw them from my window every day, sitting primly on a bench or hooting scandalously to a friend—but I had never learned, close up, how deformed they were. While I was solid bone and made floorboards creak and hammocks sway, this boy seemed like a bird, or a bag of twigs, his limbs bending impossibly like those Oriental boxes that fold and unfold endlessly upon their cleverly ribboned hinges. I was stunned and mute.

Impatient, he asked again, "What is it?" because he wanted to know and here I was, an adult.

I stammered for a moment. My parents had begun to argue in whispers—I learned later that it was about whether it would be too much for Father to buy me something so exotic as a banana wrapped in foil—and so weren't paying attention to my predicament. I had mixed so easily with the other children that day only because my self-consciousness had evaporated in the joy of discovery, but here, in this pause as the professor fiddled with his ropes and his flames, I could feel it beading up again inside my cooled heart.

"I . . . I don't know."

"You do," he insisted, then squinted and looked at me more carefully. "Are you a midget?"

"What's that?"

"I saw one in a museum once and he got married to a lady midget, and there was, there was the tallest man in the world who married them."

This meaningless information passed through me like a gamma ray. Upset and confused on my first outing, I forgot the commands my parents had given me, and for the first of three times in my life, I broke the Rule. I told him the truth:

"I'm a boy."

"You're not. You're a midget. You're from Europe." Apparently, that's where he thought midgets were from.

"I'm a boy."

He smiled broadly, showing a gap in his white teeth. "You're teasing."

"I'm not. I'm six."

He held up both hands and made that number. "I'm six!" he

announced, and suddenly the idea of this, the newness of himself, overshadowed any further curiosity about me. "I can count to a hundred because my dad's a tutor and he taught me."

"I can count to fifty." This was the amount Grandmother found decent for my age.

Hughie considered this and seemed to find it adequate. He looked up at the people wandering around us in their thick black clothes. He seemed to be watching them intently; later, I was to learn he considered himself to have magical powers and could, if asked politely, cause the trees to sway just so across a field. Then he looked at me with the face of a man who has made a decision.

"I eat paper."

"You do?"

He nodded, growing in pride. "I eat it all the time."

I won't bore you with the rest of the conversation. Like the tribesmen you hear of in the Southeast seas who, upon meeting a stranger, go through long and ritualized recitations of their ancestors, we enacted the childhood ceremonies in which two boys agree they will be friends and not enemies. Just like the tribesmen, in fact, we ended it with a spitting contest that, since I won, put me in a place of love in Hughie's mind that would endure, despite any intervening unkindnesses, all the fifty-odd years of our friendship.

"It's time!" the barker shouted from his spiral tower.

And the miracle occurred.

Professor Martin threw his weights onto the sand below and the balloon, quivering, began to rise into the air. The little man, hoisted on his quicksilver moon, kept feeding the roaring fire at its base, lifting them even higher—though the ropes still dangled, held at each end by a strong man to prevent the professor from floating away—and then he turned and opened a bag of rose petals over the cheering crowd. When the clouds of roses cleared, we saw he was even higher, releasing great colored streamers that we reached to catch. And still it rose, the marvel. It was like nothing else on earth; it had no parallel in any animal I had read of, any fairy tale or fable; it had no precedent even in my dreams. This was the human mind made real, overshadowing even the birds in its longing to be free. Are we the only animals that must escape ourselves? Because, seeing that balloon, I could imagine my own soul, trapped in the dusty acreage of my old body, burning with a flame like this and lifting away from me, just as silvered, just as new.

I felt a prod and was handed a phallus in foil.

"Little bear, this is a banana."

Many years later, when we were both getting tired and forgetful, I reminded Hughie about the afternoon at Woodward's Gardens when we first met below Professor Martin's marvelous balloon. We were sitting in a roadside diner at the time, and I was getting hungrier while Hughie read the sports page of a local paper, grinning at the high school teams, his glasses down on the tip of his nose. He put down the paper and frowned.

"Balloon?" he asked. "I don't think so."

"Yes, it was an enormous silver balloon and you asked me what it was."

He considered it. We were both in our late fifties, and Hughie had lost his beautiful red hair by then and gotten a bad knee that never ceased to bother him. "No, we met when my father was your tutor."

"You're forgetting things, Hughie. You're an old man."

"So are you," he pointed out. He was right, of course, but old for me meant I looked like a small, freckled boy. I grinned my stupid grin and went back to my milk shake.

"A balloon. That's how we became friends."

"No, I showed you a magic trick on the stairs."

"I don't remember you doing card tricks."

He removed his glasses. "I came in with my father. You were trying to hide behind a door like a baby, even though you looked like Senator Roosevelt in a sailor suit. You were ridiculous. I made the queen of spades appear from the fern and you have admired me ever since."

"Well."

"Well."

We both looked out the window to the parking lot, bored and restless on our travels, hoping to see something familiar out there. We went back to the paper and the growling stomach and did not speak for another hour. That is what it means to have an old friend.

We did hire his father as my tutor. I think it must have come from a conversation beneath that amazing balloon at Woodward's Gardens. Mr. Dempsey arrived every weekday, and the most surprising part, looking back, is that Hughie came with him. I think my mother felt a child of wealth deserved undistracted tutelage, but my father finally persuaded her that I would never be an ordinary child of wealth, and that to enjoy life I would need more than one kind of tutelage. Education, yes, and language and the arts. But perhaps I also needed to learn how to be a little boy.

Hughie had figured it out without a single lesson. He arrived in his little suit and hat, smiling politely, but the moment I appeared in the hall, my books in hand, he immediately transformed into a raging bull and headed shoulder-first into my side, knocking me over and spilling papers all along the polished floors. "Man overboard!" he would cry in delight, "man overboard!" then go about picking up the papers and asking me about my day. All this was a surprise to me, and I could never think of any better response than to bean him on the head with a book of poetry and whip his arm with a book strap. Of course I was larger, stronger, capable of lifting him above my head and dropping him over our back fence and into the pastiche little Oriental garden in the house behind ours, where I was always careful to drop him on a pillow of wild grasses. Oh how he would laugh and scream, then scamper back with a water lily behind his ear. Yet I always thought of him as the stronger. Throughout that time, I strove to impress him, to be as clever or as wild, and though I ran faster than he ever could for years, still I could never quite keep up.

You'll say I'm lucky to have found him as a friend, a boy so willing to accept an ogre as his companion, but of course that's the only person I would have found. A sort of crazed child. But I wonder why Hughie accepted me so quickly. It could be that he had his own oddities, of course, a clumsy sense of reality, or even a boyish self-absorption so immense that it towered over even my hulking, hound-eyed self. Perhaps he thought himself lucky to have found me, too.

But what did he think I was?

"Oh you were Max," he told me several times over the years. "I don't know, just Max, the way Mama was Mama and nobody else. Who knows? You were never a thing, you know. Like a toy or a dog. I knew you were a person, but not like a kid, and not like a grown-up. Something else, who knows what, I didn't care. You're still just Max, you idiot, now give me a cigar. No, one of the nice ones."

Childhood is remembered in the marrow, not the mind. I can't tell you for sure what happened one day or the next, which birthday it was when Hughie wrapped a frog in ribbons and set it loose across the tea set, causing Maggie to drop the milk, screaming, or what age I was when Mother refused to change from a dress too low-cut for Father's taste and, seeing that he would not win, he took the sugar bowl and emptied it into her décolletage, forcing her to laugh. Or when Father took me to Meigg's Wharf and we saw our old maid Mary, in bright makeup, holding an iris, and she ran up to us and cooed over how much younger I was growing. "You don't look so old now, you wait, dear, your time will come." My father made us move on without a hello. I remember how Mary stared as we left her, how she dropped the iris and it looked, there on the sidewalk, like a frozen kiss.

I could never write a true history of my childhood, because everything happened before I knew what time was, the point in my life when a promise to pick berries on Saturday would cause me to ask every few minutes, "Is it Saturday yet?" Life had no before and after, was not yet strung upon a thread, and thus cannot be brought out from the drawer intact.

So my memories of that time are of Mr. Dempsey visiting and Hughie drawing with chalk across his shoes; Maggie and Nurse gossiping in the hall; a series of turtles in the terrarium who lived and died just inches from my glass-pressed nose; the vegetable man banging on the back door each morning; the song of the grinder's cart—"Any old knives to grind, any old knives to grind?"; fountains of smoke rising from the side-wheel steamers in the harbor; the flies and acrid odor of the horses, how pained they looked and how sorry I felt for them as they rested in the carriage house; the wet-wool smell of my bathing suit drying in my room; the old women on the street dressed from eras past in frightful wigs and hoopskirts; Mother and her balms; the rasp of Father stroking his whiskers; the smell of the gas which was the smell of the night. These were the Years Before Alice.

❧

I want to note that I am no longer sleeping well.

The bunk below yours, Sammy, could accommodate a little

boy's nightmares and late night reading of cowboy books, but not this old man. And the odd little night-light in the corner, besides being a waste of electricity, reminds me too much of the electric gem my father tried to add to my mother's jewelry box, glittering so falsely from the baseboard. The whole house, so modern and efficient, so slick and wallpaperless and fine in the daytime, loses every one of its charms at night and leaves me feeling lonely beneath the dry husk of its walls. It could be, too, that all this writing of the past, like scratching a bite, prolongs the pain. So I am not sleeping.

One night a few weeks ago, I got out of bed, careful not to wake you, and crept into the bathroom where a window opens onto the sky. I climbed onto the toilet and stood there, staring at the stars and trying to make out their patterns one by one as my father taught me. I found Orion; one can always find Orion. I found the Dipper. And bloodshot Mars. I tried to convince myself that, even though my hands had shrunk into tender starfish, the stars were unchanged, and their light pulsing across the universe was the same as ever, and that if I stared unblinking and let it pool into my eyes, I might close them and keep that same light, like a mouthful of milk, trapped inside me for a moment. Then I might feel the way I used to feel, full of this same light. But this was not the sky I once knew; there was a new planet out there with a new light. Pluto, I think they've called it, the planet of the underworld. And if I closed my eyes, that would be in there as well, a drop of violet poison clouding all the rest.

"Hello?" The light came on.

I turned and saw my mother.

No, it was your mother, Sammy. It was Mrs. Ramsey with her hand upon the switch, but the light fell over her so unnaturally that it showed every line on her face with the harshness of a rival who does not forget. She stood and stared at me with the face of an insomniac, and for a moment I was afraid somehow she'd caught me, seen an expression on my face that no child of twelve could have. Instantly, though, I saw that it wasn't discovery in her face, and it wasn't pity for an odd child who couldn't sleep. It was grief. For here was another burden in her life, the burden of a little boy standing on the toilet to look out at the sky, on top of all the other burdens she had carried. A woman in her mid-fifties, nearly my own age, wandering the midnight halls in grief; I understand her better than she can ever guess.

"I'm sorry," was all I said.

Mrs. Ramsey smiled; the look was broken. "What are you up to?"

"I don't know." The answer I knew a child would give.

"That makes two of us."

Mrs. Ramsey shifted her weight in the doorway and looked out at the stars herself. Her dressing gown fell open at the neck and showed a constellation of freckles across her breast. "Want some milk?" she asked. I nodded and took her hand.

The day that Father disappeared, long ago in San Francisco, I awoke from my unmade bed to find another, formed in snow outside my window. Like a health-crazed mother who feeds you on a steady diet of grains and crackers but one morning produces a sugared white cake just because she's missed it for too long, the world had happily shrugged off all expectations and given me a snowy day. I had read about it, and heard my father's recollections of the castles and dragons carved from the banks of creamy Danish snow, how he and the other boys would slide on wooden boards all the way to Prussia, but I was not prepared for the real thing. I thought it would be like a toy left in the yard; I was not prepared for snow to erase the world entirely and leave a crisp, blank page. I stared out at the mansions that were not there, the horses, the surreys, the work-bound men I was so used to seeing. There was no sky; there was no city. I gasped as we always do at the unnatural.

I was not a child anymore. I was sixteen and a little sullen, full of self-pity for my dreadful fate, forced to wear old-fashioned clothes so I would pass more convincingly as a man of fifty-four. Hughie, of course, wore anything he liked: a sack coat, loose pants, wild paisley. All I could be proud of was a beard as thick and luscious as any poet's. I had it shaved and clipped just under my chin; each night I stroked it in the mirror like a pet. It was even losing its gray at last (through the help of some dye my barber happily suggested). I was, however, no closer to being a real boy.

But despite my appearance, I was merely sixteen, and, bookish and lonely as I was, I felt the thrill of the day's change as much as anyone; maybe more so. It seemed, somehow, as if it had leveled the world; from my window I could see men in frock coats and ladies in bonnets throwing heaps of snow at one another. Magically, a carriage came by done up with boards to reproduce a sleigh, and couples were lying inside, laughing under a layer of fur. I dressed in my shabbiest clothes, kissed a bewildered mother as she stood holding the curtain back, and was let out into a world turned deaf and blind to what it was before. Children were being led, dazed, through the haunted paths of a dead and crystal world, but older boys (more my own age but grown into wild, handsome lads) were drawing on boyhood novels to produce snowballs that, correctly aimed, were knocking down the top hats of old Nob Hill swells. It was no world, that morning, to be old and tired.

And I, for once, was not; with the grin and dyed-brown beard of a young man, I was no target for young rascals. I was able to con a sled ride from some boys who had nailed old skate boots to a crate, and found myself sailing to the bottom of California

Street where the streetcars were running on their tracks as usual, having already kicked a morning of snowfall into slush and dung.

They say some young men, older than I, put stones in their snowballs and aimed them at politicians, Supreme Court justices, even our dear Mayor Pond. They say the tax collector and assessor's offices went to snowy war in the corridors of City Hall. They say Chinese who were caught outside of Chinatown were pelted with rocky snowballs and that, in retaliation, all whites sneaking through Chinatown's alleys looking for a smoke or a crib-girl were thrashed with bamboo. They say the buffalo in Golden Gate Park finally looked at home with powdered-wig hides, but I saw none of this. I only know that I found Hughie sledding through the cemetery near the old Mission Dolores, skipping his school-work just as I was, and that together—old man and young boy—we bruised our legs into bouquets of violet and gold, scarified the clean white hill, and yelled our voices raw with joy.

They say the most that fell that day was a foot of snow in Golden Gate. About three inches fell in the city itself. I have since learned in my travels, especially during a hip-high whopper in Colorado, that this is nothing; this is a mere extravagance of frost. But for us it was as thick and bright as luck.

When I came home that night, trudging through a wet and sodden twilight because most of the snow had melted downhill and out into the bay, I found a house of dimmed gaslights and worried looks. Mother sat in a shawl in the back parlor, doing her needlepoint. A canary cage sat behind her, empty as a winter tree.

"Max," she said as I stepped in, "we don't know where your father is. He hasn't come home."

"He's late at work," I offered.

"We sent a boy, he's not there." Her face was one of infinite patience, an expression she had readied hours ago just for my return. I saw a spot of blood on the flesh of her thumb; she had pricked herself just before I came in.

"I'm sure he's okay, it's the snow," she informed me.

The image of Woodward's Gardens came to me, and Father walking among the snow-powdered dromedaries, searching for the great silver balloon he'd loved so much. But I knew it was ridiculous.

Mother took my hand. "Don't you worry," she said. "John has dinner out for you, and do your lessons for Mr. Dempsey because he'll be able to come tomorrow . . ."

"What if it snows?"

"It's already melted," she told me evenly. I saw the pinprick welling, now a red pearl catching the light, quivering on her skin; she did nothing and only looked at me. "And Father will be home later, but don't you wait up."

"Mother."

"You need sleep, dear boy."

"Mother."

"*Kiss me*," she whispered. I did, catching some of her powder in my beard. And after I left the parlor for the dim light of the hall, I thought I heard the clatter of needles falling to the floor, and then the soft noise of a thumb pressed against a sucking mouth.

But he did not come home, ever again.

∾

For the first few months, we had the frozen hearts of people kept alive on hope. But all the police ever found corroborated what they'd known at the outset: that Father had never gone to work the day he vanished, that he had worn his black wool suit and top hat but not taken his cane, that he had bought a fine cigar from his favorite store on Clay, had a whiskey at the Bank Exchange on Stockton and enjoyed a free lunch, tipped his hat to a judge outside the Main Library, and was never seen again. The dotted line connecting all these witnesses with our own house led nowhere convincing at all; it led in a straight line out of San Francisco and directly into the water. No body was found, nor was there any evidence to show it might be, and I remember thinking it strange that on the one day a father might leave a trail of bootprints through the snow, mine had not left one.

After a half a year, however, the visits from our accountants outnumbered the visits from the police. They sat with Mother and myself in the parlor, where the coal fireplace caused their middle-class brows to dampen with sweat. Mother, dressed in the deep purple of uncertain mourning, listened while I tapped a pen nib on the table (they took me for a freeloading in-law). "Things are complex, Mrs. Tivoli," they told her. Father apparently liked to run his finances with an element of risk, and so everything he made always became tied up in some new venture; very little was saved. Without Father at the helm, the fleet of these astounding little projects was floating wide of its goal and a few had sunk to the bottom. Add to this the lack of income after the brief pension from his business had run out, the missing body that gave insurance no reason to pay, and thus, the accountants told us over greasy spectacles, "the books grant you one year to live as you are doing, in this house, and then there will be nothing." They told us to sell the house for what we could.

"We will speak plainly, Max," Mother told me once they had left. "They're right." I would not look at her; I sat in what doctors now would call an adolescent anguish. I rested my head against the plasterwork, feeling the raised outline of a poppy on my temple. She continued, her hair escaping from her pins in cheroot-smoke

curls: "We'll sell the house. We'll sell the love seat and the gentleman's chair of the second parlor, the clocks, the lamps. Some
furniture in your father's study, the desk, the chairs, the moth collection. Maybe the geode. The duplicate silver. We'll keep Maggie, I think, if she wants to live in South Park again."

"South Park?"

"Where else are we going to live? Besides, I need to be at
home." For a moment, as if the word were the planchette of a
Ouija board, moving without her power, she took on the lilting
strangeness of my father's voice: "We will speak plainly, Max."

She explained the plans to me in phrases that seemed to come
from a distant star, so bright and clear but already old. Someone
had to fix them, our new plans, as calm, real, and undesperate as
we could make them. You see, a phoenix was rising within my
mother, or, as the good mothers of this small town might put it,
a miracle. Sammy, I'll use your gross twentieth-century term: she
was pregnant.

❧

"I like you better poor," Hughie said when he arrived on moving day.

"We're not poor."

I could hardly talk to him. I was so ashamed at our change in
station. I stood among the old ornamental iron dogs of the yard,
and Mother stood at the upstairs window looking down. For we
were to live upstairs this time, with another fatherless family—the
Levys—living a quiet life in the flat below. I faced away from
South Park itself; it had changed so much. The little wall and
fence around the park were gone, leaving it a stamped green oval
among houses that no longer even resembled the beautiful old
ones such as ours. The trees in the park seemed to be different as
well, less maple and elm and more eucalyptus, following the re-

cent misplaced craze for the trees that left the city smelling like a medicine chest. In fact, it had even lost its old name; some of the new people were grimly calling it Tar Flats.

Hughie smiled. "Well, anyway, like you used to be. Nob Hill didn't suit you. You were starting to look like a bank president, old man."

"You look like a music hall singer."

That made him laugh. He was done up in lavender and gray, with the dandyish ill taste of a seventeen-year-old with some pocket money, wearing—just to spite me—a velvet vest that I had told him time and again made him look like an organ-grinder. Hughie never cared.

I noticed a movement in the downstairs apartment; the white flash of a dress, but in a moment it was gone. I hoped our neighbors would not come outside until we were moved. Those first-floor renters were the last people I wanted to meet. I noticed a wasp's nest had formed under the eaves since I'd been gone.

I said, "You know what Mother's telling everybody?"

"No."

"That I'm her brother-in-law."

"But that's stupid! So she's your brother's wife?"

"That I'm her brother-in-law come over from the East to help her run the household. Now that Dad's gone."

"But that's stupid. You used to live here. Won't people recognize you? I mean, the little freak?"

"Nobody recognizes me. When I left here, I was five feet tall with white hair. Now look at me." Newly seventeen, nearly six feet, with a full head of brown hair and a gorgeous streaked beard, I looked positively presidential, but dressed in Dad's old clothes, I felt I took on some of his European glamour and held my thumbs in my waistcoat pockets, preening. I said, "I think I've improved."

He winked. "I think so, too, Max. Soon you'll be a handsome old man."

"And you'll be an ugly one."

Hughie swatted at a passing wasp and then turned to where Mother looked out from the window. The wasp flew on. "Hello, Mrs. Tivoli!" he yelled.

"Don't shout, you plug-ugly," I told him.

"I ain't ugly," he informed me, smoothing his vest.

Mother shook from stillness at her post, held one hand to her hair, and waved with the other.

"How is she?" he asked, still looking up at my mother while she smoothed her best black dress, the one she wore to present herself to her old home the way one dresses for a dinner knowing an old lover will be there. She disappeared into the darkness of the upper room.

"Pagan," I said.

Now he was interested. "How so?"

I kicked the dry grass. "She's reading tarot cards. She's burning a spirit lamp all night in her room."

"I guess she still has a lot to say to your dad."

"Oh she doesn't talk. She's listening."

"What does he say?"

"Nothing," I said firmly. "He's not dead."

He nodded and looked back out at the park, arms crossed. "I agree."

We had come up with our own idea (not shared by the police) that what happened to Father was happening to men all the time in those days. We were convinced he had wandered into a bar on the Barbary Coast, drunk down a mickeyed beer, and, fallen into a drugged stupor, been dropped through a false plank in the floor onto a waiting Whitehall boat. There, he was taken out in darkest night to a clipper waiting outside the Golden Gate, the fees exchanged, and awoke to find himself headed on the sunny ocean towards the East, part of a whaling crew. A captain would be shouting orders into the prevailing wind, and pigtailed, tattooed crewmen would be shuffling by, eyeing their new mate. A trip backwards into his own salt-rimed youth. In other words, he'd been shanghaied.

But what I secretly thought had happened was even more obscene, fantastic. I imagined some Norse enchantment that had trapped my father so he was unable to reach us; I thought of some old ghost come round Cape Horn to haunt him and how, like Merlin locked by Nimue inside the rings of an oak, Father sat in a green coil of fire, waiting for me to speak the exact phrase to break his spell. What would it be?

"Hap!"

The sound came from behind us. A girl nearly my age had just come out of the first-story door but now lay anguished in the grass. I could not imagine what she was doing. She was all in white lace and held her hand to her neck, waiting, almost listening to the seconds passing, and we stared at each other in the wake of her odd cry. Then, slowly, in terror, she removed her hand, showing me *first*: a bright kiss of pain on her neck; and *second*: rolling in her outstretched palm, the gold-black liquid body of a wasp.

Alice, are you reading this? It's you!

I had seen girls before, of course. Not only from that nursery window where I watched them in their little-lady dresses pointing at the birds, but, later, I saw the girls of Nob Hill on their way to school, kicking pebbles at each other and laughing; I saw young ladies coming home past curfew in their beaus' phaetons; I even spotted some kissing in the parks until the couples, noticing a leery old man, took off for thicker bushes. And I had fallen in love with the everyday girls: the girl at the newsstand with a shine above her lip, the girl with sad eyes selling pineapples stacked up in a pyramid, and the German butcher's daughter who came with him to our back door and translated. But I never said a word to them. I merely nodded from the kitchen, or tried to hide my nervous sweat by tossing down my coins and rushing away. It was a thrill, an agony.

I hadn't yet met a proper girl. All boys are primed at seventeen, ready for love. And I, imprisoned in that awful body, was sure to fall for the first one to meet my eye.

"I've been stung!"

And so had I, Alice, seeing you for the first time. Worst luck of my life: I was struck dumb by my heart.

Hughie ran to her. "Are you all right?"

She blinked as the pustule at her neck began to swell. "I've never been stung before," was what she said.

"You'll be all right," Hughie told her. "Lie down."

She refused, sitting there and looking at the poisoner in her palm. "It hurts."

"Well . . ."

"More than I expected. Mother got stung once and I thought she was making too big a deal of it, but . . . oh, it hurts."

"It's swelling, too."

Now she turned those soft brown eyes, those ageless eyes, on me. "Sir, your son is very kind."

I tried to speak but nothing happened. I was a mute old man and she looked away.

"Mother!" she yelled, then looked again at the wasp. "Poor little thing."

"Hmm," Hughie said, getting up.

"You're going to leave me here?" she said.

At that moment, I was opening my mouth to say the words I'd

been trying to speak for almost a minute. She seemed to notice and looked right at me. I blinked. There, they came out at last:

"He's . . . he's not my son."

But the words were drowned out by a shout from the side of the house. I looked and it was merely a woman, a mother. Alice, you turned away and never heard me.

I would like to call it fate, but I should call it chance, that put you in my yard at the time my heart was at its most tender. I suppose I'm lucky it was you and not someone crueler. Still, if it had been anyone but you, Alice, I would have loved again, and plenty, before this ripe age. Cursed by your eyes, however, I never have.

"Mr. Tivoli!"

Her mother rushed out of the house and kneeled at her daughter's feet. She held a cloth against the girl's taut neck, pressing against that tender skin with the casual efficiency of a nurse. She was a fine woman, moving so naturally with her sticks-and-bones daughter as the girl hissed and struggled. Mrs. Levy wore clothes from the final years of widowhood, and she had the careful beauty of an older woman. She dressed for her face, with a collar of pearls, and for the things that do not age: a discreet folding bustle for her womanly silhouette, and a creased shirtwaist for her impressive bust. I am not good at age; what was she, Alice? Forty-five or -six? She had a dark-complected face shaped like a hazelnut, with a bow hairline and uncolored lips. She smiled and scolded as she daubed the girl, but she was not looking at her. She was looking, with those deep brown feminine eyes, straight at me: "Mr. Tivoli, it's wonderful to meet you at last, don't flinch, Alice, it's not that cold."

Alice! I had her name, and now she was twice the girl I'd known before.

"I hope you're happy with your brother's old home, we just love it here, don't we, what were you doing, you foolish girl? You slap them, they sting you, ah well, I hope it won't swell, and if it does it will remind you, won't it? Alice, sit still. Now you've got your dress wet, and we'll have to air it. I met your sister-in-law, Mr. Tivoli, and she's a charming lady, so sad, so sad."

Hughie snickered. "That's right, Mr. Tivoli, your lovely *sister-in-law*."

It was all a scene that Alice's mother was directing. Every moment that I stood there, seeing Alice, the girl was growing ever clearer to me, ever larger; I watched her blinking her tears away, red with anger, and sighing as her mother held her hair. Yet Mrs. Levy was pulling me in the opposite direction, taking away my right to have a schoolboy's heart, replacing it with the leather flaps of an old man, someone whom stung-Alice could never love.

"Alice, be quiet, this is your landlord, Mr. Tivoli. He is old South Park, aren't you, Mr. Tivoli?"

She was crumbling me before her daughter's eyes. My hat felt far too tight and it occurred to me that it wasn't mine; I must have picked up the wrong one at some party.

"Not old at all, Mrs. Levy," I said, then, "Hello, Alice," which had no effect on the girl, who was staring elsewhere with a riveted gaze, but which made the older woman laugh in a downward, separating scale like a string of pearls.

Alice turned to me at last. "I hope you don't make noise upstairs like the last couple. They sounded like cattle."

Mrs. Levy attacked her daughter with a reptilian noise. "Besides, Mr. Tivoli," the widow added, "I noticed the beautiful rugs you've brought from your old home on Nob Hill. What a soft, lovely household you'll have!"

Mrs. Levy had a charming way with conversation, and I was a

child of seventeen, so I could only follow where she led. I spoke
of rugs, Brussels rugs, their color and feel, and I could almost
taste them on my tongue as I kept up this dusty, woolen conversation while all the time I could have been asking Alice about her
schooling, her piano, her travels; I could have been hearing Alice's voice. Instead, I had to watch the sweet girl staring off beside
me and falling ever further into her own thoughts. The pain of
the sting must have subsided under her mother's care or the dull
growl of my voice, and dear young Alice was dropping, dropping
into some imaginary life I longed to share.

"... I think, I think it's nice to have rugs around."

Alice: "Ugh."

"And damask love seats, I saw them too," Mrs. Levy said, as
proud as if they were her own. "I'm impressed, Mr. Tivoli. You
seem quite taken with the household, for a man."

But I'm not a man! I wanted to say, but she had already paused
politely and then asked about the person beside me, whom I had
completely forgotten.

"I'm Mr. Hughie Dempsey," Hughie said with all smoothness,
tipping his hat to Mrs. Levy and her blinking, dreambound
daughter.

"Ah, Hughie," Alice repeated.

"He is a close friend of the family," I said.

Mrs. Levy was gathering her daughter together by the waist, as
one carries cut flowers to a vase. "Wonderful, wonderful. I should
get poor Alice in and treat her neck. I hope to see you visiting,
Mr. Dempsey. And of course, Mr. Tivoli, we will have you and
your sister-in-law over for dinner soon."

Bows, nods, smiles, and as the girl was carried into the house,
worrying once again about the sting's poison, I stood as still as
any of our ornamental iron dogs. Some people were making a
commotion in the park behind me, and through my haze I could
make out a man walking along, waving a flag of caution as a

steam-powered carriage made its exhibitory circle to general shouts and jeers, but the wonder of it was lost on me, for I was working to think how I could get into our lower story without my mother, find Alice alone, and convince her of what I truly was.

Beside me Hughie's amused voice: "Mr. Tivoli, I believe you are wearing my hat."

All of a sudden, life was gorgeous broken glass. There was no moment when I did not feel the pain of Alice's presence underfoot, and sometimes when I stood in the parlor listening to Mother's explanation of our accounts, or weary recitation of her night beside the spirit lamp, I stepped to different places on the carpet, wondering, Is Alice underneath me now? Or now? And so I would move across the parlor like a knight on a chessboard, hoping that when I reached the point above Alice, when I stood in shivering alignment, I would feel the warmth of her body, the scent of her hair rising upwards through the house.

Hughie thought I was acting like a fool. "Don't think about her," he said. "She's fourteen. She wears her hair down and probably still plays with dolls. She doesn't know about love." Then he would flip another card into his hat across the room, intimating that he knew—as we often do at seventeen—all about the matters of the heart.

But I could not be stopped. She swam like a mermaid in the swamp-tank of my dreams. I lay in bed with the window open, hoping I would hear the sound of her voice screaming at her mother from the kitchen—"I'm going crazy in this house!"—and it would enter like a sweet poison into my ear. Or I would hear faint footsteps, and I'd picture my girl in her black stockings and white dress dipping her finger into a fresh-baked chocolate cake and then trying to cover her crime. I plotted all sorts of ruses in those weeks and months as I listened to her below me, singing to herself like a phantom lady, or waking from a nightmare with a shout. I thought perhaps I'd come up with some household repair that needed doing. Normally, of course, we got some local men to help with the house, but maybe I could convince Mother that I was the one to do it. Hughie shrugged his shoulders at this, sniffing to say it just might work. Some minor task, a peek behind the wainscoting for mice, a paint touch-up. Anything so I could be near her.

Not that things went well when I did get close. I charted her movements with the science of an astrologer, and knew she went to Mrs. Grimmel's Girls' Academy each morning at exactly eight with a bow in her hair and cake crumbs impastoed on her lips, and returned each afternoon at two; sometimes she did not come until much later, in another family's yellow surrey in the company of two other girls with wine-dark hair and glasses. It was only on those occasions with her friends that I saw my Alice truly happy, waving her arms to part the waters for her story, because after she yelled goodbye on the dark stones of 90 South Park, she always turned to face the house with the jaded expression of late childhood and the loathing step of a golem. I often tried to put myself in the garden just as she might be coming home, but I could never time it right and Mother was always calling me inside for some chore.

I did place myself correctly once, pretending to fix the iron gate. I had just returned from a job interview at Bancroft's—a job that would keep me for over twenty years, filing documents for a thirty-volume *History of the West* that Mr. Bancroft was publishing—and I looked down the street to see moody Alice stomping along the two-bit boards of the sidewalk. The light went whitewash for a moment.

"Hello, Mr. Tivoli."

"Hi, Alice. How was school?"

My eyes had cleared enough to see she wore my favorite hairdo:

barley-sugar curls with a floating lily. She pinched a sly corner of a smile.

"Idiotic, Mr. Tivoli," she said. "As always."

"I'm . . . I'm sorry."

"But I did decide never to marry."

"What . . . never?"

She shook her head, sighing. "Never. We were reading Shakespeare, and I think *The Taming of the Shrew* is a real tragedy. There's a waste of a good woman."

"Yep," I said. I hadn't read this one.

"Miss Sodov didn't agree. I had to rewrite my essay. How crazy! Now there's a shrew." Suddenly her tone became conspiratorial: "Mr. Tivoli, I wanted to ask you about—"

"Max!" my mother said from the doorway. "What are you doing there? The gate is fine. Hello, Alice, don't dawdle with Max there. I think your mother especially wants to talk to you."

Alice rolled her eyes and moaned, then lumbered into my house. Mother stood there, smiling without an idea of what she'd done. For a moment, I plotted matricide.

*

There is a little lie in here. I have made my heart into a camellia floating in a bowl of clear, pure water when in fact it was a dark and bloated thing. It was absolute pain to watch my Alice pass under my window every morning and never once look up in curiosity or tenderness at the gargoyle perched above her. And it was not with stars set in her hair that I pictured her while I lay in bed each night. No, my thoughts obsessively recalled a single base moment.

It was late in the evening, after supper, and I had slipped out into a corner of the back garden because I couldn't read my book, or think, and had to go to the rosebushes there and crush a little flower in my fist. I had been weeping for a while when you arrived. Alice, you were in your chemise and pantaloons. I think you were worried you had dropped something earlier in the day, a valuable pin or brooch your mother would scold you for, and so you slid through the back door, closing it carefully, and hurried into the darkness of the grass, whispering, searching every blade, heedless of how you looked. I stood unbreathing in my dark corner. On your knees, cat-stretching your arms into the yard, I could see through the neck of your loose cotton chemise a pink landscape of skin. You turned and writhed in your cloud and I turned and writhed in mine. I saw your legs stretching and tensing as you hunted and jerked your body in hope; women's pantaloons were devious things in those days, split down the crotch with overlapping fabric, and once you shifted just carelessly enough to allow the veil to part and I glimpsed the vulnerable blue veins of your thighs. A cat leaped in the yard; you froze, the chemise settling off one shoulder. Then, abandoning yourself to fate, surely imagining a lie that might save you, you ran to the back door, opening it to make a bright square and then, closing it behind you, a dark one. I spent all night looking for your jewel, darling, but found only a hairpin, a bird's egg, and two battered coils of grass where your knees had been.

The agony that one night caused me! The blueness of those veins colored everything in sight, and every night I had to rid the world of you just to sleep, just to survive another day. Sammy, close your ears. I did this in the most obvious, the most boyish of ways. I'm sure you think no one was ever like you in the world, and that young men in my day, adrown in love, secured their wrists in wolfman-chains until the dawn. No, we succumbed like all young men. Forgive my crudeness, Alice, but I was crude, and I hope you'll find it flattering, now that you are old as well, to think of me in bed, staring at my memory like a French postcard, watching the starlight trickle into the darkness of your clothes.

I did not climb down the trellis to peek into her window; I did not hang a mirror discreetly from a tree so I could see every holy one of the nightly hundred brushes of her sweet hair as she stared bored into the looking glass; I did not sneak into the carriage house to touch the seat from which she had just descended, feeling the startling warmth my fidgeting girl had made there. I imagined all these things but did none of them. No, I was left standing on the carpet and trying to feel her soul's vibration (damn those Brussels rugs) and holding the memory of what I considered to be the closest I would ever get to love.

"Don't go on so much," Hughie told me when we went out on our bone-shaking bicycles. "You'll get love. You'll get better love than she has to offer, I can tell you. I've got some books you can read, but don't keep them too long. I think my father knows I took them."

I read the books. They had nothing to do with love, but they kept me up very late night after night. One, perhaps acquired for the collection by Mr. Dempsey to convince himself this was a form of study, turned out to be a tract on spermatorrhea and terrified me for almost a week, but the others were a source of great knowledge and fascination. I especially enjoyed the pictures. I returned them all to Hughie and we did not speak of them, just exchanged an understanding flick of the eyes. I had been distracted, at least, but I still was no nearer to love.

The opportunity I was looking for came through Mrs. Levy herself. Desperate, heartaching, red and ugly from lack of sleep, I decided I had to take a chance; I had to have another photograph to fondle in my bedroom. I rashly decided on the house-repair idea and went downstairs in shirtsleeves, a badly tied cravat, and with a yet-unformed idea about needing to examine a leak in her daughter's room.

"Mr. Tivoli!"

Mrs. Levy stood at the open door, smiling only faintly and touching her hair, which was middle-parted and done up with surprising sloppiness in puffs on either side of her head. A few presses of her experienced hand put things in place, and she stood slightly away from the door, embarrassed or signaling me that I was welcome. The sun pinkened her face. She was in unwidowlike green and wore an old-style bustle high at the back of her skirt. Mrs. Levy seemed conscious of her artificiality and straightened herself slightly. She made these small but profound adjustments in the first moments I saw her in the doorway, distracting me from her maneuvers by light, intelligent conversation:

". . . something about the evening positively Shakespearean, don't you think? Something about being in a grove of trees, like Arden? I wonder if that feeling will ever change. I wonder if a hundred years from now people will be standing at their doorways looking at the trees with that comical sensation of being in love."

She had transformed herself into the old Mrs. Levy again and gave a light rendition of her laugh—that descending string of pearls. "I'm being stupid. Please come in, Mr. Tivoli. I'm sure Alice would love to see you, too."

"I've come to check the paint," I began, but found I was already inside the house, inside my own old hallways repainted in dimmer colors and sectioned by various wallpapers, dadoes, and friezes so that it was like coming upon an old friend done up for some event—a state dinner or a chowder party—looking so unlike themselves that you blink awkwardly and turn away, kindly refusing to recognize this strange person attached to a beloved face. I found no scent of my childhood here. This was not like walking through a pyramid tomb of the past, knocking against my old relics; this felt very new; someone else had cracked and repaired that porcelain figure; it was a museum of Alice. For there she was.

"Alice, Mr. Tivoli is here to check . . . the paint you said? Say hello, dear girl, and maybe wipe your hands, thank you."

Alice's deep brown hair was up; she looked like a woman. She stood up from the settee and set down her book (*From the Earth to the Moon*, the distance between us in that room, my dear).

"Well, gee, hi there, Mr. Tivoli," she said mockingly as she smiled and shook my hand. These were the most ordinary gestures, given to me as she gave them to all others. I searched desperately for some sign that something dear was hidden for me in this routine, but very quickly she was sitting back on the couch, lifting her book. She wore the strangest dress of gossamer satin, which had a sheen of age about it that had probably gone unnoticed in candlelight. Some hairs clung to the fabric, burnished gold hanging on a sleeve. The light was ribboned throughout her hair, which was parted and coiled elaborately around her head as it might be for a dinner party. These were not the costumes Mother and I had seen them wearing that morning on their way to temple. They had been playing in the closet, and they had done each other's hair. So this was what lonely women did the whole Sabbath day long.

"You both look nice," I said, and grimaced, trying to shake the burlap from my tongue.

Mrs. Levy smiled conspiratorially at Alice, who finally turned human in my presence: she blushed. She touched her hair, sighing and looking everywhere but at me and her mother, as if searching for some escape from the room in which she had been caught playing dress-up with her old mother. I had done this; I had made a little flame under her skin. I took the moment—snip—and coiled it in the enamel locket of my heart.

Mrs. Levy sat, motioning for me to sit as well. She turned to her burning daughter. "You know, Alice, a cup of tea would really hit the spot right now, wouldn't it?"

Alice said, "Ugh," then stared angrily at her book.

Mrs. Levy looked warmly at me. She sat perfectly motionless and lovely, knees to the side so that her dress could fit in the chair, and I saw she had already loosened her bustle so that it lay more naturally. It must have been an old dress, something from her courtship with Mr. Levy long ago in Philadelphia, a shimmering vestige of girlhood and vanity.

And she continued to look at me, signaling something from deep inside her eyes. I looked back to Alice, who sulked in the settee, then to her mother and that mysterious smile.

"Where's Tillie?" I asked, referring to their maid.

Mrs. Levy shook her head. "A family emergency. Somebody's died, I think, or is going to die. In Sonoma, so we're all alone."

A tilt of her head, a blink of the eyes. What was she trying to tell me?

"Shall I make tea?" I ventured.

The room released its breath. Mrs. Levy laughed again and Alice let out a little snort of amusement, shaking the ebony wreaths of her hair, twisting the ribbons of light all over.

"Wouldn't that be wonderful, Alice?"

"Oh, absolutely wonderful, Mother. Stunning."

Her mother shot her a mean look. "I appreciate it, Mr. Tivoli."

I went into the kitchen, utterly perplexed. There, the tea things were already set out on a silver platter. I lit the gas of the stove in that old kitchen where I used to sit beside John Chinaman as he haggled with the bread and fish vendors who came to this back door. I boiled the water and made the tea while Mrs. Levy stood there in the room with me, humming something under her breath. And then, with no help from her at all, nothing but the encouragement of her pearl-drop eyes, I arranged the tea things in the parlor directly in front of Alice, who gave me a little breath of gratitude before setting at the cherry cake. I sat back. I realized they had been sitting in the parlor all afternoon, distracting themselves with hair and costumes, weary, thirsty, and half starved.

I was a fool; I had seen so little of the world that I didn't know what the Jewish Sabbath might mean to the Levys. Hughie, who had somehow heard of these things, informed me that my Levys had to get gentiles to do for them what they could not do for themselves. Heating or even serving tea for themselves was forbidden, he said, shrugging his shoulders. Another boy of Hughie's acquaintance knew even more, earning his pocket money by working at Temple Beth El as their "Shabbos goy," as he called it. "They pay me to put out the candles," he said, smiling. "Or take tickets. It's crazy. And they don't even pay me, they leave the money in a little pile, like they forgot it there." This boy (red-haired, skinny, whom Hughie liked but whose name I have forgotten) told me their holy book forbade my Levys from even enjoying a candle that one of us had lit unless we lit it for our own pleasure before they entered the room. I imagined Alice waiting in her dark bedroom for me to enter, pretending I had lit the candle for myself. There she would sit, gauging my own pleasure at the flame before enjoying it herself—would this be nothing less than love? It was as close as I dared get.

In reality, I did very few of these tasks for the Levys. Their maid, Tillie, though Irish Catholic, was a veritable clairvoyant in their household, understanding the least squint or shiver to mean the fire must be built again or the gaslights brought up a little. She knew which sighs meant tea, which tosses of the hair meant bathwater should be run, and though sometimes I heard the furious shouts as Mrs. Levy caught her stirring beef gravy with a milk spoon, and watched as the angry mother stomped out back to bury the defiled object, Tillie kept the Levys in the same great middle-class comfort that we, upstairs, Protestantly free to boil Saturday tea, were enjoying. I wonder, though, how devout they really were; I've learned since that some of their practices were unusually lax, and that neither of them really believed in God. But they did keep up this Sabbath ritual, even if, in truth, they rarely needed me to aid them.

But memory reverses, sometimes. The things we did every day diminish into specks and unequaled events, chance encounters, bloom like ink spots on the page. So while the Levys only needed me on rare occasions, these are the times I remember from those months at South Park when they lived below us. I usually brought Hughie along for reassurance, and once he even came with Mother, on one of her few outings in the months before my sister was born, to a meal at the Levys. We all dressed carefully and had a few sips of sherry before we made our way down, and I had the time of my life because, somehow, with joke-cracking Hughie to distract the mothers, Alice at last began to notice me. Seated between me and my friend, she paid no attention to the younger man but kept drawing letters in her potatoes that I tried to mimic in my own, and while I knew this was a childish game we were playing, I pretended that these were messages for me, and that if I paid attention she might spell out some urgent call for love.

"Alice! What are you doing! And Mr. Tivoli, I'm ashamed of you. A man of your age. But you're forgiven as long as you tell us the story of that chain around your neck."

Alice leaned forward and touched my necklace. "Nineteen forty-one. What does it mean?"

"Nothing."

"The year the world's gonna end?"

Hughie broke in and said it was the number of stagecoaches I'd robbed as Black Bart, which made the women laugh and forget my little golden tombstone, which I now hid under my cravat. I looked away from the conversation. Mirrors were set between the windows of the room and so gave me a view alternating between a scene of the backyard—in which an orange cat crawled across the lawn—and each of our reflections:

There was Mother, in her pearls and a jacketed charcoal dress that she had altered following a pattern in *Godey's Lady's Book*. She had an air of such elegant patience in the lustred light of the room that, rather than looking like a woman on hard times, she seemed like a duchess fleeing from her country in the costume of her maid. There in the window was the cat, padding through the grass. There was Mrs. Levy in curled Roman hairdo, canted forward with her head on her gathered hands, touching everybody with her intelligent eyes, as in a ritual. Now she looked at me with those light-catching girandole eyes, now she turned them on my mother. There, in the next window, the burning tail of the cat on its quest. Hughie, florid and sweating a little, was dressed all in butternut as if he were a Rebel soldier or a man heading out to picnic, touching and adjusting his oddly small-knotted bow tie in a gesture that might have been uncertainty or pride. In the window, the cat was on the fence, hovering, considering a leap into the darkness of the next yard. And there was Alice. Plainly dressed, neck long as a plume, hair up and womanly, she fondled her borrowed earrings with polished fingers, turned away from Hughie's joking as if from a burning thing. I froze and tried not to let her know I saw: there was Alice, sideways in the mirror, looking at me at last. The cat leapt out of sight, a flame off to another hell.

I should explain the wetted ink; these are not tears. Last night we had a thunderstorm.

We never had these in my San Francisco, so I hope I am not revealing my location too much by saying the hills east of this flat town act as nets, bagging us eel-swarms of electricity. I am unused to storms, and tend to bark and huddle like the family dog. In a way, this is useful, since it keeps my childish cover, but I don't want to be this sort of child. I want to be your sort, Sammy, the shouting kind, the brave kind. But there I am under the bed with Buster, both of us bristling and shivering away until the woman of the house comes to flick on the lights. Is it old-fashioned of me to abhor the electric?

Last night it burglarized the middle of a dream. I was with Alice again, in love again. I won't give you the details, doctors. All I will say is it was a lily pond of Alices, old and young, in aprons and dresses and pearls, and I was happy in my dream until it was bloodied by a stab of thunder.

"Alice?" I cried without thinking.

"Shut up," Sammy called from his bunk above me, and went back to sleep.

Light bloomed across the ceiling. The dog and I froze, awaiting the end of the world. A wait, a wait, you can never be ready enough, then it comes on—gotcha!—fresh as hate.

I must have screamed a little. Sammy groaned and called me a filthy name.

Buster was in my bed now, skinny and quivering like a tuning fork, staring at me with his little-girl eyes. He smelled of garbage but I could not put him out, so I pulled him towards me. He was operatically grateful but got nervous, lost his footing, and fell on top of me so doggishly that we both yelped and, embarrassed, scuttled in the sheets before the next blast of the fox hunt. A flash, a roar. We were a pile of fools.

A light went on in the hall; at least the current was still on. "You boys okay?" came your mother's voice.

"Yes!" I said.

Sammy: "Duckbrain's pissing his pants."

She came to me and held me. She smelled of sleep and cream and singed electric bed warmer. She cooed a boy's name in my ear. Then she patted my arm three times and left, taking tremulous Buster with her, and I felt, for once, as if it might have all been worth it.

"Jesus Christ," came your voice, Sammy, from above. You sighed, fell back asleep in the snore I know so well. The thunder made a long, dull quake in me.

I will keep writing. These are not tears, these are not tears.

Mrs. Levy always let me know when Tillie would be gone. She had all kinds of ways, but mostly she left a card with a corner torn, and every Saturday when we returned and went through the silver card receiver in the front hall, I longed to find her little message there. The moment I found the card, I went downstairs and, often as not, discovered the two of them in some kind of desperate situation that needed the slightest help from a gentile's hand to set aright.

One Friday evening, for instance, after I had been dining with Hughie on Market Street, where we'd glimpsed Mammie Pleasant, the voodoo witch, Maggie opened the door for me and showed me the card receiver, knowing I was always eager to find a message; I think she knew it had to do with a girl. I found the card with some excitement, but first I went to Mother in the sewing room and exchanged versions of our days while her sewing bird held another golden gown so recently dyed widow-black. I listened and nodded and finally withdrew and raced to the Levys' door, but no one answered. I rang a few times, and was about to give up when I heard a gleaming voice coming from around the side of the house: "Mr. Tivoli! We're out back!"

And there they were, sitting in the chill of the San Francisco summer night, in their warmest clothes. It was a sad scene: they had dragged their parlor's tête-à-tête out into the yard and were sitting on it doing embroidery by the light of the moon. Mrs. Levy wore beautiful furs I had never seen before, one of those enormous hats that ladies wore in the eighties, a dark tornado of feathers, and pale suede gloves that did not match. Alice was also in fur, a thin sealskin much too large for her, and a fur cap that made her eyes, in moonlight, seem like precious things brought round the Horn. They dropped their threads and laughed to see me. I discovered later they had been like this for hours.

It was unclear what had gone wrong; they knew Tillie was away visiting a dying relative, so Alice had lit the gaslights just before sunset and they had sat down to a good briskety Sabbath meal. Then—perhaps the gas cut out, or an open window brought a breeze—every light went out and they were thrust into cold and darkness; they had not even built a fire. So here they were, too tired to go and visit friends but too bored to sit in a dark room, talking to the taciturn ghosts of my grandparents through the walls. They had gathered their warmest family furs, carried the tête-à-tête into the moonbright yard, and continued their evening's activities, laughing and telling stories to each other in the brisk night air.

"I think I'll light your gas again," I said, having learned the way to phrase this thing.

"Oh no!" Mrs. Levy objected, this time more seriously than usual. "No, it's lovely like this. Bring a coat, Mr. Tivoli. And wouldn't a cup of hot coffee be wonderful, Alice?"

"Yes, oh yes," Alice panted through her skins.

I went upstairs and found my best frock coat with buttonholes of twisted black silk I thought might shine in moonlight. I boiled coffee and poured it into the electroplated Oriental samovar set on the table. Outside, I saw that Mrs. Levy had moved from the sofa to stand in a spotlight from the moon where her fur seemed to bristle with the instinct of its animal past.

"How gorgeous you look, Mr. Tivoli," she said, leaning against a tree and smiling as if about to start an aria. I poured the coffee into the queer glass cups they owned, and the ladies dipped down with eerily identical flower-plucking gestures and began to sip. I made some mmm's of pleasure and they laughed again, free to love the coffee they had both been craving. Mrs. Levy motioned ghostily: "Please sit beside Alice, she's a ball of warmth."

"I couldn't . . ."

"This coat itches," Alice explained.

"Please sit, Mr. Tivoli, you've worked all day and now all night."

I don't think people own these tête-à-têtes anymore. Some minor god must have been punished for bringing them down to us. A tête-à-tête such as the one I found wet with moonlight that evening was a sofa shaped like an S, made of two armchairs facing in opposite directions but sharing a middle arm. You must picture it: a couple sitting ear-to-ear, glove-to-elbow. So when I began to take my place as Mrs. Levy instructed, and looked straight at my befurred and itching Alice, I was closer to her than I'd ever been. The wind blew and a hair floated out from her hat, stretched into the air, and landed on my lower lip, sticking there like a fishing line. I felt the hook bleeding into my mouth. Alice did not seem to care or notice but merely smiled.

Mrs. Levy was posing against the tree, her fur falling open to reveal her scarlet departure from widowhood, which had taken place in the last few weeks. Jasmine bloomed around her. "Shakespearean again, isn't it, Mr. Tivoli?"

I dared not move or speak but stared straight at the mother, blinking. I noticed it was a full moon tonight and her movements cast shadows along the grass as if it were bright day. It occurred to me, as she talked, that she stood directly over her buried spoons.

Then luck broke over me. There was a sound from the front of the house and Mrs. Levy bowed theatrically before doing the unthinkable: leaving her daughter alone with the neighbor, this kindly, elderly man.

Alice said, "I think maybe I was born in the wrong time."

"What?" I tried to speak softly, not wanting to detach the hair from my lip.

She stared away from me to where the moon was cresting the trees. Then she said, "Tonight, for instance. I love it tonight."

"Well, yes . . ."

"Nothing modern. No kerosene lamps smelling things up, or gaslight. Hurts your eyes. No groups of people crowded around a stereoscope, or a piano singing another round of 'Grandfather Clock' for heck's sake. I wish every night was just starlight and candles and nothing to do. We would have so much time."

I was afraid any minute she might turn around and the hair would fall away, uncoupling us. I wanted to say something to keep her talking, looking at the moon, traveling back to her simpler age, but I could say nothing. I just kept still, looking into her eyes.

She continued in her slightly hoarse voice: "It's hard to imagine such a different life. We'd think about light all the time. You know that when it got dark in winter and there wasn't much light, you would have to do everything before sundown, well, there weren't any streetlights on country roads back then, were there? How frightening. And you couldn't read at night except by candlelight, and you probably saved your candles very carefully. Not like us. You made your own, they were everything to you, if you read books. And you had to read, what else was there to do? They had so few nice clothes they never went out. They didn't have parlors or nonsense like Wardian cases and kaleidoscopes or watching magic lantern shows. There wasn't any of that to do. There were just . . . people. Think of it."

Alice lay silent and I worked my nerve up to say something: "They went to balls."

She shook her head, still facing the moon. "I mean a long time ago. I mean before kerosene lamps, and I don't mean special evenings like balls, I mean evenings like this. Ones we like to kill with a parlor game." Then my young love looked at me at last and my chest went cold with fear: "How could anyone fall in love by gaslight, I ask you?"

"And yet they do," came a voice behind us. Her mother was back.

Alice was still looking at me. "Was it like that, Mr. Tivoli? Candles and long hours in the evening? When you were a boy?"

"No," I said softly.

"Mr. Tivoli isn't that old, Alice! Really! We had kerosene lamps when I was a girl, you know. And pianos."

Alice blinked for a moment and faced the moon again. "Too bad. I'm in the wrong time. I want all my nights to be like this."

Mrs. Levy seemed to be smiling. "I do like the moonlight."

Alice considered this. "The dark, too, and the cold," she said. "And the silence."

The last word came almost as a command; we were silent. Alice closed her eyes and breathed in the night air, and this action, just the contraction of her shoulders under the oily gleam of sealskin, detached the invisible hair. I was alone again. Mrs. Levy stood before me against a tree. She was looking up at the stars; you could just see her breath forming in the chill air before her face, a ghost mask. We were all breathing, all wearing these masks. It was like a play of some kind, with the bright moon and the furs and hats and the little audience of spoons below us; I did not know what it meant. I saw Mrs. Levy lower her head and smile; I saw Alice breathing openmouthed up to the stars, her cheeks webbed with color; I saw my old hand resting against her sleeve, desperate to tap a code of some kind to her. I saw how the moon had dropped into her cup of coffee. It struggled there like a moth. Then I saw her lean forward, her mouth in a silent kiss, and as she blew on the furrowed surface to cool it, I saw the moon explode.

⁂

Later that night, after I had lit the gaslights, carried in the tête-à-tête, and started a fire in the Levy house, after I had lit the short-burning candles in their rooms, I went upstairs to find Maggie standing like the sewing bird with a sealed note in her grip:

> Max: *It's more than I can bear. Come to the garden at midnight.*
>
> —*the girl downstairs*

Some things are so impossible, so fantastic, that when they happen, you are not at all surprised. Their sheer impossibility has made you imagine them too many times in your head, and when you find yourself on that longed-for moonlit path, it seems unreal but still, somehow, familiar. You dreamed of it, of course; you know it like memory. So I didn't hesitate. I took the note from Maggie and threw it on the fire. I changed my clothes to finer things and blackened a wet handkerchief by wiping the day's soot from my face. I remembered the moon in a cup of coffee.

She was there in the garden. The moon had set; I could only see the glow of white showing from under furs. She was sitting on a bench beneath the trees. The twigs cracked under my feet in the dark garden and she stood, silently watching me approach. Off far away a fire engine sang in steam. A night-blooming cactus in the yard was on full show for no one in particular. I came closer and I could hear her gasp; I could see her holding her hands together and then, when I was close enough for her to see me clearly, she took my arm and whispered something before she kissed me. I was still and quiet and shocked. Seeing my frightened eyes, the widow was unable to hold in her laugh; she leaned back her head and out it came, that string of pearls. Reader, I was seventeen years old.

❦

Dear Mrs. Levy is dead now, buried south of San Francisco in the Jewish part of Colma. She died in her seventies, after a prolonged illness in Pasadena, where her good daughter tended to her almost daily. Her skin became spotted and pale and she allowed no visitors in her last years; she took to wearing her old widow's veil when her lawyers would come with documents for her to sign. She died without a penny to her name, and I picture an older Alice weeping by her mother's bed, holding a hand so thin that the rings no longer fit her fingers. The cold hand of my first lover.

I will be discreet. We must be gentle with the dead; the dead can say nothing for themselves. I will only tell you she was kind and generous with me over the weeks we spent together in the darkness of the garden and, more than once, in the midnight dangers of our South Park. She was confused and touched by the innocence of old Mr. Tivoli, and I think she took my trembling and moodiness for love, because after we were done and I lay shivering and gasping on the ground, Mrs. Levy would stare at me and, just for a little while, her eyes would star over in tears. She was a woman, not a girl, and though she had often been lonely, our nights were not desperate ones for her. They were simply "a little honey for my heart," as she always whispered in my ear. Mrs. Levy, you never said it but you probably loved me. You were kind to me and I treated you badly and in some hell you are all smiles today, measuring my private seat of fire.

Why did I do it? Why, when my poor eyes squinted into the garden and saw not my sweet Alice's face among the fuchsia but her mother's, did I not step back into the house? No one would have been hurt; it could easily have been construed as nerves or, better still, propriety calling for nothing further to be said of women in dark gardens. And nothing magic happened; the strands of starlight did not bind me to the spot; I could have left at any moment. But I was young. She thought I was an old businessman with a butterfly heart, but I was an ordinary boy of seventeen who had never known what it was to smell a woman's hair that close, or feel a hand brushing his skin, or see a face unlatched with longing. It is almost another kind of love, being loved. It is the same heat but from another room; it is the same sound but from a high window and not your own heart. Brave or carefree people will not understand. You, Sammy. But for some of us, the young or old or lonely, it might seem a palatable substitute and better than we have. We are not in love, but we are with someone in love, and the spare dreams of their days are all for us.

Think of it: I had never been kissed. And I had no sense, from my life as an old man, that I would ever be touched or loved by a woman. I was unprepared for my own body; Hughie's books had taught me what was what, but not what I might feel, and it all happened quicker than my dull mind could handle. From the moment Mrs. Levy took my arm under those trees, she moved without doubt—my very presence there meant I was willing—and I, heavy with doubt, could not keep up with her hands and kisses and her little whispers like folded birds placed in my ears. I could not keep up with the heat under my skin, or the scrape of her nails as she undid my shirt buttons and I was bare to the night. The body, that pale spider, stuns the mind; it wraps it up in silk and hangs it from a corner so that the body is free to go about its business. I awoke to find myself lying in the phlox, hardly able to breathe, while Mrs. Levy sat above me, glad-eyed, lunarly bare-bosomed, stroking my hair and whispering: *You're a good man, Max, don't worry, you haven't touched a woman in a while, have you? Max, you good, good man.*

I was Mr. Tivoli on the steps and in the mail, but I was Max in her arms, dear Max, handsome Max, strong and eager Max. I had never heard my name said so many times, in so many ways, all of them tender and good, as if that name—which always tasted of hard tack in my mouth—were so rich it could only be indulged in quietly, carefully, within the secret antechamber of my ear. It was the first and one of the last times I heard my name said like that, because though women have gasped a name into my ear, it has seldom been Max. Sammy, have you heard it yet? You have had so many Sammys said to you—the "Get in here" Sammy, the "Aren't you a laugh?" Sammy, the "Come out and play" Sammy, the "Don't bother me" Sammy—but are you old enough, reading this, to have heard the very different and surprising Sammy that comes from a girl in love? For once, someone is not calling you or informing you or addressing you at all; it is not talk. She is saying it for her own pleasure, because though you are there before her, saying your name calls forth not the past Sammys she has held, but a future Sammy she imagines still kissing her like this. So Mrs. Levy conjured up a future Max, a strong man always lying in the phlox and breathing hard, and I was so unused to the feeling that I accepted him; I became him for a while, for I still answered her notes and, after a time, recognized the signal of shades in her window: one up, one down. A wink in the night; for young men in old bodies, my God, isn't that reason enough?

Of course I didn't forget my Alice. It took everything I had not to let the *ah-hiss* of her name escape into Mrs. Levy's ear, and I considered it a kind of tribute that Alice's face often played fairy-lamp-style in my mind while I trembled in her mother's embrace. Also, my situation allowed me greater access to the household below, and Hughie and I (complicitous Dempsey always came) spent many an evening carving at a fat, hard roast and surviving the older Levy's version of "Listen to the Mockingbird" in order to delight in the pleasures of the younger Levy's piano renditions of Civil War marching songs. *Peas! Peas! Peas! Peas!* we would sing. Alice stuck her tongue into the air as she pounded the piano, Hughie would bellow along and punch the air to break his boredom, Mrs. Levy blew every word like a kiss to me, and dear old page-turning Mr. Tivoli harmonized with a smile. I had one hand on the music and one pressed decorously against Alice's lacy back, where I felt the buttons of her spine beneath the buttons of her dress and, on every blessed *Pea!*, the sweet convulsion of her frame.

Mother did not come to these events; she was laid up the last weeks of her pregnancy and took daily doses of whiskey to keep her from the dangers of hysteria. Before my evenings at the Levys I would bring her dinner up to her and tell her, as always, about my day at work in the belly of Bancroft's brick whale, how the funny white-haired hatless man sold me the *Call* and I read about the three Haymarket Square anarchists still waiting to be hanged. Together, as always, we went through the cards from the receiver. She told my tarot. I read to her from a *Cosmopolitan* magazine that she was perfectly capable of reading herself, but she always closed her eyes and listened. Later, after the parlor entertainment and before the tumble in the phlox, I came upstairs to kiss her lips and snuff out the smoking candle beside her.

I was sent out of the house when she began to go into labor, and Hughie and I found ourselves in an old banker's bar drinking growler after growler of ale. From the ceiling sprang a Hindu serpent of paper, endlessly writhing down into a basket, and men picked it up from time to time to read the latest world events. Hughie wore a new mustache and was all in black; it was his uniform at the Conservatory of Flowers, the park's greenhouse where he worked.

"Have you seen the Victoria Regina?" was his new line with girls, referring to the popular name for the gargantuan water lily he tended, and they always blushed. You see, Sammy, in those days this was a racy thing to say.

"How's the Leviathan?" Hughie asked that evening, as always using his filthy term for my good neighbor.

"Oh come now . . ."

"The boys at the conservatory want to know if it's true about Jewesses."

"You told the boys?"

"Oh not the details. But are they the hottest?"

"Hughie, I don't know any other girls. In fact, I don't know girls at all. Mrs. Levy is a woman."

"You don't still call her Mrs. Levy."

"I wish I called her Alice."

"Not that now. Think of nice things. Tell me about your Mrs. Levy . . ."

I was wracked with guilt. I might pretend that this was all a way to bring myself closer to Alice, but every time I saw her on the lawn pulling weeds from her wilted helianthus, every time she turned that worry-pleated face to me, I went hollow. I was betraying the very thing I meant to save. I was unraveling from one end everything I wove from another. "How Greek," Hughie would say. I suppose it was an oft-told tale; I suppose I was not the first to make a mess of love, but it never matters, does it?

I told Hughie all the things I cannot tell you, not from bragging, not from adolescent pride, but because I dared not keep a diary in my mother's house; I had to scrawl my memories in him. For instance how Mrs. Levy prepared for our evenings by wearing a kind of sponge with a long thread for removal, how she eventually produced a pig-gut device for my own use. Hughie was fascinated. He was my great companion, after all, as mystified by everything as I. All we knew of sex was in his father's books, and I now realized they were mostly aberrations. Of course, what was I? Would my Mrs. Levy ever have loosened her corset for a boy of seventeen? It was my deformity that drew her, my mild monsterhood. Yes, Hughie always knew the whole of my life. Well, almost the whole.

The men at the ticker tape muttered and growled over news of

a dam break back east, covering a town in thirty feet of water, killing thousands. The bartender asked if I wanted another for my
son and myself.

I began: "He's not my—"

"Dad needs another," Hughie broke in, grinning, then said to
me: "Drink it down, Dad. I have to tell you something."

Off in her high room, that instant, my sister was being born. I
am glad to report that no one screamed except the newborn girl
and nothing was smothered except a mother's worry; red gleaming Mina was lifted into the world gulping like a lungfish, coughing, and then as the cord was severed and she was made as lonely
as any of us, she sang out and Mother could see through the
green mist of the chloroform pills that here was her baby. Here
was a thing that would grow old; here was a thing that would turn
beautiful and lose that beauty, that would inherit the grace but
also the bad ear and flawed figure of her mother, that would smile
too much and squint too often and spend the last decades of her
life creaming away the wrinkles made in youth until she finally
gave up and wore a collar of pearls to hide a wattle; here was the
ordinary sadness of the world.

And I myself was growing a little older as I listened to Hughie's
story. What he told me loosed a loneliness I had not expected.
Hughie sat all in black, a grave man telling a grave thing, pausing
only to accept his steam ale and to blow the foam from the top,
turning back to me with the soft eyes of a temple cat. "Don't be
angry," he kept insisting, tapping his nail on the bar just below a
carved insanity of hearts and thorned initials. "It's nothing to me,
I swear, it's nothing." From above, the smoke-trail of paper floated
down into the basket, as if returning to its burning source, as if
something other than myself were running backwards in the world.
But nothing else does; the world falls forward when it falls apart.

They were a few brief words. A cluster of glass. You see, while

I was romping with Mrs. Levy in the corner garden, my Alice had fallen in love. Simply, brutally, in love. With whom? With Hughie, of course. Who else?

Doctors, an update:

I have survived an examination just this afternoon. I avoid physicians as much as I can, and especially since I have become a little boy, but the thunderstorm of the other night has given me a sore throat. I tried to hide it with lozenges and smiles, but swallowing Mrs. Ramsey's cooking has gone from a small torture to an impossibility. All I can do is moan and grimace. The dog is terrified of me. And you, Sammy, have been teasing me mercilessly. So I have been taken to a little bungalow in the nice part of town, a windowless place with movie posters and a spool of gauze to play with. Mrs. Ramsey, that kind woman, bathed me in her concern, gave me a dry kiss, and said she would be back. So for almost an hour it was just me and the gauze and the movie-poster nurse. I have memorized the snowy battlements of her cap.

Dr. Harper turned out to be a jokey fellow with the stained-wood look of a Hollywood leading man. He stared into my throat and squinted for a while before he spoke to me.

"You don't feel well?"

"I'm fine. It's a sore throat."

He shook his head and took some notes. "It isn't. It's something very different. I've never seen anything like it." A little laugh.

Was it possible? That half a century of doctors, who had bled me, blistered me, purged, sweated, and electrocuted me, could not discover what this man caught in an instant? I have withstood Rushians and Thomsonians, Grahamites and Fletcherizers and Freudians—so had I become an old lake bass that, lazy with slipping so many barbed nooses, gets landed by a schoolboy? I am an

old man; I do not understand the world as it is, and it seems entirely possible that the new century has found an X, Y, or Z ray to
sound out a man like me. Still, in this small hamlet on the plains?
I calmed my impulse to confess; I sat still as a child.

"I need some measurements, old man," he said, smiling
mysteriously.

I shivered, then he took my height, my weight, the length of
various bones, peered into my ears and eyes and listened thought-
fully to the off-key radio of my heart. I noted the numbers myself,
but knew he could not tell that I had shrunk two inches in the
past year, lost a proportional amount of weight, and now owned
only a tight snail-wad of genitals. I lied about my medical history,
giving myself an infant hernia operation, chronic bronchitis, and
a handful of allergies, just to handicap his game. Throughout, he
tried to interest me in little jokes, but I was elsewhere, floating
above, terrified that my choking swallow was that clue, in boys'
detective stories, that always reveals our young hero to his foe.

"It's all very clear, old man. Let's find your mom and dad."

"She isn't my mother. And my dad's dead."

"Oh," he said, startled for the first time.

"What are you going to tell her?"

He grinned and tousled my hair. "I'm going to tell her everything about you."

They spent a good ten minutes in his office while I waited in
the outer room again, dead or dying of something, thinking how
to interrupt their conference, perhaps counterfeit a yellow fever
attack, and realizing with a dull laugh that I was showing my age
after all: the disease had been wiped out by 1900. That very moment, I heard the movie-reel sound of adult laughter in the hallway and there they emerged, my Mrs. Ramsey looking so young,
amused, and aglow. I was handed a green candy wrapped in
paper; Mrs. Ramsey wrote down the name of a novel she recom-
mended; Dr. Harper took the note, then gave a wink and a seri-

ous wave before departing again; and before I knew it we were out into the always-fresh sun of my new hometown. I put the candy in my pocket beside the pills I had carefully pilfered from the exam room. Then she told me my lot.

With men like Dr. Harper around, I will be forever safe. It turns out I showed early stages of what doctors call parotitis. That is to say: the mumps. A child's disease. If the quack proves to be right, I have swollen glands to look forward to and days of fever in my bedroom. But he is certain to be wrong. Have you ever heard of mumps in a man of nearly sixty?

Mrs. Ramsey took me to the drugstore and bought me a chocolate bar, a pair of roller skates and a silver toy army pistol much like one Hughie used to own. For you, Sammy, she bought the Ruf-Nek chewing gum you love. For herself, she browsed the cosmetics aisle and laughed and giggled over the potions before choosing an erotic shade of lipstick and two kinds of eyebrow pencil. She examined the scents, frowning, and finally learned from a pink-eyed clerk that her favorite cologne had gone out of style and had to be specially ordered. I asked her what it was. "Rediviva," Mrs. Ramsey replied with a sigh. I produced the doctor's prescription, which I had enhanced with my own forgery, and she took it dutifully. Then it was an easy trip to the pharmacy counter, where this little soldier became the proud owner of potassium, quinine, and a lovely blue bottle of morphine. We live in a golden age.

It was almost a week before I had him break her heart. Your heart, Alice, your bruised-peach of a heart. I did not do it out of spite; I did it because it was absolutely necessary. Now, looking back, it would have been far wiser to have Hughie run into her arms and bedevil her with cheap diamonds and carnations, and whisper sticky things into her ears; nothing turns a girl like an amateur's heart. She would have dropped him in a fortnight, I think, and not because she was stupid or fickle, but because sometimes we are frightened when the bomb we're planting goes off in our own hands. And if I had done this, what would have come of it? She would have hated Hughie, and probably me through association; she would have fallen for the next handsome boy she saw, at one of those dances she loathed attending, gone out with him, and, finding herself waiting on a foggy corner one afternoon, her heart would have been broken after all. At least this way it was managed by someone who cared.

Hughie agreed to do just as I said. He was to meet her at the Conservatory of Flowers, where she had taken to visiting him after school, and break her little heart with the sharp crack one employs to split a geode. He was to be gentle but firm and leave no tatters of love hanging in her chest; she was to be cleansed of this ridiculous sensation and thus find herself open to, even grateful for, the love of an apparently older, more considerate man. Hughie wondered at the plan; he thought it was remarkably cruel to such a pretty girl. "Pretty?" I asked, suspicious. "Did you . . . did you do something to make her feel this way?" He denied it and agreed to the task. At first I was going to hide behind a fern to watch my bit of theater, but he said this would make him nervous and he'd probably foul it up. So I was sent home and there I waited for word from Hughie that he'd cleared the brush for my arrival. I sat in the parlor and tried unsuccessfully to read; I set out a card game for myself but kept losing. I ended up finding one of my father's whatnots—a monkey's head encased in glass—and stared at it for over an hour, finding in its grotesquery a brief escape from my own.

At four o'clock, the front doorbell rang and I heard Maggie speaking to someone in the hall. I had told her I would be in for anyone except those calling on my mother. Presently there was a knock at the parlor door: Maggie, telling me there was urgent news. I waved my hand and poured a glass of whiskey for myself and one for Hughie. I steadied myself, looked out the window to where two squirrels were at war. I heard a wretched voice:

"Mr. Tivoli, I need your advice."

It was Alice.

We have no heart at seventeen. We think we do; we think we have been cursed with a holy, bloated thing that twitches at the name we adore, but it is not a heart because though it will forfeit anything in the world—the mind, the body, the future, even the last lonely hour it has—it will not sacrifice itself. It is not a heart, at seventeen. It is a fat queen murmuring in her hive. I wish I'd had it in me, when Alice stepped into the room looking so drowned and desperate, when she fell to her knees and sobbed so hotly into the wool of my pants, to send her back to Hughie. To stroke her hair (though I did that) and cup her chin in my rough hand (that too) and tell her he would kiss her in an instant; he was a boy, after all, and she was a thicket of beauty. To say "He'll love you" and "There are ways" and turn into the tilted light of the room as she wiped her face and blinked and readied herself for another battle. To let her go. But there was no heart in me. When do we grow one? Twenty, thirty years after we need it?

Instead, I looked at the head shuddering on my knees; I stared at the pale furrow between her braids as if searching for the source of a lost river. I waited until it was time to touch her, and then I did, and she did not shake my arm from her shoulder or my hand from her head but emptied herself even more into my lap. Without knowing it, she and I were conjuring her father, and we each played our parts—Alice weeping unashamedly, Mr. Tivoli hushing and shushing her—until her sniffs and gasps meant it was almost over.

She began to speak: "It's Hughie, Mr. Tivoli." I slipped my finger into the loop of her hair ribbon.

"I know," I said, then added too silently for her to hear: "Call me Max."

"He was a monster, a monster, he said . . ."

"What did he say?" With a tug from my finger, her ribbon fell out of its knot; I shivered; she did not notice.

"He said . . . he said he wanted us to be friendly. Idiot. He said he didn't want to spoil a sweet moment."

I sipped my whiskey nervously. Hughie had improvised from the script; he had treated my Alice like any girl he met on the street. "Where were you?" I asked quietly, wondering what else he had added.

She sniffed and sat back, letting my hand fall from her; the spell was undone. "It was at the Victoria Regina, like always. I always meet him there. He can usually get away for a minute and it's quiet there and you can just stare at the lilies. I was . . . I thought I'd be brave and ask him when he was going to take me out. And he said . . . oh, he said I was just fourteen. And that he wasn't interested in girls like me. At fourteen. Not that way. Girls like me? Are there really other girls like me?"

This was a little off the script, but close. I imagined Hughie getting a little stage fright, there in his uniform beside the enormous lily pads, and whispering whatever came into his head; possibly, he was truer than I'd intended. "What else?"

Some memory cut her and she winced in grief. "He said he loved me like a sister. I'm not an idiot, Mr. Tivoli."

"Max. You're not, no, no, Alice . . ."

"I know what he was saying. He was saying he can't ever love me. Wasn't he? Or . . . was he maybe . . ."

"No, no, Alice, sit here beside me . . ."

"I don't understand," she murmured.

I touched her shoulder again. Then I made a mistake: "Just forget him, Alice."

She pulled away and I saw that she hated me. It happened so quickly; one minute I was an understanding friend, a father almost, and then the next I was an old man who knew nothing of love, nothing of passion, a man who could offer only his own sad poison. But to see that hatred in her eyes; it felt as if she was gone forever and no plan of mine would ever bring her back. Hughie might wreck her heart a hundred times, but if I told my Alice to forget him, to find a sweet and loving boy nearby (perhaps nearer than she ever imagined), she would send me out of her life. She would turn again into the sullen downstairs girl who never thought of me. Those eyes, threaded with hate like opals, burning off the tears; I would have done anything to change them. So I sputtered as she looked on. And then I discovered what she had come to hear:

"I'll talk to him, I'll tell him . . . I'll mention you . . ."

"You will?"

"I'll tell him how beautiful you are."

"Does he think I'm beautiful?"

"He does. He thinks you're the most lovely girl."

"Oh my."

"Yes, the most lovely girl he's ever seen."

"The most lovely girl . . ." she repeated.

Alice left my parlor happier than when she entered it; she left with all these stupid promises of mine, done just to keep her in the room, just to force one more occasion for us to talk and to make a secret between us, for this was to be kept from her mother at all costs. I nodded, pursing my lips. When she left, she kissed my forehead, and as I smelled the soft cotton at her throat, I thought of how I was more than a confidant to her, more than the sharer of a secret; I was her only route to love. As she had once depended on me to light a Sabbath fire, so now she depended on me to bring some word to warm her heart. And though I knew the smile faintly forming on her face as she left was not for me,

and the sleepless night she would spend was not over my bearded
face, still I was there in it somewhere. I was a houseboy of her
heart. When we are very young, we try to live on what can never
be enough.

Alice, what are you thinking, reading this, now that you are old?
You know where this is leading and I'm sure you have a different
story. One, perhaps, in which you are more lost and innocent, a
little piece of Alice-glass chiming in the window, or one full of details I can never know: how Hughie laughed at your cleverness;
the thick, erotic pads of the Victoria Regina; the angry way you
missed your father; the weird sensation of that old man undoing
the ribbon in your hair. While in my version Hughie is just the
man who happened to block the light, in your memory I'm sure
you loved him for specific reasons, as we think we do; you still
warm your hands over the ember of that early love; you could
never be convinced, in your old age, that it was only chance.

I told your mother—did you know? Of course I did. I told her,
as a secret between us, that you were in love with Hughie and that
he did not deserve you. This was not a lie, but it was cruel; it was
meant to make her huff and sigh if you ever mentioned Hughie.
Looking back, this could only have made you love him more.

One night, you were different. You will remember this. One
night, Maggie let you in and you were a stone daughter striding
into the room. You didn't sit on the rug and blush; there was no
blood in you that night. You chose my father's old chair, arranged
your braid, then stared at me and said, with no accusation in your
voice: "He doesn't love me." You waved away every one of my
words, wincing just a little, and kept repeating what you were
now too smart not to see. He didn't love you; no, of course he
didn't. It had been clear from the beginning. You wore a gaudy

young girl's necklace and cheap shoes that fell from your heels. You produced a cigarette from a reticule and it was as if you said: *I am now a woman who does these things.* At fourteen, a woman who does these things. I stopped talking and let you build this other woman from smoke, breathe her into being there in the room. There was silence while she turned, all hair and tendons, in the slant of moonlight. When she was gone, I was the one who fell to the floor at your knees and wept; I can't say why. You were the one who touched my hair and said soft things that gave, as always, little comfort.

Then I heard you murmur something I cannot forget. You said, "I feel so old."

I lifted my face. "What?"

You shook your head, latching the thought back in.

"You can't feel old," I said.

You just rocked a little in your chair, your hand on my head as you lit another cigarette. The room held you in the curve of some shadow. You looked as old as you would ever be. You said, "Like I'm floating above my body. And I watch myself and my little stupid movements, how I put the kettle on for tea or brush the dust from the braid on my dress, complaining how it gets so filthy, sitting with Mother and reading the visiting cards. It takes so little to be myself, and I've done it for so long, being so little, doing such little things. But most of me is floating above, watching. As if it weren't my body. Part of me knows something that it can't bear to tell the rest."

I sat, stunned, feeling the burn of your words. A woman whose body wasn't hers, floating outside her life; you would understand, I thought. You would know what life was like for the sick, time-twisted boy who was in love with you. I watched you smoking, as if the smoke could keep the coldness in your face.

"I want to tell you something, Alice."

"I don't want to talk."

But it was too late; I had begun to say the thing my mother taught me never to say. It felt like the first words of a spell, though, the kinds of words that try to lift a curse. "I have to tell you. Listen to me. You don't have to talk. Just listen."

You took your eyes down from the gaslight and they were alive again, for a moment, and I think you hoped I was going to say something about Hughie; I think that even after this last *no*, still it was not beyond belief that there would be a *yes*.

"I'm not . . . what you think I am, it's not what I am. I know what I look like." I was speaking roughly, between hard breaths. My throat was gagging on this foolish thing, but I went on: "Alice, I'm . . . I'm seventeen. Do you see? Alice. I'm just a boy."

I felt a little rapture when your looks broke open. I think you had never considered me to be another person in the room; here I was, listening all this time, the messenger of renounced love; here I was, kneeling before you on the carpet; and all this time I had been as wretched as you.

"I'm just a boy."

I saw a sadness beating at the back of your eyes, an insect dying behind a screen.

"Do you believe me?"

"Yes."

You will remember: you held my face with both hands and, thumbs out, wiped the tears from my cheeks. There was blood in your face again; your eyes were moist like my own; you were my old Alice thinking, *Let's one of us be happy*. There in the parlor you saw through me and knew how young I was, younger than you; you gripped my face and were the soothsayer for both of us, pursing your lips over something bitter, then nodding your head in slow degrees before you kissed me. You will remember: it was you who kissed me that evening in the parlor. I tasted that last coil of smoke held in your mouth; it tasted like a word, like a *yes*. From some other room we heard a baby's undulating *oh*. You kissed me and did not pull away or change your mind; you drank from me like a thirsty girl. I was the first to say he loved you. You will remember.

I wanted to see her first thing in the morning; I could not wait. It's true I had not slept since she whispered, *Mr. Tivoli, Mr. Tivoli,* and stood to rearrange her hair and calm her swarming breath (I did cause something there, at least) before leaving me. I sat in my chair as my sister wailed into the night, and of course in my imagination I continued that evening with Alice as far as a moral man could, and then I set the cylinder back in its cradle and replayed each moment in the music box of my mind.

As I lay in bed, I went over the scene I had been rehearsing since dawn: what I would say to Alice. I had an addict's rage against himself, the rage of a reformed man waking to the evidence of his night—a scorched pipe of opium, a cold and beaded vial of ether—but feeling inside him, gnawing past his first reproach, the love of those long-desired objects; his arm is already reaching across the bed. I had to see her. Why had I told her I loved her? It might have cost me everything. But no, I rationalized, no, she needed to hear about love; everyone does. Don't they? Didn't she? Oh God, and I had said I was just a boy; she had believed me. Had she? Perhaps it was sweet, or perhaps for her it was just as it seemed: an old man wetting her face with his gross kisses. But as much as I tried to search the details of her face in the gaslight of the evening, I lost her more and more. The past had its back already turned; there was no speaking with it.

I plotted as well as I could. I would smile and laugh and pretend the night was nothing in particular; that I, like her, was baffled by tangled human moments like ours. I would apologize; no, that would give me away. I would pretend it was a private joke of ours. The old man, the old neighbor, a private joke. Unless, of course, unless I could make out on the surface of her face some ripple of hope. I got out of bed, eager to see her as soon as possible, if only to know of my fate.

"Mr. Tivoli?" Maggie's voice came from the door.

"Yes?"

"I have your coffee and a note."

On custard stationery on the silver tray, beside the toast. One edge of it was dark with spilled coffee; I glared at Maggie and she left. A note from Alice, I thought, and felt relieved. What a coward I was. Now I would not have to confront her; I could know, in a few lines, what that first kiss had meant for both of us. Here is how it began:

> *Max,*
>
> *You are a monster of the lowest kind. You are a false, betraying criminal. You are a sick, blackened, evil old man and I cannot believe I ever cared for you. To have betrayed me is nothing. To have seduced the mother is nothing, used me up, is nothing. You may toss aside my old broken heart, it doesn't matter. But Max. You have touched my girl, my Alice. And if this mother ever sees you again, I am sure to tear your eyes out.*

It was only much later, of course, that I pieced together what must have happened. Alice, late at night, arriving home in a teary whirlwind of confessions. And Mrs. Levy, sitting in a black nightgown, listening, feeling her heart fall to pieces inside her. She saw only an old man, her lover, pawing her daughter with reechy kisses. She could not have understood it was a boy of seventeen, like in a song, stealing a kiss.

But I was thinking of none of that. I was reading quickly, trying to figure out what I'd do now. Maybe a full confession, disease and all, with Mother as a witness. Maybe have Hughie talk to Alice once again. And Mrs. Levy; well, perhaps she was still in my thrall. A few perfect words and I might be saved. So I read on.

More hateful, overwritten stuff, pulled from the deepest well of a mother's rage. Some upsetting parts about the police, immediately retracted. And then a final bit that chilled me:

> *Enclosed is a check for our last rent. Our furniture is all taken care of, but there is nothing to reveal where we are going. Oh, Max, this much I will ensure: you will never see Alice again. Nor me, my moonlight love.*

Overwritten, yes, but I could tell at last what I had done. To have peeled her clothes off in the garden, night after night, and listened to her giggling in my ear. Her moonlight love. I had never thought about her, in all my worrying over Alice; she was an adult, of a different world, and I'd never considered she might be just as fragile as her daughter. And yet it seems quite clear that I shattered poor Mrs. Levy. That I took perhaps the last love in her old heart.

I heard horses breathing and battling their reins out front. A panic seized me, and I ran in my nightclothes to the window. That childhood sound of hooves and springs and leather, that old carriage noise, and below me I watched a hired two-in-hand clattering away. Black and dull, it rattled slowly across the light, the isinglass unrolled so I could see two faces in the window. There she was. My love, my sweet girl, shaking in the cage of the carriage, in traveling clothes, a bag on her lap, eyes closed against the dust cloud of her future. That was the end of the first time I loved Alice.

❧

Sammy: this is a letter from the front lines; I write this with you in the room. With you asleep beside me in this bed, muttering through some shallow dream just as Buster twitches through his own there on the floor. My writing may be shaky, for it turns out Dr. Harper's right, after all:

At nearly sixty, I have caught the mumps. And you, poor Sammy, have caught them as well.

At first Mrs. Ramsey, feeling my improbably swollen gills, sent me alone to the "sewing room," as she calls it, to suffer in solitude among the scraps of her unfinished dresses—I can see fabrics of cherries and corals and reclining geishas; or are these perhaps my fever's inventions? I have been so sad in my sickroom, writing in my journal, burning in and out of my fever like a lighthouse. But today I awoke to find a brightly opened door and another little boy being shoved inside.

"Better get it over with," your mother said as she dragged you to the bed, poor Sammy.

"Jeez, not with the duckbrain!" you shouted.

"With the duckbrain. In you go," she said, and folded you, still complaining, into these sheets warm from my sickness. That old folk wisdom, that it's better to catch it as a child than as a man—well, everything's reversed in me, I guess. I remember fifty years ago when my mother took me for a carriage ride and I was thrown into a goose-down bed with hot, irritable Hughie. Mumps again, but that time I was no child; I did not catch it. I remember Hughie's moans and mutterings made it impossible for me to read my *Boys' Life* in peace, and I lay for a week beside my best friend until he reached a level of sanity to throw me, perfectly healthy, from his bed. You, Sammy, burn brighter.

You lie asleep in the bed beside me, in an equal fever. Earlier today, after another throat-probing from chuckling Dr. Harper, we stared at the ceiling and tried to name the shadows we found there. We like to guess from sounds in the hall what your mother is up to, and from sounds outside what the ridiculous neighbors are arguing about, and you make up fantastic stories to soothe our hot brains. We are forbidden sour things, and so eat gruel night and day until we are fairly sick of it. I am your friend again, Sammy, the only other boat on this particular sea, but I am worried. When I wake from a hot sleep, I find you watching me curiously. I hope I have not been mumbling. I hope that in my fever I have not given too much away.

But what a lucky chance this virus turned out to be. To lie so close beside you, Sammy; to time each breath to yours. Fathers have traveled this far for less; dying fathers, we have traveled across the world for less, for glimpses, for the carried voices of our sons.

II

Forgive the gap in these pages; I have finally recovered from my illness and have found myself, once again, in school.

It is a humiliation, to say the least, to recite my times tables with this Midwestern crowd of children—five times twelve is six-ity— but the hardest part is to keep my voice as quiet as I can, my profile low, so that the teacher (a woman exactly my age) won't notice that odd boy in the corner scribbling his life's confession. I'm not the only child who hides this way. Some of the poorer students, with cardboard shoes and nits in their hair, sit in the back with me and glare out the window, or at the wall where seven chromolithographed presidents stare down, each with his signature hairdo. We try to fade into the plasterwork; we are the classroom ghosts. "What's the capital of China?" the teacher will ask one of us loudly, and we will quake and pause and answer, predictably: "France." A smirk from the adult, a laugh from the good kids up front, including my own dear son, and we move on to history. In a moment, I will move on with my own.

But first, Sammy, let me put down that you love me. Something in your long fever must have burned away your doubts and, after the gauntlet of the hotbed, I am once again your bosom friend. You pass me notes while our forefathers dump tea into a Boston bay; you blink and feign narcolepsy while redcoats march in lines across distant states; you allow me to see your pencil art—the automotive wonders you would produce, all bristling tubes and fold-down gadgetry—as Valley Forge swallows its frozen victims. This morning you were the ink monitor and soberly filled our clay inkwells to their brims before gaily dropping a tiny frog into mine. Until it perished, gagging on the lampblack, the creature left a leaping pattern across my lesson book so exquisite—a hail of dark roses falling from the sky—that I will try to place it here in this memoir as the only evidence that I am not lying, Sammy. Your father was beside you all along, grubby lad. And you did sometimes love him.

Onward.

⁊

I was a dead thing after Alice.

I turned eighteen, nineteen, twenty, entering the first chill of adulthood, losing the last of my gray hair. I went to work each morning at Bancroft's, I coughed at the dust of books and came home late each night, the man of my own family. I took care of Mother, little sister Mina, and the receipts and details of 90 South Park Ave no. 2. I was also in charge of no. 1, that ghost-rapping flat below us, dealing with the new renters; they were gentile and I was never called down on Fridays to pour a forgotten cup of tea or light an untended fire. Instead, I was the dispenser of paint and polish, the boss of the chimney sweep.

Alice's departure led to a maniacal obsession with the trivia of their escape and the discovery of their trail. I spoke with other Shabbos goys I had run into, badgering them until they agreed to ask around the Jewish homes, and the temple the Levys frequented on their well-dressed Saturdays. I had Hughie stalk the dress shops where the elder Levy bought her clothes, dropping flirtatious hints about his missing aunt, her lovely girl; I found myself prying open the floorboards in the bedroom, convinced I had heard the creak of a hiding place; in short, I lost my mind. But there was no trace.

Hughie tried to help me. He took me to see Lotta Crabtree perform her leather-lunged parodies of Jenny Lind, all burnt cork and fright wigs; he bought me tamales on Market, strawberry sodas at Slaven's, milk baths at Anna Held's in the Baldwin, and a nickel peek at the grand full moon one drunken night on O'Farrell.

But Hughie had his own concerns. By twenty, he was no longer the lanky custodian of the great Victoria Regina, dusting that vegetable vulva with a long-feathered mop, but had become something else entirely. He now sipped brandy in warm libraries and sang foul choruses of "Goober Peas!" in arm-over-shoulder quartets; he sewed initials into his old bright blouses and bought new ones, brighter but finer, and new collars, stays, and spats and various tweedy, glittering things. Hughie took up a clever and cruelly argumentative style of talking, a handsome sideways grin, and a few phrases—"Ye gods!" and "I swan!" and "exflunctication"—that confused the rest of us. He had all the excitement of someone newly allowed into a great country, all the tics and warts of pride, and the glow of someone happy and relieved. You see, without a word to anyone, a mention of any hopes or applications, Hughie had landed at Berkeley on scholarship, and now he had become that rare thing in my South Park: a college man.

A neat fold in fate, I think, for Hughie to climb from tutor's son to starry student while I, the once-rich monster, burrowed ever further into the honeyed Bancroft warrens. But as a dear soothsayer told me once: every face card looks back underneath.

My beard turned an autumnal chinchilla blond and I wept when Hughie told me to shave it off. "You have to decide," he said, "whether to be old or young, and I think you've been old long enough." It was a disaster. The beard, it's true, had made girls turn away from my grandfatherly face, but the mustache I kept made them laugh; I seemed too much like those widowers who brush hair over their bald heads and dye their skin a summer's bronze in winter. An antique gigolo; a joke. My waist was thinning with the receding tide of my twenties and I looked less and less like a *burgermeister* in a Brueghel, but these changes seemed impossible, artificial to anyone who knew me more than a year. *Does he wear a corset?* I could hear them snickering at my workplace, so I had myself reassigned, and spent the rest of my career at Bancroft's in solitude, hidden by old books. Hughie's taste in dressing me was hopeless, and after stepping out proudly one sunny day in one of his inventions—shirtsleeves, a cap, and white belt-looped trousers—I soon realized I looked more like a tightrope-walker than a gent. Mother, of course, agreed; her wordless face repeated: *Be what they think you are, be what they think you are.* I went back to my frock coats and opera hats and hid, once again, in the anonymity of old men. I would be old until I was young, no sooner.

As the years passed, my only companions were my sister, my mother, and Hughie. I was the priest of Alice, keeping the sacred embers glowing until her return, and then, when I could learn nothing of her whereabouts and as the years passed on without her, I became the widow to my own hopes. Like many men before me—like my missing father, I believe, and perhaps like my dear Hughie—I numbed myself to life.

And there was Mina, my beautiful and ordinary sister. At six, seven, eight, she never wavered from the charts of typical height and weight, had as much talent at the pianoforte as any young girl should have (none!) and, in short, was never precocious or particularly bright. The only thing she could draw with skill was our carriage horse (shivering Mack); any other subject became a bristling slide of paramecia. She was polite to a point, but also liked to scream in a rage before bed. In fact, her moods were not recognizably adult in any way and seemed more like the facets of a con man's dice—gorgeous piety, prim respect, bitter tears, wild lava-spouting ire—that could be weighted to fall wherever most suited her. My point at last: she was not a real person. True children never are. She was a fraud striving to be human and was, therefore, simply (and printer please put this in your plainest type) a regular girl.

Despite this blessing on our house, I was not allowed to be a regular man. Remember that to the rest of South Park I was still Mrs. Tivoli's brother-in-law, living out the last years of his bachelorhood in plodding duty. Mother decided very quickly that no chances could be taken with a child—especially not chatty Mina—and so I was introduced to my own sister as Uncle Max. "Mina, give your Uncle Max a kiss before he leaves, no, don't pout, dear girl, that's it." She didn't call me Uncle Max, of course, because from some odd church lesson she felt that, like Adam, she should give every man and animal her own proper name. She began by calling me Uncle Bean, and through a series of edits, I became Beano, then Beanhead, and eventually my final name: Beebee. She would shout it with joy in the morning—"Beebee!"—and the same way at night when I returned, with attention-getting volume at dinner when she wanted the gravy, with sorrow when I took a vase from her shattering hands, and last of all with wistful remembrance at night when I pulled the counterpane to her chin and sang to her, which she used to love.

I was envious of her youth. You can't imagine what it was like to hear girls screech at her from across the park and find that same, bloodlusting shriek coming from my sister's lips—and to realize with a shock what childhood was for her: belonging. So new to the world, she was already a part of it. To be so favored by nature; to know of no reason why anyone would not love her—in fact, to have no suspicion that one single person in the world did not love another—made her into a creature so enviable that, at times, I hated her. Each morning, I would stand in the doorway of her room watching as her eyes blinked at a day as standard and blessed as the last. As with so much else, of course, I hid these occasional splinters of hate within my flesh. "Good morning, little one," I whispered.

"Oh Beebee!"

I am a kindly monster, of course; I do not deny the world its lovely things. Its Minas.

Mother had changed, too, over the years. She had been brought up carefully, trained to be loved, so I could never have blamed her for practicing her birthright. Men came by now and then: a banker, a saloon owner with a gold cane and vulcanized rubber fillings in his smile, an actor who wore a wig. They were not so bad, but they did not stay. Instead of turning to a man, the last of which had abandoned her so ruthlessly, she turned to her daughter. Mina became the purpose of my mother's life, and that, of course, meant money. So Mother went to work.

For a while she kept her occupation secret. It wasn't seemly for a woman to work, and the career she had chosen was out of the ordinary. Her clients usually came when I was at work and Mina was at one of her dance classes, but nothing can ever be secret for long in San Francisco. The first clues were feathers left in the front parlor from very expensive hats belonging to ladies far richer than Mother was used to seeing. And then, one morning, a strange woman appeared at the front door and told me she had an appointment.

"With whom?"

She wore an expensive outfit of fur tails. "Madame Tivoli."

"*Madame* . . ." I repeated.

Mother was already rushing to the door, saying, "You're early, you're early!" and quickly got rid of the woman. She walked back into the parlor and it was there that I confronted her.

"Mother, what is going on?"

"Nothing, little bear."

But I was the man of the house. "Tell me now."

She did. In a voice so drained of life that it implied an anger too great to be expressed, she explained exactly why a rich woman would stop by so mysteriously in the morning, and why another was due this afternoon. She said this, handed me her card as proof, and then told me: "Now don't ever talk to me that way again. And I don't want to hear that you are embarrassed, upset, ashamed. This has nothing to do with you. This is about Mina. Take this tea into the kitchen and wake your sister or she'll be grouchy all day." She sat sideways in her chair as if she still wore a bustle; she was of a generation that had learned to sit this way in their youth, so she still did it out of habit and out of a sense that this antique pose was the essence of beauty. The women who sat this way are all dead now.

Her calling card said it all, as strange and simple as electric light: "Madame Flora Tivoli, clairvoyant." After so many years in the sewing room trying to speak with the past—her lost husband, lost girlhood, her son growing backwards in time—now, for the sake of her good, beautiful, ordinary girl, she would make money in commune with the future.

As for Hughie, he and I were closer than ever, and had our own adventures. We were young men, no matter what my looks might have implied, and we did live near one of the crudest, filthiest, liveliest places on earth: San Francisco's Barbary Coast. It was located east of Chinatown, where the old town square used to be, just close enough to the docks for sailors to stagger off their boats, spend all their dough on drinks and whores, and stagger back by daybreak. The kind of place where bars offered any man a twenty if he spotted a waitress wearing underpants. Our parents had warned us against it since we were boys, at church the preachers spoke in low tones about the vice that went on over there, and local leaders were always making up curfews to keep young boys away. Of course we went as soon as we could.

Our first couple of times down at the Coast were innocent failures. We were young dupes, of course, and when a beautiful blond waitress offered us her house key to visit her after work hours, we gladly accepted. "Shall I trust you, sirs?" she asked, biting the lipstick from her lips, and we nodded our innocence. "Well, I can't have you keeping my key, so what will you give me to show trust?" We offered a little money, finally settled on twenty dollars, and she smiled and dropped the key onto the table with a whisper of her address. Hughie and I were all giggles and liquor when we made our way to that boardinghouse at around two in the morning, but by two-thirty we were sober and solemn. The key did not fit any lock of the building, and we were halfway around the block, trying every door we could, when people began to yell from their windows and we realized we had been taken. Later, on our way back from drinking, we would see young men like ourselves trying keys in doorways all across the city, and by then it was our turn to laugh at youthful lust and folly.

I do remember one detail from those drunken days that drove me mad: in every bar, every deadfall tavern, I saw advertisements for Klondike suppliers for the new gold rush: Cooper & Levy. Levy, Levy—that name, blazing at me nightly. I took it as an emblem of my own insanity, a concoction of the chemicals of my brain. How maddening: I could not forget her, still, even here!

One night, Hughie's college friends (who thought I was his uncle) took us to an actual brothel. I cannot remember what the outside looked like; they were all the same. You rang the bell and some sweet Negro woman answered and led you into a parlor which opened wide onto your left and there—it was always the same—the room was decorated so richly and gaudily you would think you were among the wealthy on Nob Hill who, by coincidence of their taste and budget, bought at the same furniture shops as the madams of Pacific Street. There in that parlor the lady of the house would greet you. They were always lovely in the way women used to be—not slender and breakable, Sammy, as you seem to admire—and always blond.

"Gentlemen, what would your pleasure be this evening?" she asked. She was in a long yellow gown covered in a fine black netting on which were sewn, as if plastered there during a storm, large silhouetted leaves. A thistle pendant lay between her quivering breasts. She was as stout as a bottle but had a pleasant lightness in her movements, especially the way her hand kept brushing at her cheek at if performing some private spell under her ear. Her eyes picked every one of our pockets and I seemed to sense a relief in her; here were a few boys who would be easy to please.

"Perhaps a virgin?" she offered slyly. "We have a sweet girl staying with us, she's in the bath now, so it will be a moment. She is of course much more . . ."

"No thank you," Hughie said sharply. We had all heard this ruse before.

She blinked and smiled; his whipcrack of defiance seemed to amuse her. No, that's wrong; it touched her; it softened her. She gave us a new, lower voice with the boozy grin: "Then, boys, maybe you'd like a better deal. I've got viewing holes in her room. A country gentleman has just joined her, he's quite excited and may not last long, so I'll give you a very good deal."

Hughie's good friend Oscar, a tall dragoon of a fellow, thanked her and declined for us all, though Hughie seemed nervously intrigued. The woman tried to interest us in bottle beer and half pints of liquor at bad prices, and then showed us the intriguing automatic harp on the sideboard, which took only pennies and nickels. This was another way to lose money in a brothel and we had enough only for one thing. Hughie said what one always said in these places: "May we see our choices?"

To which the woman—Madame Dupont was her name—turned and shouted out what madams have shouted in San Francisco for all time:

"Company, girls!"

The other boys had their heads bent back to watch the girls descending the rainbow of the stairs, but I was oddly captivated by Madame Dupont. As she looked up at her harlots, pleased by her collection of youth, the shadow they cast on her thinned her face, darkened her salon-treated hair, and in an instant I recognized her. The thistle pendant. I must have made a noise; she turned towards me, her face warped by time as through a quizzing glass, and I nearly laughed aloud to think who this proud and powdered woman used to be.

∽

"So, Max, you've been in love!" Mary remarked, for surely you've guessed it was my old gossiping maid, who, accent shifted slightly south to French, hair bleached "back to its natural color" as she said, now went by the name Madame Dupont.

"I what?"

The boys were already upstairs, having taken their time in choosing among the girls who—in this particular house—all wore satin negligees to just below the hip and little stocking caps as if awakened from their sultry beds. I waited for the last ring of the register before revealing myself to my old servant. Her maquillage crumbled for an instant and the old Irish servant rose like a Gaelic witch from a lake, but soon Madame returned and took my face in her hands, kissing me in leopard spots across my forehead. I was given a free bottle of champagne (quite an honor; these were her most lucrative goods) and she informed me I had been in love.

"How old are you now, Max?"

"I'm twenty."

"Twenty, God, you still look . . . I mean, it's something. If I didn't know I'd think you were a man my own age." She blushed, a finger to her nose, "Which ain't much more than twenty, a course." There was the old accent, springing up like wild thistle.

"No, I'm really twenty."

She lifted her neck and my old maid was gone; she was once again a woman with an unbreakable heart. Her pearls dropped into the rolls of her neck, those signs of beauty that we used to call rings of Venus. "Should I envy you, Max?"

"What?"

"You should have been a woman," she said, looking at me intently as I imagine she must have examined every one of the girls upstairs, the girls who, like her, had fled from bad domestic jobs, or men, or families. "I know, I can tell you. A woman, all she has is her youth, and if she's smart she invests in it, gets all the jewels it can earn her. I have a sapphire from a prince, Max, and I got it when I was twenty-six. That's right, when I was working for your family. When your parents went to the Del Monte hotel for the weekend, I used to have men up to my room to make a little money. Don't be shocked. Every girl does it, even maids in good families."

I tried to turn the conversation my way. "When did you stop being a maid, Mary?"

"A maid, what a question! Ha! Oh, you mean a servant. After your grandmother threw me out."

"But I saw you at Meigg's Wharf."

She cocked her head. "Was I wearing a servant's dress?"

"You don't remember? I was with my father, and you had an iris—"

"That's an old trick, Max. I earned a lot more pretending to be a servant girl than I ever did being one. Rich men, they liked to pick me up. That was a little gig I did for a while before I got in a house. And then I got this one when Madame Dupont died. But we were talking about you."

"You've had a hard life, Mary?"

She slapped me down with a stare. "You don't get to talk about my life. Whatever it is, it's all I could make of what your family left me."

"I wasn't—"

"Your grandmother's dead?"

I nodded and told her my father was gone as well, that Mother and I lived in changed fortunes in the old South Park house. "I guess you wouldn't know. We live in different worlds . . ."

"We don't. You're in this parlor, I'm in this parlor. That seems like the same world to me."

"I . . . well . . ."

And then she changed again. "More champagne, dear?" she asked, smiling. It was like this the whole time, with old gay Mary coming into view and fading like the streetlights we had seen along Pacific that very evening, glowing and dispersing in the gusts of fog. Perhaps this was what she had become: a trick portrait flickering among the women she might have been. "I was saying you'd have been better as a woman. You'd have been ugly when you were young."

"I was ugly."

"You're still young, too, but for a girl it'd be lucky. I wish I'd been ugly. Ugly girls never have to worry about marriage or children, not unless they get desperate. And you wouldn't get desperate, Max, because you'd know your best beauty was before you. That you'd be lovely when you're old and wise. To be beautiful and happy at the same time."

"I'm not either one."

"Way of the world, boy. Should I envy you?"

Her stare, sharpened by the scattered light of her pendant diamonds, was broken by the arrival of a strange character in the parlor. At first it appeared to be a stooped-over old cleaning woman,
but I quickly realized it was a man in a plaid woman's dress, scarf,
apron, and cap, entering the room with a feather duster and an
ashcan. Madame Dupont rose, unsurprised, and kissed the man
on both cheeks, then began to give explicit instructions on which
rooms needed the most attention. She treated him like a beloved
servant, and the creature, who seemed as bland and mustachioed
as any man on Market Street, nodded faithfully as she talked.
When she was done, he handed her a gold coin and left the room.
The coin barely caught the light; she slipped it into her pocket
with the swiftness of a stage magician. Then she returned to me,
smiling but businesslike.

"Yes, Max, now people pay me to be my maid. Things change,
boy." She did not sit down with me again. She just gathered our
empty glasses and said: "Don't ever come back here."

She was tidying her parlor without a glance to me. The awful
baubles and whatnots of her professional life were being put back
in their sad places; the automatic harp was relieved of a fingerprint
on its gilt back. And within Madame Dupont, the bars were going back on the windows, prepared for the next ringing bell, the
next entrance of the Negro maid and some covey of snickering
men. She spoke and she arranged the room: "A woman like me
enjoys believing she was always the way she is. And when I'm legitimate, I'll believe I was always that. Don't come back here."

I wordlessly took my hat from the post. I fit it onto my old
man's head and—I can't explain it to you—I began to cry. Monsters will do this. Mary softened at once.

"I'm too rough," she said, frowning, touching my arm. "It's
because of how you look, like a policeman trying to strike a deal.
Oh, don't take it that hard. Look how unhappy you are. Did she
love you back? Of course she didn't. Not you, not any of us, they

never do. Oh all right, I'll get you a girl, not that it ever helps, Max. And next time you pay like everybody else." She was true to her word, of course; I paid each one of the many times I visited her house over the years.

Within a moment I was at the stairs, being directed towards the landing where a young woman waited with a smile and jaguar eyes. I don't recall her very specifically; she held a long feather and kept waving it lazily through the air; her hand appeared and she crooked a finger towards me. I do remember I was magically drawn to her, for I was still young and sad and eager for comfort. "Max," I heard behind me, and I looked back down at Mary. Curiously sad, the old blond gal, and who knows why? Perhaps it was the wasted opportunity of my condition, the poverty of advancing age, or maybe just the sad gold-dusted air around her.

"You know I'm glad you came," my old maid said at last, chin lifted in the gaslight. "All my life I thought time was not on anybody's side."

My writing has been interrupted by fortune, and I must write it down. Sammy, it's wonderful news: I may soon be your brother.

Mrs. Ramsey, the lovely lady, has said nothing yet, but during one of my long sleepless nights (old age does not reward all the frankfurters I am fed) I decided to rifle through her desk. Don't think this was the first time it occurred to me—I long ago became a juvenile delinquent—but I only recently discovered where she keeps her key. Have you found it yet, Sammy? Or are you one of those boys, those happy boys, who are incurious to all the secrets hidden around them? If so, it explains how I have managed to keep this journal for so long. In any case, you may find the key in the linen drawer beneath the Christmas cloths. That is where I found it last night, with Buster as my companion, and he dutifully padded downstairs beside me to the study.

There, in her desk, I found something astonishing: a set of adoption papers. She had filled them in only as far as printing my name in her formal Victorian hand. I believe my date of birth must have stumped her; there is only a scratch of ink as if she were thinking and let the pen's weight fall onto the page. I will try to let my birthday slip—I am supposedly thirteen in September. I held the pages to Buster's nose and he sniffed them with admiration in the moonlight. "It's going to happen, Buster," I whispered to him, rubbing between his eyes so that he closed them in delight. "I'm going to be with my son." A little groan of pleasure from the dog.

Brothers! Would you like that, Sammy? Sharing your knee pants? Breaking your sled? Doing your homework for you on the brisk walk through the February slush? There is no use asking you, even in the privacy of our room, even as we lie submarined in the zebra-striped midnight. You are the kind of boy—you are, Sammy, you are—the kind who will break any heart he's handed.

So tonight, I celebrated a little; a mistake. Having cased this house thoroughly in my midnight tours, I knew the hiding place of the bootleg gin and mixed myself a tiny little Martinez (their proper name in San Francisco, where they were originally made with maraschino, an ingredient that seems to have been lost along with the *z*). I sipped it out of a juice glass while Mother prepared dinner. Now why did I do such a thing, I who had not had a drop of booze in some time? I don't know, my nagging Reader. Perhaps the old man was weary.

The liquor made me warm and kind. All through dinner, I silently smiled and found myself staring too deeply into my future mother's eyes. I kept thinking of those papers, the possibility of a family, a home. Mrs. Ramsey squinted, concerned, and smiled back. When you started telling jokes, Sammy, I laughed with your mother, but for some reason both of you looked at me strangely.

I discovered myself to be sitting with my feet on the table, juice glass raised high, giggling as hysterically as a harlot in a pub. Reader, I was blotto. I quieted, pulled myself into a more sober position, but I was disturbed. Clearly this new body of mine had never heard of a Martinez.

Luckily, Mrs. Ramsey went to get the ice cream and, when she returned, opened up the topic of my stay with them. I was over-joyed when she turned to me, saying, "Hey, kiddo, you've been with us awhile now. Hasn't he, Sammy?"

"He sure has," he growled, mushing up his ice cream with a spoon.

"You getting along, you heathens? Staying up late whispering? You know I hear you."

"He's the one whispering. In his sleep. A complete freak."

Mrs. Ramsey: "Sammy, hush it."

"What do I say?" I shouted. Too loudly, I think.

Sammy spooned some of his cream, slurped it down, and became an astonishing mimic-mask of my face: "*Please stay, oh stay, stay!*"

The ice cream coiled like a cold snake in my intestine. I decided it would be best to laugh but I lost control and became a chatter-ing hyena.

Sammy snickered: "What's up with you, duckbrain?"

Mrs. Ramsey stared at me with sharp interest, then gave out a bemused little laugh. "Oh my Lord, he's drunk."

My glass was found and in it she smelled her old friends, gin and vermouth; Sammy launched into his own fit of hysterics; I was taken to the sink and given a short speech and a tablespoon of black pepper to coat my wretched tongue and now here I am. "Grounded" for a week.

It's no great punishment—this duckbrain rarely ventures out—but it was a fall from grace, and worst, worst of all, was the look in her eyes: the thick thunder of doubt. Not at my behavior but at her own, for even considering taking this feral thing into her life. Oh, Mrs. Ramsey, reconsider. You do not understand how far I've come.

I must stop writing. Obviously I am still drunk.

⌖

Morning. Slight hangover; not everything grows young along with me. Sammy, oddly enough, seems wary of me and, perhaps, impressed that I found the gin. No, I won't let you know its hiding place. Let me scribble out a little history before this headache does me in.

⌖

"We've gotta go, old man," Hughie told me one evening over beers. "I mean one last time."

Years had passed, and both of us were changed—older, younger, respectively. We sat in a bar near my friend's bachelor apartment, blowing the foam from our steam ales; it was where we often met, in those years before we grew apart, but that evening Hughie had a purpose. He pulled out the newspaper, and though by then he was a man, there was something boyishly anguished in Hughie's face when he showed me an item on the third page. "We've gotta go," he said, blinking and wincing at memory. It was a former Hughie, a young and strawberry-nosed Hughie, who informed me they were tearing down our Woodward's Gardens.

The place had been closed for years. Professor Martin had sailed his last ascension long before, lifting into the air in his weightless metal droplet to the awe of those last children, tossing his last paper roses into the last leaping crowd as some still-unknown misfortune popped the dimpled fabric of his ship and sent him, a fluttering scrap of glitter, to his crumpled death on the

ground. No other balloonist took his place. Nor did any new
monkeys replace those in the Family House who, after years of
heckling the proud Victorians with their heathen commedia del-
l'arte, were found one morning on the floor of their cage wrapped
in each other's dead embrace. Woodward himself died in the late
eighties and it was only the furious infighting of his daughters that
kept the place open for a few last acrobats and flame-eaters, last
visitors to the dromedary whose hump had gone tonsorially bald.
So this was the last event, an auctioning of every piece of plaster,
and what they called "the removal of the animals."

I knew what this meant: it was my last chance to see him before
he was led away, old Splitnose Jim, the imagined savior of my
such-as-it-was boyhood.

We arrived just in time to see the coyote cowering in the three-
cornered amphitheater. Men lined the stands, suffering the soft
streamers of rain, and Hughie and I took our seats and watched as
a young man holding a dog's muzzle approached the lean and
mud-streaked animal. "The removal of the animals" was mostly a
rodeo, of sorts; we had all come to see our favorite wild animals
roped, corralled, and penned for their new homes. To our surprise, the coyote made no move; it just stood there as the man
inched closer. Every moment we thought it would hear the pack
howling in its blood, but it never did. It shivered in the rain and
sniffed a stone. It bent its head to be muzzled and was led off
through the stands, licking its new owner's hand. We were not
pleased. Next came the lioness, which had been sold at auction to
a Chinese highbinder (whom you would call a "mobster," Sammy,
and admire as a hero). The lioness and the Oriental entered the
ring together, as if in some odd Roman ritual, and I was surprised
to see both the poor girl's lazy walk and the object that the highbinder produced from his suit pocket: a pistol. He brought it to the
animal's soft, squinting face and fired only once before she fell in
thumping misery to the dirt. He did the same with the jaguar and

hyena, the latter giving just a little chase and gargled song before submitting in a heap against the wall. Hughie and I sat steel cold with shock.

"Oh my God it's a slaughter."

"Hughie . . ."

"They're just killing them one by one."

"Maybe just the wild ones," I said, watching the tall Chinese man ordering the hyena dragged out by its legs, its spotted hide covered now in dust. "Maybe to keep us out of danger." But another minute proved me wrong; they had brought out Split-nose Jim.

I did not want my bear to be that slow or old. I did not want to see him roll his feet across the wooden planks as he entered from the grate; I did not want to see him sway with sniffing, senile pleasure at the meal set out before him—enough carrots and soup meat for a den of bears—or see into his mouth as he stared out at us and yawned, showing how his old man's teeth had worn down almost to the gums. I did not want to see him blinking as the sun came out, licking at the air until he decided to lean back against a fake stone and enjoy the warmth. His keeper had thrown a piece of rope into the pen and Jim kept glancing over at it while he tried to doze, finally deciding it was worth investigating, but I did not want to see the way he swatted at the knotted hemp, curious, until submitting to some long-bred playful urge, sitting on his rump and batting it back and forth as if this were any day of his life. I could not tell what kind of pity to feel for Splitnose Jim; he, at least, did not know if he was young or old. He was merely a paw with a rope. Liver was set out in a silver bowl but he ignored it. The sun arrived again and brightened his fur. Moments later, the German stepped out with the gun.

The crowd began to scream. Hughie and I were pounding the air with our voices, trying to stop him, but the rest of the men shouted advice: "Get him closer!" "Move the liver!" "Shoot for the head, the head!" "Get his legs!" This did nothing to Jim, who was used to crowds of all kinds, but the German got nervous. He was a butcher from North Beach and planned to sell Jim's meat to specialty restaurants at a hefty profit. With his beard and chapped hands, he would have looked more at home in a back room with a bloodstained mop than beneath five tiers of half-drunk onlookers. He stood wide-legged in the arena and glared out at us with his gun by his side.

"Be quiet, you! I know all about it!" he shouted to the mob in a thick accent. "I don't need no advice! I shim him right in the butt of the seat!"

And this was what he did, just as Jim dropped his dainty tongue into the liver bowl. The butcher cocked his gun, shaking nervously, and after a fast exhalation of air, fired off a shot that hit Jim somewhere in his haunches. The old boy gave a long, rough bellow, turning around and around, coughing and grunting. Blood smeared the planks in a flourish. The German watched, startled, while the crowd shouted gaily to the bear the way people do to poor women standing on the ledges of high buildings, urging something to happen, something terrible, anything to happen. Jim noticed the crowd now, and barked at us like a seal; some men laughed. Then, picking up his rope in his jaws, my old friend made off towards the entrance to his cave and slipped inside. Across the stage, he had left a long rubrication in blood.

Now the crowd went crazy with advice. The bear was gone, hibernating from death; the German stood frozen except for a nervous lip-twitch; the hour of battle was passing and the audience would have none of it. "Scare him out!" they shouted, or "Let him sleep!" or "He's dead, go get him!" One man yelled out, "Sing 'Oh, Dem Golden Slippers'!" which made the crowd spew laughter, since this was what audiences commonly shouted to dull minstrel performers. But no one moved in the pit below us.

Years later, when talking over this memory in a tent somewhere in Nebraska, Hughie bald and gray-templed and myself boyishly blond, we agreed that the image that stayed with us was not of Jim roaring out of his cave a minute later, terrifying the poor gun-happy German and staggering blindly around the perimeter of the stage. It was not my bear shitting the floor as a new hail of bullets pelted him, or how he fell in a whining, terrified mound. It was not the ten minutes or so we spent watching his gore trickle across the wood, damming up in a clump of leaves before soaking them and running on towards the wall, that stinking eternity it took for Jim to bleed to death. We best remembered the stage before his reentrance, empty except for a hunter and a shining flourish of blood. A scene from a children's opera. How the sun spotlighted the very sawdust point where Jim would make his curtain call. How we all shouted for him. The straw, the beer, the hopeful wait for the star. The thrill when his shadow hit the floor where he would die.

We left while Jim lay on the floor in the pile of his own blood and shit; I could not bear to watch. I only heard the German shouting and shouting, and the crowd applauding, and I imagine they must have dragged my old Jim out of the bear pit where the creature had performed for twenty years. I'm sure he died in confusion; I'm sure he could remember nothing of his youth in Yellowstone or wherever he was born, or his life on the streets with a ring in his nose. I'm sure he did not know he had grown old or that nobody loved him anymore. He died in plain confusion, perhaps thinking that all this would go away if he performed his old tricks for the audience, balancing a peanut on his nose or roaring to the sky, but he was surely tired; or perhaps he thought that when he opened his weary eyes, he might be in a forest full of trees and creeks of salmon, buzzing bees, and roaming bears. For I am sure he had not seen another bear for thirty years or more.

∽

Hughie was married in January of 1898 and went to war three months later. It was a sweet and informal ceremony at the bride's parents' home in the Fillmore; the time was half past three. Hughie and I wore frock coats, striped cashmere trousers, patent leather boots, and tan kid gloves—as well as top hats, of course; I can hear you snickering, Sammy—and in his buttonhole he wore an enormous sprig of stephanotis in the accidental shape of Prussia, which, like that dead nation, threatened to invade the rest of his coat. The bride was a plump-cheeked beauty with the strained eyes of a devoted reader; the daughter of a newspaper editor, the young woman, like those strange creatures who exist only at the salt point where freshwater meets the ocean, dressed and walked like a society girl but nudged and guffawed like a seamstress. She wore a white dress and a bonnet, not a veil, because soon after the ceremony the couple departed in a coach bound for a destination known only to me. I went ahead to handle the luggage and pay the porters, and when Hughie and his new wife arrived, they seemed in awe of themselves as if they had done something never before accomplished. The coachman said that the wedding guests had thrown slippers and one had landed inside: good luck. A left shoe, the bride informed me, was even better. The coachman produced the item: left indeed. There were kisses, solemn promises, and with an exhalation of steam, my youth departed.

Why did he marry? I don't know; for love, I suppose, or something like it. Young men do marry, after all. But there was something hard won about Hughie's marriage, almost as if he were closing his eyes and diving backwards from his life. Something sad, you see? I can't describe it. All I can give you is a small moment I remember, one of many from the blizzard of days, a night of no importance at the time.

I was drunk and angry. It had begun earlier in the evening, when I came home from a miserable day at Bancroft's—walked home, in fact, to save on money—to find a piano recital in full flower within my parlor, all ladies in taffeta and stiff aigretted hats and a corps of girls in lace berthas. Some confident child was at her instrument, tearing Mozart all to shreds, and I watched her white-gold curls wriggling in the electric light before I realized this was my Mina. Happy, beloved, ignorant of life: my Mina. I felt a presence beside me; it was an ugly woman in heavy brocade. She looked over my thin clerk's clothes, then said, "Here, man, get some more cake for the girls," and stepped away. I did not know her at all, but I knew the tone: it was that of a woman used to talking to servants such as me. I was twenty-five.

I fled to Hughie's. He was a lawyer by then and owned a building so ridiculously small and fairy-tale that I referred to it as "the Pumpkin." The streets were dark, as was his house, so I rapped lightly on the door. No answer. As his best friend, I had a copy of the key, so I let myself in. I thought maybe I'd help myself to his sherry and a snack. "Hughie?" I called, and there was no response.

Then I saw light glimmering from the library—the light of a fireplace, wavering like water in the hallway—and I wondered if he was simply asleep. And so I stormed down the hall and into the room. I was so selfish a young man it never occurred to me that Hughie might not be alone.

He was not; there was a letter. He held it before the fire with two hands as if it were the tiny dead body of a lover, and he stared at it as if some new breath might bring it back to life. A simple letter; a page. Hughie was dressed in just his suit pants, shirtsleeves, and an undone cravat, leaning into the sphinx-headed arm of his ridiculously Egyptian chair with the posture of something firming up against collapse. The fire sent its apprehensive light over the room, polishing and tarnishing the objects around us. A noise came from the chair as if my friend were gently choking. I admit I see these details only in retrospect; at the time, I had nothing on my mind but the sherry in his cabinet.

"Ah, Hughie, got a drink for your pal?"

He shook, startled, and I was such a fool that I laughed. But he was not facing me; he was facing the fire now, and just as he might drop it into a mail slot, the letter went neatly into the flames. He jerked back when he had done it and almost immediately his hand went out again to catch it. But the letter was buffeted by the waterfall of fire, and except for one small fragment, it burned into a kind of fragile film that floated up the chimney in one piece.

"Hey, what was that? Ain't got a log?"

I heard him laughing now. "Get us a drink, old man," he said.

"Who's the host here?"

"You are for once. I'm dead tired. Hey, I'll find us some H and we'll have a little party. I feel like a little party."

We had one. By the time I was back with the whiskey (I had changed my mind, as always) Hughie was up and dressed again, bearing in his hand a vial of his wicked hashish and two pipes which lay bedded together in their velvet like the beginning of a grand quotation. He was all aglow from the fire. He found us some cold beef and potatoes, then entertained me late with his liquor and his pipe. At first, the smoke was pleasant enough to send us both into a calm stupor. I looked up into my skull and it was as plain as the interior of a parasol, as full of indistinct shadows. We both lay there in solitude, together, as friends will, but soon we were restless. We set up a game, but as the hours filled with whiskey, as the cards were dealt and foolishly laid down, I fell once more into my own worries.

"I'm unhappy, Hughie."

"So am I," he said without looking up.

I fiddled with the pipe lying there on the table. "No you're not. You've got a lucky life. I want your life."

He spoke in bitter tones: "You may have it."

I did not notice his voice. I never thought of Hughie as unhappy for a moment, and it would have annoyed me, I think, for him to take on such a new role so late in our friendship. Melancholy was my birthright, not his. I lifted my hands into the darkness above the globe of lamplight. I said, "I want this stupid house, and your stupid girls." I waved towards him, saying, "I want your young looks. I want nice clothes that people my age wear instead of . . . my God, look at me, I'm still wearing my dad's pantaloons!"

He smoked without expression. "I don't want to talk about your clothes."

"You get along so fine. Most of us mope around about some woman or another our whole lives, nothing can make us happy." I fell into a momentary pause as I considered what I meant by this. I looked back at him and said, "But you're happy even if nobody loves you."

Oh, he looked up now.

"Shut up, Max," he said.

I laughed. "I mean who would love you? Your Pumpkin House. Imagine some woman in here yelling at you to get rid of your smokes. Get your feet off that ottoman! Where's your good coat? Not here. You don't need it," I said, coming out of my dark haze and smiling. "Who could love you? You're inhuman."

He said nothing but just looked away from me, down to where the one unburnt scrap of letter lay on the hearth as white as youth.

"I'm wrecked. Can I sleep here tonight? I won't vomit this time."

"No," he said, standing up and going to the scrap of paper. I could have read what was on it if I'd wanted, but I didn't care back then. I was too concerned with myself. The scrap went into the flames, unnoticed, and Hughie stood with his back to me, staring at the fire. He said, "The maid comes in the morning and she gossips with the neighbors. She already thinks I'm a lowlife. I don't need drunks on my sofa." I heard him laughing now. "And you *will* vomit. I'll call you a cab."

"It's Alice I miss."

"I know."

"It's Alice."

"Okay, Max."

"Thanks, Hughie, I love you."

I could see his whole body outlined by the lightning flashes of the fire. He did not move for a while and neither did I, intent to sleep there in my chair where I was happy. The fire spoke, chattering like a madman, and then quieted again in a helix of sparks. My friend, so still and copper-outlined in the dark, said something so softly that I cannot, even more than thirty years later, hear what it was.

It takes too much imagination to see the sorrows of people we take for happy. Their real battles take place, like those of the stars, in some realm of light imperceptible to the human eye. It is a feat of the mind to guess another's heart.

In the morning, I would remember very little of that night, and Hughie never mentioned it to me; I'm sure he had heard many stupid rants from drugged and drunken friends in his days, and forgave me, of course.

And that first afternoon of his husbandhood, he waved to me gaily from the window of the train. I suppose he married for love, a little, but largely he married for fear, as most men do. But it is not for me to describe Hughie's heart. He met his bride within months of our chat, took her out in streetcars and carriages all over town, ate Chicken in Cockleshells at that old great San Francisco restaurant, the Poodle Dog, and asked her to marry him within a year. I was not consulted on any of this except the color of his gloves (tan, as I told you). But how funny it is with men: they will beg you loudly not to leave them at the pub, but they will go off and marry without a word, as if it did not concern you in the least.

Hughie took his commission right after the wedding and headed to the Philippines, where his captain took Guam from the Spanish in a single afternoon. Meanwhile, Mother's business did well, mostly because she had the brilliant idea (or vision, as she put it) to become a specialist in Civil War dead. Women in old lace caps came by the hundreds, sitting in our darkened parlor while Mother summoned up the horrors of Cold Harbor: "There's dead men a-lyin' in over five acres here, and I'm among them, Mama . . . I ain't got no legs." She gave it in such detail that the stunned women often forgot to pay and had to be reminded by post the next day.

By the time I was twenty-five, I seemed to be in my mid-forties: plump and elegant with waxed mustaches. I looked like my mother's generation. In 1895, in fact, we appeared to meet each other's age and, nodding as we passed, continued in our opposite directions towards age and youth, respectively.

What I did not realize was that, as Mother and Mina were growing older—the former with her graying chignon and the latter with her flirtatious laugh—I was getting closer and closer to my real age. While at twenty I had been far off the map of youth, now that I was nearly thirty I looked nearly right. Perhaps not quite in the bloom of youth, but approaching it in my ogreish way, and I began to get more than my usual share of glances from ladies who peered like fascinated children out of carriages, street-cars, and shopwindows. Because I saw the world only as a bored audience eager to hear the joke of my life, I thought these girls were just eyeing my odd clothes, and that their pink-orchid smiles were just amusement at my ugliness. I did not understand these women were speaking to me in silence. I did not understand that my glands, like those fine tubules that twine down a silkworm's back, were spinning from my ugliness a face both young and fine. The century turned, the seasons changed, but little changed for me until a lucky and terrible disaster.

∽

What a hidden blessing to be grounded, Mrs. Ramsey, for now I have the time to put this down just as it happened:

It was in March of 1906, on the three-penny planks of Fillmore Street. The morning was a surprise to me; so warm and fogless for March, so lovely that people floated almost in a daze through Golden Gate Park, carriage tops down, and one could see women on the promenade in the palest of summer dresses, never worn before or since, women grinning in the glory of light fabric but still—cautious girls—carrying a fur wrap in case this miracle should turn on them. A bright, hot sunny morning in San Francisco! Imagine! The shock was akin to that of buying, out of duty, a novel written by a dull and uninspired acquaintance and finding there passages of heartrending beauty and rapture that one could never imagine coming from such a tedious person.

A street scene like any other, though, of course, from a time that now seems forever lost. There were dray horses hauling goods to the rich folks up the hill; there were Chinese lugging vegetables across their shoulders, traveling the back alleys and shouting to the cooks in the kitchens; there were men and women by the score out on that gorgeous afternoon. Another great change in me that year: I had shaved my beard at last. I walked along dressed in a plaid bow tie and a porkpie hat, looking every bit a man in his mid-thirties and glad of it because, for this brief moment of my life, I was the age I seemed.

There came a scream from the street. I turned my head so quickly I lost my hat: there before me was a carriage piled full with a picnicking family, and coming towards it down the hill hurried a brakeless gasoline automobile. I remember how the little girl in the carriage stood up, pointing at the beast that would kill her: some monster from a dream, a book, from the flickering gibberish of a magic lantern show. I remember how the ribbons in her straw hat coiled back in the wind like snakes about to strike, how the family stood in mute tableau, the horse twisted eyes-white to the death machine, how the car driver slumped, jerking in the spasms of his stroke while his shirtwaisted passenger climbed over him in a frankly sexual way and fought with the controls. One could make out the mother in the carriage grabbing her girl's waist, about to throw her towards the sidewalk. The father, thrusting one defiant palm to stop the oncoming machine. I did not see the awful moment; or perhaps our brains erase these things for us. I recall a sound that I do not have the heart to describe.

But it is not of the accident that I want to tell. I have seen worse human horrors than these, and more than my share. What's important about that sunny afternoon of death was that I turned away, and this choice to turn has made my life what it is. I turned away from this awful sight, towards the hot, bright, impossible sky, and there, silhouetted so crisply, I saw a hot, bright, impossible sight:

An eye. A clear brown eye on whose surface was reflected the scene of death itself. The star-lashed eye of a woman.

Who? Oh Reader. Oh careless, careless Reader.

It was Alice. Time, that unfaithful friend, had changed her.

Not cruelly, as you're thinking, but in the most ordinary of ways. Standing on the street beside me: taller, hair darker. Shoulders broad, neck long with a little softness under the chin, face full and clear, unmuddied by the baby fat of fourteen. Faint lines around her eyes, as expected, tracing every expression I'd known in girlhood. Unexpectedly pale and powdered, yet a drop of sweat sat on the wing of her nose like the jewel of an Indian bride. The girl I remembered was not there. The face so soft and full, incapable of any hardness no matter how strongly she hissed or hated, it was not there. The cheeks so soft with down, the clean eye blinking in wet fronds of lashes, the restless breastless body; all that was gone: the softness, the pink, the girl.

And yet. She was both more faded and sharper all at once; the dreaminess of the eyes was lost, but a clarity that was dormant at fourteen had come into gradual focus, giving her a new kind of beauty. This was no girl of fourteen, breathing a curl of smoke into my mouth; this was a woman over thirty.

"My God!" we both shouted, and for a moment I thought we were both gasping at this reunion. I realized, of course, that she was speaking of the little carriage girl, now entombed in rubber and splintered wood. I turned and saw men running to pull metal aside. The car passenger was already on the street, alive enough to accept a young man's coat and wrap it over her tattered skirt. The horse, now in the last hours of its life, nodded its head hopelessly from its place beneath the wreckage. I could not make out who else could be saved. A tire and a wheel rolled together for a few feet before falling in endless spirals to the road. There was no sound to be heard above the noise of panic. Well, perhaps one sound: an inhuman heart rejoicing.

"Come," I said, and offered my hand, which, in the atmosphere of disaster, I knew would not be rejected. I was right; Alice stared at me, squinting, then took my hand in her gloved palm and ran with me. I had not yet had time to feel my luck, that I had found her at last; after all, true believers are not amazed by miracles.

But look at this unexpected fortune: *she did not know who I was!*

This was the witching hour of my life—the only time when I was exactly what I seemed to be—and God had brought me, at this golden time, the prize I wanted most. I found a little tea shop for us, something with red "flock" walls and café curtains pulled shut so that the shadows of passersby formed a kind of Balinese shadow play on the yellow fabric. Somehow, as we took our seats and ordered, I was so stunned by my good fortune that I could say nothing. Here it was, the prize. To sit across from Alice one last time. To hear her sigh when the tea arrived in an opium-cloud of steam. To see her eyes close voluptuously when she took a bite of cake. To notice a spot near her ear where she had failed to powder and the skin—that old pink, glorious skin—showed through. We chatted and I was grateful. If fate had handed me a body always in disguise, and if disguise alone would let me be near my love, then I would accept it. She would never need to know. She could not love me, you see. I had noticed the golden ring on her finger.

"I didn't expect to see someone die today," she told me quite plainly, after we had finished our strangers' chatter and settled for a moment in silence.

"No one could."

"I expected a totally ordinary day," she said, then smiled with that old glow. "Excuse me, I can tell I'm going to babble, but it's just nerves. I came out here to buy a camera. I spent an hour looking at all the different kinds, and the man, who'd been so nice, he became concerned when I told him it was for myself. He said, 'Oh miss, ladies can't use these, their fingers are too small.' I got so angry. I stormed out of there. I was furious over this ridiculous man . . . this stupid comment. That's what I was doing when we saw the accident. Fuming. Making a whole speech to him in my head. And then. Well."

"I was eating a pickle."

"Was it good?"

"It was."

"See, isn't it extraordinary these little things? How you wake up in the morning and think everything's going to be fine."

"Yes."

"I mean, you don't look in the mirror and think, Okay, get ready, just in case you see something horrible today."

"No."

We both stared into the cups, at their tidal pools of bits and leaves; I had learned enough from my mother to tell a lover's fortune in that cup, but said nothing of what I saw. I poured out the tea. After all, to my beloved Alice I was nothing more than a stranger.

She took a breath, leaned back, looking around her. "Well this is very strange and awkward. You know what, I'm going to go, thank you."

A panic. She couldn't go, not yet. Alice was married; she could never link her life to mine; I could not even hope to have her as a friend; but it was not enough just to see her and know that so little had changed. Despite all their fears, we ask very little of the ones who never loved us. We do not ask for sympathy or pain or compassion. We simply want to know why.

"You should stay a little bit. You're pale. You nearly fainted, you know."

"You saw that?"

"No, well I . . ."

Alice smiled and met my eyes—ah the tea leaves there! "It's terrible when you realize what you've become. So I'm this. I'm a woman who faints." Laughter, brilliant as water.

"No," I said. "That's not what you seem like."

"I've become something I used to despise. A heroine in a bad novel." She spread her hands, laughing again, as if her fate were now complete. She looked like no such heroine: my Alice was dressed all in black, shirtwaist and skirt, bright white cravat, hair pulled into a very masculine driving cap. At her throat she wore an old-fashioned brooch that I recognized as her mother's; I knew it contained a lock of Mr. Levy's hair. But she also wore some kind of jacket I had never seen before: wide-lapelled, fitted, embroidered in Oriental coils and arabesques. It wasn't really that it was too fashionable; it was simply bizarre. Other women in the shop were staring, whispering, perturbed. Alice did not seem to notice. She knocked against the table with a fist, saying, "But I shouldn't faint! I shouldn't be that kind of woman! I've seen people die before."

"Don't think about that. Drink your tea."

Her eyes were off in the corner of the room and she herself was far away: "In Turkey—I traveled to Asia years ago—I saw a man stumbling, poisoned, through the streets and he collapsed onto a carpet, dead, just a few feet from me. His face was curled up in . . . well, in anguish, I guess. The Mohammedan women were wailing in that way, you know." She did a startling imitation, dovelike and plaintive. "I didn't faint then."

"You traveled to Asia?"

"With my husband," she said, touching on the sad fact at last. I have no idea why she stayed and drank her tea with me, why she told all this to a stranger, but she went on: "That poisoned man, I sometimes wonder if he did it himself, put arsenic in his own mint tea. Over love, I guess. That he didn't suspect poison would be so painful, so awful, so stupid and unromantic. The moral is: it pays to do your research." Another laugh, full of chimes, and then—oh wonderful thing—she blushed.

What I wanted from Alice was modest and easy. Not to have her love me—I had no hopes of that—but to answer one question that had maddened me for years after her disappearance. Like the audience member who watches a magician take his silver dollar and make it vanish into a handkerchief, I did not need it back. I only wanted to know how she did it. I wanted to know where Alice had been all of these secret, hidden years.

She was still talking: "You know, I don't think I want this tea. It's not enough of a vice. Now's the time to indulge in a vice, don't you think? After something horrible."

"I don't have many vices."

"That's because you're a man. Everything is a vice for a woman. They don't have wine here, do they?" She raised an arm and caught a waiter, demanding a glass of wine. They did not serve wine; it was a tea shop and, besides (his face seemed to say) she was a lady, and it was only the afternoon. Alice seemed annoyed.

I said, "We can go somewhere else."

Her eyebrows worked in a private fury. "No, forget it. Since no one knows me here, and since you're a complete stranger, I'm going to have a cigarette. Don't be scandalized, I'd think less of you. And don't tell my mother."

"I don't know your mother, so I won't."

"You're sweet," she said, and I lit her cigarette. It was then she noticed my lighter, something Hughie had given me long ago, and its engraving of a lily pad. "Is that from the Conservatory of Flowers?"

I fidgeted with the lighter and slipped it into my vest. "I—I suppose so. It was a gift."

"Hmm, the old conservatory. Do you know, is the Victoria Regina still alive? Does it still bloom?"

"I haven't been in a while."

Alice looked into her tea and her expression stilled completely. She said, very quietly, absolutely to herself, "I've been gone so long . . ." Then she retreated into a place in her mind where I could not follow. With that look on her face, she was indeed a stranger.

I was not saddened by how Alice had changed. Any of her former lovers might have looked at this beauty grown from fourteen to thirty-two, full of such strange and pensive expressions as this one, and felt a watery sadness at what was lost. But I felt no sadness; I was different. I knew more than the easy aspects—her eyes, her voice, her joy—that time leaches from the body: I knew the ominous little cough she gave when she was bored; I knew the smell of the anise seed she used to cover her cigarettes; I knew the tremble of her three visible vertebrae when an idea stirred her; I knew the flutter in her eyelids that meant annoyance at some stupidity; I

knew the tears that came to her eyes the instant before an out-
burst of laughter; I knew her quivering night-cries, her bathtub
operetta voice, her bitten fingers and her snore. The things I
knew, the Alice I knew, could not be touched by time.

"It's strange. You're very familiar," she said. "Are you from
here?"

"I've lived here my whole life."

Her eyes widened. "Don't tell me it was South Park . . ."

"Not South Park," I lied. "The Mission."

With no forethought at all, some part of my brain had decided
to erase South Park, Grandmother, Father and Mother and Mina
and the rest of it. I did it instantly, with no regret. In fact, it was
with great relief that I murdered Max Tivoli. It was my first homi-
cide. Alice, of course, did not notice a thing, not even the bloodied hands clasped so calmly before her on the table. Instead, her
face brightened at my words.

"The Mission! Did you know a boy named Hughie Dempsey?"

"Not that I recall."

There, my best friend was gone as well. Corpses were amassing
at our feet.

"Oh." She sniffed and shook her head. "Well, I didn't go to
the Mission much, so I don't think it was there."

Alice, you were always so bright and careful in your dealings
with the human race. Didn't you recognize that old neighbor-
man who smiled at you each afternoon as you came back from
school? The old fraud who made you Sabbath tea? The bearded
humbug who held you to him one night and who tasted, I would
guess, like tobacco and rum? I suppose that, for all you knew, the
old horrible man was dead or dying in his room in South Park.
Before you in the tearoom was no one at all.

"And yet you seem so . . ." she continued dreamily.

"You said you'd been gone so long. You used to live here?"

"I was born here."

"But you moved away."

"Yes," she said, holding her cup gently, as if to protect it. "We moved away when I was fourteen."

"Fourteen, that's young," I said.

A little chuckle. "Yes, it was."

"Where did you go?"

"Pardon?"

I could feel the pulse of my heart in my neck. "*Where did you go?*"

Alice seemed to notice my too-loud voice. All these questions, from this oddly familiar stranger. Then, because of course it could not possibly matter, she told me.

But all I said was: "Ah, Seattle!"

"Maybe that's how I know you. It's a small town."

"No, I've never been farther than Oakland. I've always been intrigued by Seattle."

This amused her. "Intrigued by *Seattle*?"

"Why did you go there?"

She considered this and held her fingers tightly under her chin. There was a stain of longing in her face that she blotted in an instant. "Family," she said. "My uncle ran a supply business. We ran all the supplies for the Klondikers, maybe you've heard of us. Cooper & Levy."

Cooper & Levy. Did she even realize that her hiding place was posted in every opera house and evil bar for her foul villain to see? And I had seen it. I had noticed that maddening name Levy shouting at men nightly along the Barbary Coast, but I'd ignored it. Only in the tea shop did I see that I'd been given—plastered before my very eyes—the one great clue I sought. I had merely been too sad to see it.

I said simply: "I've heard the name."

She smiled and shook her head. "Well that was us." Eyes on her tea.

"Tell me more."

Alice plucked another cigarette from her reticule and put it to her lips haughtily. She examined my face as I held out a flame. She said, "I'll tell you for as long as this cigarette lasts, and then I'll have to go." She put her lips to the cigarette, the cigarette to the flame, and when she was done she told me all that had happened in the years she spent without me:

"I went to Seattle with my mother. The boat pulled up and the town was smoking. Just tents and scorched buildings, most of the place had burned down a week before—it's that kind of town. My uncle's shop was fine, and we bought into his business just in time for the Alaska gold rush. Let's see if I can still do it." Then her tone descended into a standard shopkeeper's recitation: "Cornmeal, dried whole peas, lentils, lanterns, lye, summer sausage, and sleds for sale."

"No dogs?"

She laughed. "No, they had to find their own dogs. Thousands of men gave up their lives to come there, ready to dig up some gold, all those dreams, it was . . . well, it was boring. I used to hide in the back on the grain sacks and read, or I'd sneak out with my best friend, the two of us on one of those bone-shaker bicycles— one time we came across a cougar down from the hills! Green feathers in his mouth like he'd eaten someone's pet parrot. I remember thinking, That poor parrot, still he's seen more of the world than I have. Mostly it was dull, though, rainy and dull. I was lucky to meet my husband, that's when I stopped working at the shop. A few years ago we sold the business to the Bon Marché and Mother and I came back."

The cigarette was a third gone now, faintly crackling. I noticed a detail she had left out. "What about your husband?" I asked.

"He didn't come."

"Why not?"

"He's been dead five years now."

❧

"You're a widow. I'm sorry."

She fingered her mother's brooch and I saw what I had been too blind to notice—the black skirt, black-bordered handkerchief, jet earrings—that she was a widow many years out of mourning. My heart came alive within my chest.

"He was a professor at the university. Because of him, I saw a little of the world. Turkey, China. And I went to college."

"You've been to college?"

All of a sudden her entire face tensed angrily and she drew back. "You think no woman ever went to college?"

"No, it's wonderful!"

Coldly: "My cigarette's almost out."

I smiled humbly and urged her to talk again, in this brief time while I had her. "Tell me about your husband before it's out, tell me, please."

She said it was tuberculosis that killed him. Professor Calhoun, her mustachioed husband, respected anthropologist, dead by the age of forty. There was an ordinariness about the way she said this that shocked me, gave me a sick hope, but then I realized it was something she had been saying almost every day for five years. She wore his hair in that brooch on her lapel; she prayed for him at temple; she was still his loving widow, but time had at least taken the tremble from her voice.

"He used to take long walks in just his shirtsleeves," was her answer to my unasked question.

"He couldn't have known." I pictured poor Professor Calhoun being taken in a carriage down to the stables, taking the common cure for his consumption: hot blood sipped from a tin cup. I pictured the doctors and their illusionist devices, their purges and plasters. I'm sure bedbound Calhoun looked up at his young wife and despised himself for his deadly cold-weather walks, and for dying so quickly and losing so many days lit by the lantern of her face. We waste so much time within ourselves. Alice's hand must have smoothed the hair on his brow as he breathed through his rough lungs. The second man to die before her eyes.

"The saddest part is I have no child to remember him by," she told me. "I was ready to leave Seattle. Mother was ready, too."

"Did you miss your old life here?"

Something odd appeared in her eyes. She stubbed out her cigarette. "It went out a while ago, and I've been so boring. Thank you for the tea." Alice stood up and gathered her A&P bag and parasol. "I must be going."

One minute later, she had left my life forever.

I mean, such were the thoughts in my head as it spun in panicked circles, trying to find some way to stop her. Alice was standing oddly, looking at the shadows of the people passing by. A particular profile now appeared against the curtain; a man in an odd hat. Alice seemed rapt. I was speaking this whole time, excusing my presence in her day, mentioning the coming chill outdoors, or the police scene she might want to avoid, anything to keep her there, but something kept her there already, and it had nothing to do with me. She was not even listening to me. Then, carefully, she slid the curtain back on the rod and daylight dissolved her face.

"Are you all right?" I asked.

She smiled at the view before her; it was just a young man in an old-fashioned derby, chatting up a threesome of "hello girls" coming home from the phone exchange. She turned from that ordinary scene of youth.

"The world's haunted," she said, and winked at me mischievously. "Don't you think?" Laughter, more laughter; I loved her. She produced a glove and spread her fingers to put it on. "You don't have to sputter. You can see me again if you want to. Except you've been rude."

"What? Really?"

Cleverness was on her face. "Well, what's my name?"

"Alice."

That startled her and I realized my mistake at once, but it was too late. She studied me, saying, "I was going to say you'd never asked, but . . . now how did you know that?"

"You said your husband called you Alice."

She blinked. I sat in that anxious silence like a man in a waiting room, hoping he will be received into the house. It took only a moment for the answer: "Oh. And what do they call you?"

We were assaulted at that moment by the very "hello girls" whose shadows had played before my Alice's eyes so intriguingly a moment before; now, having escaped the masher on the street, they were babbling and laughing and full of the kind of life I don't remember having at their age. I might have been annoyed by their noise, but they bought me a little time with their loud stories. Some murderer; I had devised no alibi, no alias. Alice seemed irritated and captivated by their dither over ribbons and diets, but they finally settled their identical-shirtwaists-and-skirts into a booth and quieted over the menu. And that supposed stranger, my life's love, turned her eyes again to mine.

"I'm Asgar. Asgar Van Daler."

She laughed impolitely, then sobered as she slipped a card into my hand: Alice Levy Calhoun. "Goodbye Asgar," she said, then turned to leave.

"Goodbye, Alice."

The door caught the sunlight as it opened, blinding me in a flash, and she vanished, leaving the room just as it had been before, scented with sassafras and hair tonic. But everything was different in me, because not only had I found my beautiful, wandering Jewess at last, but now I could see her again and again for as many days as I might wish—my wild heart played this into infinity—and she would never know that I was the same monster who'd loved her so badly before.

As for that new identity, Asgar Van Daler. Well, I was no stranger to playing a part that did not belong to me. A father, for instance, my young father standing fresh and smiling in the pleasure gardens of his youth, watching the girls and tossing rye bread to the swans, my Danish father in those happy years before he changed his name. Asgar Van Daler. This inheritance was always mine to claim. After all, I do live life as backwards as a saint; like all the beatified, I consider it my duty to restore the world its losses.

I was at last the luckiest man alive. For who else in the history of time has ever had this opportunity: a second chance at love? It was like something from an Arabian tale; masked by my body, I could approach my old love—who would never accept me if she knew who I was—and I could try again. Unrecognized, better than before, I could use everything I knew to win her. Her card said she was in on Wednesdays and Fridays, and how endless the hours seemed until that Wednesday. This time, it would be different. This time, I would make her love me.

The address on Widow Alice's card was easy to find but a bit of a shock. She told me about her family's Klondike wealth, but I had not expected a two-story mansion on Van Ness, especially one so bedizened with ornament. It was a sort of collection of vertical forms, all white, tied with frippery and bows at every quoin and window, and capped with what architects inaccurately call a "belvedere." I stood hat in hand on the street for a little while; I thought I had seen every side of my old Alice, and that nothing could surprise me, but something about her house saddened me. Was this really what a rich Alice would buy? I'm not a snob, but I'd believed our home together in South Park would have seemed like a lost dreamland to her, created by my grandfather in that old elegance of early San Francisco that we have never seen again. A house of stone and modest curves. I could not imagine my Alice living like a Jonah in the belly of this whale. I had thought that, like the daughter of an impoverished duchess, she would work to buy back what had been pawned in childhood: the silver, the settings, the art. That, like any of us with a broken life, she would try to resurrect the dead.

I had to search among the medieval carvings of the door to find the electric bell—there it was, posing as a saint's head. After a bit of waiting, a stout Negress appeared with a face as wide open as someone who has just been slapped.

"Yes?"

"Is the widow in?"

"The who?"

"The widow."

She told me to wait and then left me alone in the hall. I sat on the bench, quickly going through the card receiver to see who had been there before me—some names of Jewish women, nothing more. So at least I would not sit on a chair recently warmed by some other gentlemen, handsomer, richer, and more easily loved. I at least had this advantage. Then I had the luxury of looking around the place; it was calmer on the inside, although strangely at war with itself; old, ratty books had been crammed behind glass-fronted cabinets, and though the chandelier above me was clearly electric, the hall was lighted (extraordinary, now that I look back on it) by rose-colored kerosene lamps. The maid came back through a different door and stared at me, motioning for me to enter. I smiled and nodded.

With the quick little motions of the body that we all learn in order to make ourselves as handsome as we can, I went over my posture, my cuffs, my coat and shoes, and entered the parlor to find the second shock of the day. There, sitting in a chair with a bit of lace pinned to her head, was my first lover, Widow Levy.

"Have you come from the club?"

"I'm sorry?"

"I told them I'd only pay half the dues. I don't play tennis, for heaven's sake, or swim. Can you imagine? Old ladies bobbing about like pickles in a barrel. I only go to monthly dinners and I only eat the soup and fish."

"I'm not from the club."

Mrs. Levy smiled slyly and touched a finger to her cheek. "It's too bad. They need more handsome young men like you."

She was old. Her hair was quite white and done up high on her head in rich curls, some of which were whiter than others and surely false, and over this was pinned the piece of antique lace that ladies wore to signal they had retired from the trials of beauty. She wore no corset, either, and her bodice flounced generously to cover a frame much altered from the one I'd held in the garden so many moonlit nights ago. She clearly enjoyed the privileges of age and now ate what she desired without a worry. A high pearled collar covered her neck, and over it fell two fleshy lappets; her earlobes, as well, drooped with heavy jewelry like an African queen's. Her face was broader than I'd remembered, colored an artificial pink, perhaps merely from habit, her eyes hard and dark, her lips so thin I could scarcely find in there a memory of those whispers she had given so tenderly to my young ear. I admit I was repulsed; there was no beauty in her. Mrs. Levy had dressed perfectly for her age in South Park, but now she seemed to have tired of prudent fashion, to have become almost a parody—part haggard courtesan, part countess. I realized that this queer house was her choosing, her taste. Perhaps all of us reach an age when we come to the end of our imagination.

"Are you Alice's mother?"

She said, "Ah, you got the wrong widow, didn't you? We're all widows in this house, even Bitsy, bless her soul, is a widow five years now, she lost her husband to a mining accident in Georgia. An astounding woman."

"This is a lovely house you have."

"No it is not, but I love the rooms, I barely leave it, so I never have to see the outside. Don't worry, young man, you won't have to chat up the old lady for long, Alice will be here any moment. I sent her up to change for gentlemen visitors."

"I'm delighted to talk to you."

"The gorgeous boy is delighted! My heart is fluttering. Positively Shakespearean." I could hardly breathe, watching her flirt with me like this, her lashes flicking their paint hopefully against her cheeks. But no, I was safe; she didn't recognize me at all. "What's your name?" she asked.

"Asgar Van Daler," I told her.

"Vander . . ."

"Van Daler."

"Vadollar."

"Van Daler."

"My dear man, I don't care a fig for families. Do I recognize you? Anyways, I will speak frankly before Alice comes."

"Of course."

"First of all, Alice is Jewish on both sides. I don't want you to get involved and then drop things for some blood reason."

"It's of no importance to me."

"Also, all of my money is going to the Jewish Educational Alliance. This is Alice's wish. She believes very strongly in the settlement houses, and I have to say I do too. I am being very honest with you, Mr. Dollar. Alice will only get the jewelry I am wearing on my person."

"It's very lovely."

"My person? Why, thank you," she cooed. "But if you are searching for wealth, you're on the wrong trail."

Then I made a terrible error. I was feeling the airy heart of a shoplifter and, careless, I said, "I should tell you, I'm not wealthy, either, Mrs. Levy. I'm merely a clerk at Bancroft's."

Her mood of jovial flirtation was over. Instead, she wore the old face of a brokenhearted widow writing a poisoned letter to her lover twenty years before. "Bancroft's?" she repeated. Sorrow pooled in every wrinkle of her face, but there was something alive within her eyes as well, either a buried rage or a kind of hope, one that I of all people knew too well. I was shocked to see how little dies in us. She chose her words carefully: "I knew a man who worked there. It would have been before your time."

"And who was that?"

"Mr. Tivoli. Mr. Max Tivoli."

"Max Tivoli," I repeated.

"Have you heard of him?"

I almost told her, I swear it. I almost revealed myself so that I could be forgiven, and perhaps if I had done that, I might have been kept from all the other misdeeds that followed. Instead, I was generous in another way. I gave her the lie she wanted to hear: "He died before I came."

"Ah."

"There's a rumor it was murder."

I saw the tremor of a smile on her lips: "Pity."

Then her old cheerful expression sprang back like a rubber band. "I must shut up now, my daughter's here. Keep our confidence." She turned away from me, the woman who took such pleasure at my death, to shout:

"Alice, what on earth are you wearing now?"

⚘

I wish I could remember all the details of that morning. I know we all sat in the parlor for a little while talking politics, which got Alice very worked up, and that her mother turned to her at last and said, "Widow Calhoun, get out of this house, you don't need a chaperone." Alice smiled and said, "Widow Levy, you'll be all alone." The old woman shook her head, saying, "I'm happiest alone, Widow Calhoun." They spoke to each other in this odd way, joking almost morbidly about their widowhood, and it reminded me of the nights when I came to light the fires for them and found them trying on dress-up clothes, or in the midst of charades, or painting the other's portrait. I felt intensely jealous for a moment, realizing that there was a part of Alice I might never get to know, the part devoted to her mother, and that while they had indeed left San Francisco out of love, it was only love for each other, and never for me.

"Did you get the camera?" I asked her once we were outside.

"What?"

"You were going to buy a camera before I met you. The old man said your fingers were too small."

She smiled slyly. "I guess they were big enough to hand him the money."

"You bought it?"

"Yes, I did."

"What do you take pictures of?"

"Whatever I like. Let's walk up this way, there's a hidden stairway to Franklin and I think when the roses are in bloom it's so mysterious." She put her arm in mine and, talking now and then about the subjects on her mind, led me to her secret bower.

It would be nice to tell you that she fell in love with me. There, as we took our walk among the mansions and carriages of Van Ness, the hedges that had been planted to keep us from the flower gardens, the vulgar rockwork and cast-iron fountains shaped like children—that she found the sunlight too dazzling to defy and kissed me under the rare and giant flower of a century plant. But you know better, I think; we were strangers, brought together by an accident, and once we had exhausted all conversation on cars and death and our own shock, we walked for a long time in uncomfortable silence. I tried to think of all I secretly knew of Alice, and led her now and then into topics I knew would get her talking, but mostly I think I bored her.

And I would like to tell you that she was just as perfect as I'd remembered her, but she wasn't. The tea shop had made me mad with hope, believing that everything true about her could never change for me; she had emerged from the grave of memory as perfectly preserved as love could ever be. But daylight and the lack of disaster made a difference. Alice was still my beautiful girl, even in the bright tailored suit of her "at home" clothes, the odd little toque that seemed almost like a turban; so much about her was exactly the same. But some habits of a girl are not as lovely in a woman. Her private furies, for instance, which had always seemed like a sign of character and independence, had altered a bit, becoming more hilarious from the mouth of a thirty-two-year-old, but also more sour, even petulant. How the mailman mangled her letters. The fog, the rich and stupid neighbors, their dogs. As if every annoyance of the world were meant for her.

As the time passed, I found other changes I had not expected.

"Am I still familiar to you?" I asked her.

She examined my face for a moment. I still could not believe that nothing of old Max could be found there.

"No," she said.

"Not at all?"

"I was wrong. I was a little emotional on Saturday."

She pronounced it "Satuhday." Nothing had ever flattened the vowels of my young Alice, but I suppose a life and marriage in the Northwest will do it. So there was that, and her furies; they were changes so minor that you could ignore them if you liked. After all, when listening to a symphony, we don't insist that the composer strike one chord over and over; we enjoy his skill at variation. And I had thought I'd known her so completely that I would love every variation in my Alice, every major and minor scale, because, as in a symphony, the very depths of her would never change. But there was a flaw in that thinking: the Alice I loved would never age, it's true, but still she might change. She had suffered a burning town and a dying husband and who knows what else; we cannot blame all our scars on time. Perhaps something shifted in Alice, something I hadn't noticed in the ecstasy of the tea shop.

We reached the house again and stood within the oval curve of the entrance, framed by a glazed tempest of woodwork. I was in an odd sort of panic, like a climber losing his grip on crumbling shale, not only because I had bored her so, and was not even familiar to her, but because the object I had loved so eagerly all these years had changed, ever so slightly, and I could not decide if this change meant nothing or everything to me. No one yet had ever died from not-being-in-love, but I might, if it came to that. I was still examining my heart when she spoke to me very seriously.

"All right, Asgar, tell me."

"What do you mean?"

"You've got some kind of secret. It's all over you, you're terrified to tell me, it's all you can think about. I tell you, it's a bore to be around someone with a secret. Sorry, I know I don't always put things the right way."

"I—"

"Please just tell me and get it over with."

"But there's nothing to tell."

She stared at me and called my true name: "Max Tivoli." This stopped me dead. There was a single oxygenless moment before she continued: "Did I hear you talking about him downstairs? What did my mother say? You couldn't have known him, he'd be so old. She probably didn't tell you this, but she was a little in love with him."

I found my breath at last, a lucky thief. "I'm sorry, no, I didn't really know him."

"He broke her heart. I was a little girl, there was an incident with him and we had to leave. He's a bit of a villain in our house, and we never talk about him."

"I'm sorry, I'm sorry."

"Why are you sorry? I just wanted to explain. You asked me once why we left San Francisco, and that's why. So now you know." She searched me carefully, as with a scene one is asked to memorize; that is, as if she might never see me again. "Thank you for a pleasant walk, Asgar."

"It was pleasant."

"Yes."

"I'm grateful you could come, Alice."

"It's been nice."

Dull, ordinary words for people who want the moment to die. And perhaps I did. It was too awful to think that I had preserved my heart so long ago and that now, years later, I had stuck it in my chest, smelling of formaldehyde, and found it too sorry and shriveled to work. But it's a common tale. Isn't there a statue, in Shakespeare, of a long-dead queen who comes to life before the eyes of her mourning king? The king rejoices and repents, but what does he do the next day? Does he remember how she sang off-key as she brushed her hair, how she screeched at servants? Perhaps it felt easier, in the doorway, to fall sleepily into my old life of memory and sorrow than to face my real, live girl.

We smiled tightly to each other and I saw I'd propped my walking cane beside her. Confused, hardly breathing, I nodded goodbye to her and reached out for my cane.

Alice's face turned a peculiar color, her hand went out to support herself against a column, and her eyes looked directly into mine. I had never seen that expression on her before. She stared at me for an instant—a sharp, improbable instant—then turned and saw the cane in my hand. Her face collapsed. I didn't understand any of it, the stare, the clumsy blush on her cheek. And then I realized: poor woman! She thought I was going to kiss her!

Alice closed her eyes, whispered a goodbye, and made her way clumsily into the house. I just stood there. The network of veins vibrated through my body, harp-thrummed by the impossible. Could I be wrong? That I'd seen in her eyes the same carnality I'd always hidden in mine? Alice, you will forgive my crudity, but I knew then that my luck had doubled over the years: I had become a man too handsome to resist, and you, a widow longing to be merry, had walked all those long blocks just hoping to be touched. Admit it, now that I am dead: you wanted me to kiss you. And you still did, inside the house, leaning breathless against the shut door, your heart pulsing as fast as the glands of a snake emptying itself of venom; you still saw my face inside your lids.

No braceleted ankle or can-can leg was ever as erotic as the shame you showed me in that doorway, darling. And with a great relief, everything was just as it had been before, or greater, because all at once it came rushing back—the ice in the heart, the bell in the brain—the terror of wanting you.

Now the astute reader will be wondering how I ever thought I would get away with this. It's one thing to disguise oneself for an afternoon tea or carriage ride; it's quite another to keep a lie for the length of an affair or, more improbably, for the lifetime that I hoped to be with Alice. I might change my looks and words to suit her, but how could she really love me when my truest self was buried under the floorboards? And yet, I've heard of long and happy marriages where the wife never knew of his second family, or the husband never learned that her blond hair that he so valued could be bought at any druggist's. Maybe lies are necessary for love, a little; certainly, I wouldn't be the first to create a false persona just to seduce a woman. Of course, none of this crossed my mind in the following weeks of my courtship—the visits to the House of Widows, the at homes with Alice and her mother, smiling in their ignorance—never did I consider that I might wear this false mustache for life. The heart plans nothing, does it? No, the only obstacle I ever considered was Hughie.

He was not sad in marriage; he was stable. I have to assume this made him happy, in a way; perhaps marriage was a weight, a paperweight, keeping the heart from flying across the room at every breeze. Of course we never went out to the Barbary Coast—he was married, and the place was nearing its final days—but we never went out together at all. Instead, I was invited to dinner parties hosted by Hughie and his wife. They had bought a new house on O'Farrell, something more appropriate than the Pumpkin, and I would find myself at a table of handsome, rich, and clever people who intimidated me with their clothes and their wit until I discovered they had no imaginations, that their opinions and fashions were copied from magazines they all had read. Hughie seemed perfectly at home in this crowd, but I was always nervous and drank too much. I couldn't play their games, but what saddened me the most was seeing these glittering bores lean across the wineglasses to whisper into Hughie's ear, hearing their private laughter, knowing they had supplanted me in his confidence. At least it took a crowd of them to do it.

It was only right, though, that his wife would take over all the parts I was used to playing, and she was a kind young woman, bright and pretty and never pretending to be more clever or fashionable than she really was. She was good to me, and yet we were rarely together; she always found reasons to leave the room or tend to someone else. It wasn't, as she said, because Hughie and I should be alone; I think, somehow, I scared her. In any case, by the time Alice came back into my life, I was seeing little of either Hughie or his wife; their lives were taken over by their family. Yes, shortly after the turn of the century, little Hughie Dempsey had a son.

At the time, I could not understand how the soft look on my old friend's face, which used to come only after several belts of whiskey and buttermilk, appeared so easily as he stroked his young boy's face. I couldn't see how this clever man could listen to his wife speaking of her "angel from heaven" and keep his willing smile; I couldn't fathom Hughie's belief that his son would accomplish wonders in the world, as if other worthy children, equally full of promise, were not born every minute, and failed, and turned into men just like us, who would lay onto the next generation the same hopes, infinitely deferred.

But I was not a father then. I did not know, Sammy, what happens to us in the presence of our sons. Today, for instance, when you and I built a fort among the honeysuckle and the blackberry, using an old refrigerator crate with *Coldspot* branded on the side. We shared no secrets in our little house. Instead, we lay side by side, barely fitting, our heads on the long cool grass of the forest. I felt the prick of the grass on my face and, beneath it, the moist earth coming through, smelling of blood. A strong breeze blew over a leaf, revealing the tiny husk of an insect. A drab butterfly, headed the wrong way, was being blown ceaselessly away from his goal. "Jeez, it's boring," you said, then smiled and did not speak for half an hour. Sound of desperate birds. Why would this make a father weep?

We have no right to keep our friends from being happy, and if it seemed to me that Hughie, like a man searching for a religion, had found a life that had been led before, I never took him aside and scolded him for it. He was an extraordinary man, I'd always thought, and deserved an extraordinary life. But perhaps it's the average men who need the extraordinary lives; the rest of us need the comfort of the common. He'd had fun with me, but I saw now that he'd always been unhappy, and terribly alone, even in my company. So I did not trouble his new world. I suppose in some way I envied it.

The problem of Hughie, therefore, was not his life. I could not change that. The problem was merely that Alice might come across us together, realize we were friends, and discover my true identity.

∽

I did tell him about Alice, and my old friend was stunned and happy. I gave him all the details of our meeting, her unfading beauty, and how I had worked my way into becoming a regular at the House of Widows despite the terrifying presence of Mrs. Levy. He laughed at the foolishness of my life, and had a plain and happy expression on his face, perhaps remembering how in our youth the least important things were filled with an intensity he had forgotten.

"My God, Max, really? Alice?"

"Yes, Alice."

"Well, she can't be the same. I mean, I guess what I mean is you can't feel the same."

"I do, that's what I'm telling you. It's so strange, but I never forgot. And now here she is, thirty-two and a widow, but it's like I'm seventeen."

"You're a grown man, Max. And you hardly know her."

"It's as if she's something I've wanted since I was a boy. You can't know what it's like. I mean, first love." We sipped our drinks and sat in silence for a moment before I finally told him what I wanted of him.

He looked at me for a while with a look of sadness. "No," he said. "I can't, Max."

"Come on, I need your help."

"You can't do this. A lie like this, it'll wear you out."

"You just have to forget you know me. Forget all about me. It's easy. If you see Alice and me together, just say hello to her and ask to be introduced to me. It's simple."

"It's not simple at all. We're not seventeen. It's idiotic."

"Please."

His mood changed. "Max, you have to tell her," he said at last. "You know what will happen."

He looked down at his plate because he did know.

"Please, Hughie," I told him, startling him by taking his hands. "I don't have anyone."

It was a month before it happened, but as I'd predicted, Alice and I did eventually run into Hughie. We were walking in the park to see the newly imported kangaroo, and she was telling me about a photography contest she had entered, pretending to be a man; she had anagrammed her married name and come up with the outrageous alter ego "Alan Liecouch." I was walking along and watching our shadows together on the grass when I noticed that hers had stiffened where it lay beside a stone. She had stopped laughing and I could hear the bamboo rattling in her parasol; her hands were trembling, but when I looked at her face she was smiling faintly, as if amused by her own reaction. I saw Hughie and his family coming towards us on the path. He must have seen us just moments before, because he was distracting his wife by pointing off towards the conservatory, leaning over to whisper in her ear before leading her off across the grass to follow what will-o'-the-wisp he had invented to save me.

"I know that man," Alice said.

"You do?" She rarely spoke of her life before Seattle.

"Yes, I was a girl."

"Really."

"I used to visit him at the Conservatory of Flowers."

"Oh, that's not far from here."

But she was not listening to me. She laughed a little. "I was so young."

Just then, Hughie made a mistake. He looked back, and hooked our eyes with his own: bright blue. His boater was tipped far back on his head. What I read in those eyes was an intense sadness, the kind I had only seen before that night when I got so drunk in his apartment. This was not the first time, I guess, that he had been called upon to forget someone he loved, but who can say. At the time, I was merely grateful that he had done this simple thing, this crucial thing, to make me happy.

Alice said, "He saw us!"

"Oh."

He turned away with a bitter tenseness to his mouth but Alice continued to watch him. She held her hand to the ruffles of her blouse, as if checking her own heartbeat for this reunion that I think she had been imagining for as long as I'd imagined ours. Her smile opened out and she seemed pleased, embarrassed, amazed. She said, almost in wonder, "He's avoiding me."

"Maybe he didn't recognize you."

"He's grown old," she said.

Hughie was far off now, chatting with his bundled son. I remembered our tea together, how she stared at a derbied shadow on the curtain, afraid. It had been his shadow that she thought she'd seen. I tried to laugh, saying, "Love of your life?"

"What kind of question is that?" she said, smiling playfully at me with eyes surrounded by the creases that I loved. Age will tell you what a woman is; if she has never been happy, you will know it from her eyes. Alice's eyes were full of private joys, and though I had caused none of them, still it didn't matter; I loved what they had made of her. Now she lifted her parasol again and we watched

Hughie's family disappear behind a parade of orange ice sellers
and begging children. What kind of question, Alice? Simply one
that, years later, I am still asking.

࿇

It was a week after that event, I think, that I received an interesting letter. As I opened the custardy envelope, I smelled its faint
cologne, recognized the handwriting, and was brought back to an
awful morning when I lost the girl I loved:

> *April 15, 1906*
> *Mr. Asgar Van Daler,*
> *My daughter and I are leaving this Tuesday for the Del*
> *Monte and we would be pleased if you escorted us for our stay*
> *through Sunday. Alice says you are busy with work, and that I*
> *am old-fashioned and a fool, but we have no male relatives in*
> *the area and it is always helpful, when traveling, to have a man.*
> *Mrs. David Levy*

I'm sure the Del Monte hotel looked exactly the same as it did
nearly forty years before, when my young parents met there: the
long avenue of cypresses that cut the sun in stripes across our carriage (the Widow Levy would not take a car), the great ship of the
hotel itself, barnacled with green shutters and balconies, the flag-
snapping spires, the veranda of wicker chairs where a band in white-
blue military suits played waltzes, the interchangeability of the
parasols and the table umbrellas, the ladies and the peacocks, the
people and the statues. I'm sure society editors still scribbled as
they watched the arrivals, and brothel madams passed as baronesses,
and shopgirls as debutantes, but all I noticed was the practiced
calm, learned from its guests, of a place that knew its luck would
never end.

"Are we here?" Alice asked as I was tipping the driver. Her hat had slid off to one side and she struggled with it, squinting at the building.

"You know," I said, helping her from the carriage, "my parents met in this hotel."

"What a funny place to fall in love."

"In the pool, there used to be a net separating the men and women, like a veil, that's where they met. Strange, isn't it?"

She considered me as their servant, Bitsy, chatted with the driver. "Strange, yes, that's the word for you, Asgar."

"What do you mean?" I asked quietly.

She blinked at me in the strong sunlight, smiling mysteriously, then looked up at the hotel. "Lord, isn't it ugly."

"Alice!" her mother whispered, then stepped forward and took my arm. "It's positively Shakespearean, don't you think, Mr. Van Daler? A summer house of the Capulets, before all the trouble of course, all the old families with their young daughters, a masked ball and everything." My old lover gave me a wink. Masked ball indeed!

She let go of my arm, saying, "I need to lie down after that awful carriage ride, the bouncing, I swear I don't see why we didn't take an automobile. Alice, we'll dress. Mr. Van Daler, we'll see you at supper and I hope you can recommend a book from the library as I don't know anybody anymore, and I'm bound to be bored. Bitsy, do you have my sleeping drops?"

"Uh-huh."

As the other two made for the hotel, Alice stood there on the drive, passing a glove from one hand to the other, watching her mother. The look on my love's face was that of someone solving a math equation or, perhaps, plotting a murder.

"Your mother's fascinating," I said, coming up beside her.

Her eyes shifted towards me. "I've lived with her almost all my life."

"That must be nice."

"Hmm. I can't even really see her anymore," she said, looking back at her mother.

"Well, I love her," I said, coming up beside her, and felt a blush of shame for saying so carelessly something that would have made all the difference nearly twenty years before.

Alice said something very quietly.

"Pardon?"

The Widow Levy's voice pounded through the spring air: "Alice! Stop mooning over that handsome young man! I need your help up here."

Alice turned to me with her eyes blazing in the sun. What message was encoded in that brown-white semaphore? She only said, "You better tip the driver, handsome young man," and then was off, picking up her skirt to climb the stairs, one hand keeping firm hold of her wayward straw hat with its trim as pink as ribbon candy. A peacock made its bored way across the sidewalk, dragging its gorgeous and filthy ballgown of a tail. It made a shimmering noise. I saw Alice turn back to look at me.

She was going to love me.

Even as she was stepping into the hotel, I felt the realization warming me like a new sun: she was going to love me. I looked up at the battlements and balconies of the Del Monte and realized, as the flags lashed in the bright sun, that it would be here, in the very building where another woman had loved another Asgar. Perhaps tomorrow night, in the ballroom with Ballenberg's waltzes playing, on the same balcony, with the same tolling Mission bells and the sound of the sea, the smell of Sweet Caporals. Or on the veranda, very quietly, as we sipped lemonade and watched the old maids chirping at their croquet, perhaps in that white wicker chair where I would take her hand and hear her sigh and know she loved me. Or in her room, as she sat by the window staring out at the lawns and pines that led onto the ocean, as she cranked the glass open and let the salt air into the room and began to weep.

After all these years, it would happen here. Who would have guessed it? In one of these rooms, I would take her face in my hands and kiss both cheeks, then whisper to her as I undid the buttons of her jacket, of her shirtwaist, of all the unnecessary, ridiculous garments widows wear. Her look on the stairs told me everything I needed to know, and honeyed hope—the same hope of my seventeen-year-old self, bottled and stored so carefully on that high shelf—now broke and leaked down through my body.

But how to do it? I could tell—from that look on the stairs— that Alice was lonely with her mother, and that death and time had wearied her, so that she could almost love strange, handsome Asgar who stood overtipping the chauffeur. The next few days required a delicacy of spirit that my life had rarely needed. As the Japanese will tell you, one can train a rose to do anything, to grow through a nautilus even, but it must be done with tenderness, and that was how I had to treat this time with Alice. To listen to her, smile and woo her, treat her not like the goddess I'd met at seventeen, but like a bright, sad woman in her thirties, too wise to be fooled by flattery. I had to be careful. I had to coax the thorns of my life into the spirals of her heart.

You're thinking: This doesn't sound like love. Whatever happened to the wrinkled boy who listened for his downstairs neighbor, tears in his eyes? The one who lit her fires? The innocent, pure love of his so-called youth? You're thinking: This sounds like a wretchedly broken heart. This sounds like revenge.

Perhaps. But, my readers, you people of the future, have some pity. My body may move backwards, but my heart ages just like yours, and while my simple and youthful longing had its place when she was just a girl, simple and youthful herself, a more intricate woman must be more intricately loved. Real love always has something hidden—some loss or boredom or tiny hate that we would never tell a soul. Those among you who have been rejected or ignored, you'll know what I mean. Because when she comes to you at last, though joy may burst in wet seeds inside you, still there's a bitterness that it took so long. Why did she wait? You can never quite forgive. And when she is in your arms at last, when she is murmuring your name, kissing your neck with a passion you once thought impossible, you don't feel just one thing. There is relief, of course, relief that all you imagined has come true, but there is also triumph. You have won her heart—and not from any rivals. You have won it from her.

Revenge, no, not quite. But not exactly love, either. These are confessions, so I confess everything in my heart. I do this for my penance and for my forgiveness. I do not claim to be proud.

❧

Dinner was at eight, and hoping for more luck than I deserved, I wore my favorite pearly waistcoat with my tuxedo. As I awaited the arrival of the Levys, I sat in the lobby's four-person circular ottoman—greenish, tufted, and topped in the center with a fern fountain—pretending to read the *San Jose Evening News*. I think there was a story about a Mardi Gras masquerade, a skating party, Caruso's arrival in San Francisco to perform a portly *Carmen*—it all seems petty now. But I only pretended to read. For in that setting I had my sole moment of doubt.

I watched the couples descending the staircase, prompt for dinner, the men carved from solid black, the women ruffled as sea dragons. It occurred to me that this was the scene, in those Gothic novels, where the hunchback snatches his maiden. Here with the chandelier, the glow from the newel lamp, the diamonds and the bare flesh. This was the monster's moment. Having trailed her, tricked her, now I was about to steal her—giving her nothing in return but my poisoned life, my warted lips. It was a moment of clarity. Hughie had said a lie like this would wear me out, but I saw that it would wear out everything I touched. As the clock be-

gan to strike, I had a surprisingly unselfish thought: I could leave.
I could get an auto and catch a late train, have my bags sent to me.
I could write her a note, and save a number of lives tonight. I actually rose from my seat, as if in a dream, considering whether to head
for the door, and who knows what kind of story this might be if I
had made it?

Then I turned and the thought vanished. She was there, in the
middle of the staircase. She was watching me.

Alice, it took no more time than the tick of a clock, but let me
play with time a little; after all, it has played with me. You wore a
long white gown, drizzled with embroidery and lace, the sleeves
mere veils for your arms, some kind of silver belt coming to a point
below your waist, and the long train falling behind you on the
stairs in a glittering coil; a dress that clung to you the way the del-
icate germ clings to its pale seed. There was nothing around your
neck, nothing at all, just your pale skin rippling like a river as you
swallowed—I learned later you had taken a belt of whiskey just
before—as you looked down at me beneath a pompadour that I
knew would smell of lavender, with the grandeur of a woman over
thirty, no worries of youth, no confusions or fluttering eyes, a
woman of passion on those stairs with one hand on the banister.
Alice, there were stars in your hair.

"Asgar, Mother isn't feeling well."

"She isn't?"

"That cold of hers, you know." You held a little feather fan and
tapped it on the stair rail.

"Typical."

You laughed. The net on your shoulders fell down an inch; the
belt winked in silver. More fan-tapping. Beautiful, more beautiful.

"Come down here," I told you.

You looked at a glossy set of women making their way past.
"Why?" you asked. "I like it up here."

"Come down and have dinner with me."

"I'm not sure I'm hungry."

"Come down!" I shouted happily.

You leaned back your head and laughed, every bell within you ringing. The rotund clock chimed four, five, eight thousand times. Alice, I pity everyone who has not known you.

That night, we sat together on a little velvet couch, side by side, and the waiter winked as he pushed the linened table over our laps, trapping us together just as one is trapped inside a roller coaster out at Funland-by-the-Sea. We drank a bottle of wine, unchaperoned, and chewed on the tender bones of ortolans, which I had never tasted before, and when at one point she picked up the wrong glass, I was left with hers through the rest of dinner, imprinted with the pink lunar mark of her lip on the rim. All evening I kept lifting it to my mouth, my lips to hers. And on my Alice drank, laughing more freely, staring around the room as if the golden ceiling were hers, all hers, a spot of color appearing on her left cheek like the tinted heart of a white rose. After dinner, she stood up and said we were going outside to the little stone balcony, where I sputtered into a dull and meandering story before she cut me short, asking about my first kiss.

"Oh no, I'd much rather hear about you," I said, risking the great danger of hearing your life told to you by another.

"Hmm. It wasn't my husband," she said. "Maybe it's a sad story."

"I'd like to hear it."

"As long as you tell me yours." Her smile was made more erotic by the half-closed orchids of her eyes. Then she began: "Actually, you know this story. It was Max Tivoli who debauched me, your old colleague."

"I never knew him . . ."

She laughed, only teasing; I was not caught. "He lived above us. He was an old man but he tried to act younger. He was sweet, actually, or was he really? I can't decide, it's all mixed up for me. I was fourteen. I remember he wore funny clothes, dyed his hair, spoke in a funny voice, was so strange, he told me he was really a boy inside. Not an old man but a child, like me. I was a mess that night—I was in love. I'd had my heart broken, and I went to him because—well, sort of as a father and sort of, honestly because I knew he liked me. He watched me all the time. And I was so lonely that night and I'd never kissed a man before and I wanted it to be over with, forget love, or what mothers teach us. So I chose Max Tivoli." Alice chuckled, remembering. "He smelled like an adult, like whiskey, and shoe leather. But he tasted, you know he did taste like a boy. Like oranges. He was trembling. I think— even at fourteen you know these things—that he was in love with me, in his strange way. Ugly old coot. So that was it. My first kiss. I think it's kind of sad, don't you?"

She brought her eyes back to me and they were calm; the thought of that pitiful kiss was not so awful, after all.

"So who was yours?" she asked.

"Just a girl."

"Just a girl," she repeated. Her eyes traveled in a triangle around my face. "That poor girl, what would she think if she heard that?"

"A girl I knew. She loved somebody else."

"You knew that?"

"Oh I knew."

There was that crooked little smile. She said, "You evil little man. You seduced her, didn't you?"

I could smell the jasmine from the vine, and the pine trees, and her perfume. I could think of nothing to say. For the first time, I wondered if she might be drunk. "Well, but . . . well, I loved her."

Her eyes softened in sympathy. "You really did, didn't you?"

"Yes."

"How old were you?"

"I was seventeen."

She walked a little bit away from me, as if the memory of these old loves of ours, these antique statues, had to be left behind for us to continue. "People always say the greatest love story in the world is Romeo and Juliet. I don't know. At fourteen, at seventeen, I remember, it takes over your whole life." Alice was worked up now, her face flushed and alive, her hands cutting through the night-blooming air. "You think about nobody, nothing else, you don't eat or sleep, you just think about this . . . it's overwhelming. I know, I remember. But is it love? Like how you have cheap brandy when you're young and you think it's marvelous, just so elegant, and you don't know, you don't know anything . . . because, you've never tasted anything better. You're fourteen."

It was no time for lying. "I think it's love."

"You do?"

"I think maybe it's the only true love."

She was about to say something, and stopped herself. I'd surprised her, I suppose. "How sad if you're right," she said, closing her eyes for a moment. "Because we never end up with them. How sad and stupid if that's how it works."

"Don't be sad."

"What?"

"Don't be sad, Alice."

That was when I kissed her. It happened quite naturally—after all, I had been kissing her glass all night—and afterwards it occurred to me that this was Max's second time with Alice, but only Asgar's first, so it had the thrill of an impossible moment as well as the comfort of something that had returned to me at last. I'm not sure how I did it—it makes no difference what a man does at this point; it is either going to happen or it isn't—but somehow I found my sweet girl in my arms and I tasted the wine all over again.

She grabbed the lapels of my waistcoat and I felt, in the haze of

my memory and delight, the bite of her teeth on my lips—oh Alice, let no one say that you were timid in your youth. That you
did not take what you wanted. I stood with my eyes wide open at
this miracle, but yours were closed, rose-powdered, your knowl-
edgeable widow-fingers everywhere, touching, searching, and I
was like one of those ridiculous machines that swallow a nickel and
quiver deliciously for exactly two minutes. Hell, I was like anything
you can think of: an aspen, a thundering timpani, a locomotive
boiler about to blow his gust of steam.

But so brief. A moment later she was across the balcony, flush-
cheeked, hand on her glowing breast, a look in her eyes as if she
had overheard a terrible secret.

Was it possible? That my bargain with time had undone me and
Alice had recognized me at last, had tasted in our kiss the Max I
used to be?

"Alice, I . . ."

She shook her head. I could see some complicated equation
moving behind her eyes. She gave a little smile and told me she
had to see her mother. I asked her to stay; I said I had impetu-
ously ordered another bottle and now it would go to waste. Her
cheek flushed again, and I saw now that it wasn't the wine at all
but her heart, beating too fast for her own blood. That little factory
working overtime within her breast. Oh darling, you didn't recognize a thing; you didn't mind my mouth at all, did you? Though
you would hate to hear it, you were like your mother before you,
a woman in white in the dark, body all abloom, and you had to
decide what to do with me now.

"Alice, I'm sorry, I thought you—"

She laughed. "Don't, Asgar."

"I understand."

"No you don't."

I did not know what to do; I could not explain that I did understand, that in fact I was the only one who ever would, but I said

nothing. I watched her breast go sunset-pink. I knew this was not love here, not exactly, and besides, I am no Casanova; I could never convince a woman that life is too short to walk away from moon-lit balconies.

"Tomorrow morning," I said.

She touched my face gently and said nothing. She bent down, hooked her finger into the cloth loop of her train, and walked away from me into the dining room, stumbling through the chairs and tables because, of course, she'd belted whiskey to keep her nerves up that night. My sweet Alice, she had wanted to be charming and alive. For me, you see.

I finished the wine and treated myself, in the gentlemen's bar, to a drink or four. I remember staggering back to my room, hear-ing the dogs barking from the lawn, and a milk horse whinnying in distress as he made his early rounds. I recall thinking that the world was restless and sad, and after that, I remember nothing of my waking life.

Sammy, these are dull facts, but I give them because they are my only excuse. The distance from my city, the solid bedrock of the Del Monte, the thick soup of my dreams—my only excuse for why I missed what happened next.

I awoke to a hail of splinters—the door to my hotel room being burst open at its lock.

"Mr. Dollar?"

I can sleep almost anywhere—a train, a car, and perhaps an air-plane although I have never been on one—but I can't awaken any-where. I open my eyes, unsure of where I am, and I grow briefly afraid. I am used to waking up in a strange body, but strange rooms terrify me. You will remember, Sammy, how my first week here I bumped my head on your bunk each morning, then cried out like a maiden; you never knew that I thought I was a thousand miles away, a century before, in old South Park, Maggie's sausages frying on the stove, only to discover myself in a miniature bed in the plain, plaid Midwest.

So, that morning at the Del Monte, it took me nearly a minute to register, first of all, that I was in a hotel room and had somehow ended up on the floor, cocooned in quilts, and, second, that Bitsy stood above me in a dazzle of morning light.

"Mr. Dollar?"

A bellboy was beside her, and I later discovered it was he, and not the powerful Levy maid, who had broken the door. I was terrified, as I've said, and a brief tenderness broke the hardness of that woman's face, and I swear she almost reached out to comfort me, but her hand went back to her thick waist and she shouted: "He's alive!"

"What's going on?"

She looked over me appraisingly. "You okay? Looks like you got thrown out of bed."

"Well, I've been known to sleepwalk . . ."

"Why didn't you answer?"

"Answer what?"

Bitsy gave her head that cockatoo tilt. "I been calling you."

"What's happened?"

She grinned a little and nudged the bellboy. "He wants to know what's happened. Huh."

"Bitsy, could you hand me my robe?"

She ignored my command and instead turned to the bellboy, who held my robe for me. "You got that paper? Give him that. I'm downstairs packing, Mr. Dollar. Off to friends in Pasadena if we can, and we won't be back."

I put on my robe as she left. A shout came from down the hall, and the bellboy quickly handed me the paper. It was an early edition of the *San Jose Evening News*, sparsely laid out and full of typos:

> Stanford University buildings badly wrecked, with heavy loss of life.
>
> Santa Cruz badly shaken, loss of life heavy; all important buildings destroyed.
>
> No trains from north or south had arrived at 8 o'clock.
>
> The wires being down the reports could not be verified.
>
> A man is reported to have arrived from San Francisco, in an auto, reporting that the disaster there is worse than in San Jose.
>
> Late—Thousands of people reported killed in San Francisco.

"What happened?" I whispered. "What happened?"

The answer came: a careless roll of the earth. It felt like a maid making a bed and flicking the sheet until it lies flat, a roll that seemed to come across the room towards me, sending me down face-first. I tasted dust. It was perhaps the fourth aftershock that morning, but the first that I had felt. Earthquake, of course.

It will seem brave or heartless to you, but it simply never occurred to me that Mother and Mina might be dead. I think it came from the childish notion that family is too permanent to die, or that God, knowing I had lost a grandmother and a father, would not be so wicked as to take every other lovely thing from my life. This was my hope as I lay there, my heart buzzing and oozing like a shaken hive, and I came to learn it was a common one. In the following weeks, after the fire had burned its last, you could still see sad handbills—for instance, "Missing: Mrs. Bessie O. Steele, age 33, dark hair, slender, who was to be at the Rex Hotel"—and every one of us understood it was a stupid hope, but a good one. We could not tear them down.

Of all luck, I actually heard from old Hughie two days later and learned that all of them survived. His note was delivered very formally by a member of the U.S. Post Office, and you will not believe it when I tell you it came in the form of a detachable shirt collar! As I later learned, he had been sitting in a park in Chinatown, no paper at hand, and had simply written a message on his collar and handed it to a passing postal worker. Hundreds of such items were mailed from San Francisco in the days after the fire— collars, scraps of paper, empty envelopes, cards, and bits of metal— anything to let their loved ones know they were okay. The post office delivered them all, no postage required. On one side of the collar he had written my name and the Del Monte, and on the other I read in that familiar, awful writing:

All OK, your mom as well, though your house is gone. Good riddance! Come down and watch the fire with me! We'll eat, drink, and make merry, for tomorrow we may have to move to Oakland! Love, Hughie

I like to think that it was while I lay there, listening to the murmurs of people in the hall and the clank of broken china, that a small part of that disaster took place. It would have happened at City Hall, which had lost its walls in the quake and, due to an early morning fire, was now smoldering, room by room. I like to think that the Hall of Records caught fire as I lifted myself off the floor, that the letter *T* blazed on as I dressed, dazed, and the birth records of Max Tivoli began to smolder in the box.

That's how I felt, at least. The end of Max; goodbye, old pal, it's only Asgar now. I stood up and my body seemed as light as Dr. Martin's balloon, drifting like a teardrop through the rubble and away.

∽

Downstairs, people sat in the stuffed chairs and ottomans of the lobby, stunned as hunted animals, waiting for someone to produce coffee despite shattered china and a broken water main.

It was almost an amusing sight. People who had been awakened by the 5:13 tremor had dressed in the dark, and so most of the elegant men and ladies of the Del Monte wore what we later referred to as "earthquake clothes." If I had only taken photographs for blackmail now! Exclusive heiresses, trawling for husbands, sat stupefied in evening gowns, riding jackets, and men's derbies, their bland un-made-up faces set off by their best jewels hanging from their necks and ears. Senators and millionaires sat whispering to each other in opera hats, smoking jackets, pantaloons, and slippers. One financier's widow sat in opera black, her face still masked with Le Paris night cream. Everyone looked stunned and worried; perhaps they knew that their fortunes lay in bank vaults that, while fireproof, had been so overheated in the blaze that they could not be opened for weeks for fear that the cash would burst into flames. I was staring at people who would soon have no homes and no money. It seems an excellent joke that they had dressed themselves not for the Del Monte, but for a vaudeville version of their lives.

There were rumors everywhere: a fat gentleman in a velvet suit was saying that some ghoulish man was going around San Francisco biting off the fingers of dead women to steal their rings, and that mobs had collected at the U.S. Mint, about to storm the place ahead of the fire and steal millions in gold bullion. One woman, hiding a yapping dog under her quilted robe, told me that regulars deputized as soldiers were walking among the ruins of the city, executing anyone they took for a looter. Children caught stealing were to be beaten, a sign hung around their necks reading THIEF.

"Can you even believe it?" she whispered, and naturally, I could not. I thought once again how stunned and sad and crazy we had become. Executions, indeed. It would turn out, of course, that she was right.

"Ah, your friends managed to get a car, I see," she told me, smiling.

"What's that?"

She motioned towards the window. A simple, ordinary car sat in the driveway, engine idling.

"I suppose they're not going to the city," she added.

I said nothing as I watched. A wedding-cake of luggage slipped into the trunk, a soundless slam, a chauffeur dusting off his hands. The crank went into the auto's silvered yap. I could barely see inside: a picture hat, a feathered fedora. I no longer thought of Hughie, the earthquake, of anyone but myself. Mr. Dollar. For in my panic, my stupidity, I had not listened to Bitsy's parting words. Pasadena. I watched the car as it began to vibrate, silently coughing, and then made its slow, unsteady movement down the drive and away.

The thought of losing Alice was terrible and petty but it was too much for my monster's heart. Others around me were chattering and laughing and making plans to find an auto and drive south, loading it with the idiotic junk of their idiotic lives, but I was the King of Fools because I did not want to save a single coin, not a single life; all I wanted was to keep Alice from escaping again. To keep her imprisoned within the mossy walls of my mossy life. Don't you see? She was not sitting somewhere in the hotel, thinking of Asgar who had kissed her. She was headed down to Pasadena. She was headed away from me, as she had once before, and for all I knew our city had burned to the ground and we would all be scattered across the continent or further and it would take years for me to find her again. A disaster had brought us together again, and a disaster would now tear us apart. I was a greedy goblin who could not let his maiden go.

I stood and ran through the lobby. You see; I did not have years to find her. Three, perhaps, or five. But not twenty like before, not even ten; it would be too late. My condition would betray me. Because imagine if Alice and her mother fled to Pasadena, then to relatives in Kentucky or Utah, and it took ten years—imagine it!—to find her, it would all be in vain. This was the thought in my head as I pushed aside a musician hugging a viola. Of course in ten years Alice herself might be faded into her forties, in birdlike glasses, stout and unnaturally blond and married with two children toddling by her pinkies, and I would still love her. Of course I would love her! I would still arrive at her door and bow and whisper her name and wait for the blush to cross her breast as it always did. That wasn't the problem. The problem would be that when she opened that door, it wouldn't be a man in his mid-forties, bat-mustached, grinning in her doorway. It would be a boy. A boy in his early twenties smiling in his bronze-sun of a face, stretching his sinews within his white tennis shirt. It would be too late; we would be too different. I might seduce her, of course—I might even lure her away from her husband for a weekend in a hotel, days of unspeakable passion—but it would be too late for love. Women don't lose their hearts to boys. She would drink down my youth and one morning she would pick up her smudged glasses from the bedside table and leave me forever in that rented room, thinking, He'll recover, he's young. But I would never recover. No, if I lost her now, I thought as I struggled with the crystal knob of the front door, my chances would die a little more each year as I grew younger. Oh Mary, I remember thinking in my madness, Mary, you were wrong. Time was never on my side.

∽

Mrs. Ramsey, my would-be mother, is in the room with me while supper cooks. Grounded as I am, wings clipped, I am still brazen enough to keep writing while she polishes the piano just a few feet away. Easily irritated by housework, now and then she lifts the lid and plunks out an old melody, and when she does this, she lets out a merry laugh and glances over at me. Oh, Mrs. Ramsey. There is so much I need to tell you, but not yet, of course. Not until I am nearly done.

It's death to stay so quiet. You don't know how close you've come to hearing it all, Mrs. Ramsey, for my silence nearly falls away from me twenty times a day or more. For instance: when I am reading too late into the night and that voice comes through the half-closed door, telling me in singsong to go right to sleep. When I am ill and you feed me, face-to-worried-face, those bright orange alcohols from your secret cabinet. When we stumble across each other, late at night, and I'm afraid you see through me at last, but you just whisper that you could not sleep yourself and are a little happy for the company. When you burn your awful meat casseroles, announce it will be "breakfast for dinner!" and we boys erupt in applause. When you yell in a motherly rage. When I catch you dancing all alone to the Victrola. When I watch your rapt radio-face, the wrinkles erased and the worry gone just as it was all those years ago. When I see that name on every piece of mail, Mrs. Ramsey, that name a third husband gave you to hide in, Mrs. Ramsey, Mrs. Alice Ramsey.

You cannot hide. I will always recognize you, Alice. I will always find your hiding places, darling. Don't you know that perfume gives you away?

III

I am called to supper.

From what I can smell, Alice Ramsey, you have been cooking Italian again, and waiting for me is the macaroni pie my old
wife used to make. The smell of butter and cream, the bowl like a
girl's head of golden curls—a dreamworld of memories. I can
hear Sammy already leaping down the stairs; I know for a fact he
hasn't washed his hands. Alice, I hear you speaking with him. Ah,
there: the sound of Sammy trudging back again. You are an excellent parent to our son.

So I only have a moment. Not long ago, you stuck your head
into the room to see what I was working on and, thinking it a
school project of some sort, you gave that raucous laugh of yours.
I'm glad I amuse you, Alice. Can you tell that your adopted son
is at his happiest, hidden here with you and Sammy? Can you tell
there is no more beautiful sight—no moon more full—than your
face leaning in from the hall, the skin grown a little soft and gray,
webbed with pink across one cheek, the hair now dyed, but the
same bright face I knew, laughing at this ridiculous schoolboy
who bites his tongue in concentration? At night, when I dream,
it's of that face. You, Alice, grown old in this plain bungalow. In
my dreams, though, you are lit by gaslight.

And why do you never mention the earthquake, what happened
to you there? I asked you the other day at dinner, and Sammy's

head popped up from the roast, intrigued, but you picked up your plate, shaking your head. "I'm not the one to ask," you said.

"But weren't you there? Didn't you feel it?" I tried to sound as much like a boy as I could.

You stood, the plate tilted so that it caught the flash of the electric light. "Yes."

"What did you do?"

"We weren't in the city. We were in a hotel."

"Did you leave? Where did you go?"

Alice, you simply nodded your head, smiling, and patted me on the head. "Oh Lord, leave it for the history books," you told me. "Now let's get this cleaned up before the radio."

I think I know your secret, Mrs. Ramsey. You cannot tell any stories about the fire, any stories about the Del Monte at all, because, like the blue threads woven into paper money to stop counterfeiters, there is something so integral that it cannot be removed without suspicion. He is part of every earthquake story you have, but you must leave him out, of course. You must be sure that no one can trace you back to this sweet town where you have hidden yourself and your son; you must give no scent for him to sniff you out. It's me, isn't it, Alice? I am your secret; I am your blue thread. How sorry I am that I've poisoned your stories so completely, like a well you can no longer draw from. Especially when it is so foolish, so useless, to hide anymore.

Were there still stars in your hair, that afternoon long ago? When I stepped onto the porte cochere, desperate to catch you? When I yelled to the automobile snorting and chattering along the drive, already too far away to reach, too set in its ways along the carriage ruts of the Del Monte? To my own surprise, I let out a little sob and slumped against a column, watching that gleaming green car leave me behind for Pasadena, dustily speeding through the cypress-stripes of shadow, a little hopeless pathetic sob. Alice, slipped away from me, again. My heart was picked clean at last, like a bony skull. I turned to face the white-bright sky with its crowds of clouds, its pilgrim birds, its coming locusts, and I looked away, back to the hotel, and there you were. Oh, Alice. Standing there all the time, grinning in your dust hood, lipstick perfectly applied even in the dark of the morning, waiting. Not for coffee, or luggage, or mother. For me.

You said, "Alone at last."

So plainly, as if you didn't love me. And then that dear immortal laugh, you prankster.

Weren't there stars in your hair?

I am called to supper now by two voices: careful Alice and reckless, impatient Sammy. Macaroni pie, a pleasure for an old man in his youth, remembering. I have only a moment to get this down: Alice in the shadow of the arch, willows behind her, laughing, goggles dangling from her fingers. Just waiting in the dust-dry air. The shock of that lovely, that priceless face, the one person who did not wish me dead; she had sent her mother to safety. She had stayed for me. At that very moment, her house was being dynamited by soldiers, her small fortune dying in its vault. She did not know it, giving me a flickering grin, holding out her hand. Her friends were all leaving the city, never to return; her mother was already nursing a sickness that would keep her on her deathbed for years. She did not know it. There, on the porch, pulling me towards her with a wink. Alice, whispering nonsense in my ear.

Reader, she married me. Of course she did; I was all she had in the world.

We were wed in May of 1908 and I knew every inch of ecstasy. Picture me on that wonderful day two years after the quake: a black Prince Albert coat, flared at the knee, top hat, pocket watch (hidden) ticking away the minutes until I would have my Alice, a soft smile on my face, cheeks somewhat inflamed from a departing cold but also, I suspect, from the frightened pleasure of someone about to pull off a heist. Above: the sun moving through the fog like a luminous deep-sea fish. Behind: the ruins of our City Hall, still uncleared, just the coiling staircase of the dome remaining now, the black spine of a dragon. My fiancée stood whispering with the witness—the Widow Levy, all in mauve and feathers—and I stood fretting, crushing my pocket handkerchief into a damp ball. Picture my happy heart pinned to my lapel: a bloody boutonniere.

And Alice, oh picture her, please. A seemingly plain green tunic that revealed, when she took a wide step, the shocking Turkish pants that she wore underneath. Something white in her bouquet (we are not botanists, we men in love), and on her head—my quaint and funny Alice—a tricornered hat all trimmed in lace. I can't seem to pillage my memory for any image of her face; it has been smudged from too much handling. But I imagine a clever smile bent, at one corner, into something tender.

And picture my city, with banners of celebration still fluttering from the new rooftops and church spires of San Francisco—for only a month before had marked the two-year anniversary of our so-called destruction. An adolescent, impatient town, we rebuilt as quickly as we could, exactly as before, and made all the same impulsive, glittering mistakes of a young man eager to prove he is alive. It was not just rubble that surrounded us. Besides the staircase of City Hall, the world around us looked much as it had before, but this time with new paint, modern electricity, and garages for automobiles. We were not that old San Francisco of gilt-edged gas lamps and velvet walls. We longed—as young men always do—to be modern.

I heard my bride whispering as the judge approached: "I'm so lucky, Asgar, so lucky to have found you . . ." The rest was drowned out by the black rush of blood in my ears.

I suppose Alice was lucky, in her way, to have her Asgar. I'm sure her mother, smiling beside us, thought so: he was dependable and kind; he was handsome in an eerie Nordic way; he had been a steady rock through all their troubles; and—most important to Mrs. Levy—Mr. Dollar had an income. It was not a small concern. You see, fate had dealt me one final heart to complete my flush: because of the earthquake, the widows had lost their fortune.

Only six major insurance companies honored their policies in full. The Levys had insured their house with a particular German company that, upon hearing of the earthquake, quickly closed all their business with America and never paid a cent. This was a common story. One German business even posted notices in New York proudly stating they had paid their clients in full when in fact the poor San Franciscans had to settle for a twenty-five percent discount on their losses, as if disaster meant a bulk price. I don't think Alice missed the house—it was always the elder Levy's taste—or the land she was forced to sell, but life is different for a woman. They are never as free as my Alice was before the earthquake. Think of it: wealthy, widowed, working at a charity of her own choosing. It was hard for her to realize that she had to depend on a man. That, like any poor and beautiful woman, she had to marry.

But the marvelous part, the part that warms my worst nights, is this: Alice, with a world to pick from, chose to marry *me*.

"We'll begin," the judge said, coming towards us with fluttering *Mikado* sleeves. He patted his pockets as if in search of glasses. To my horror, he approached the Widow Levy. "You are the bride?"

"No!" I shouted, perhaps too loudly.

Our witness laughed, as did her daughter. "Dear me, oh no. No, I'm the mother of the bride."

"It's me," said Alice, perfectly serious now, taking my hand.

"I see. Please stand before me. *Dearly beloved . . .*"

I was secretly happy that Alice wanted a plain wedding, with no guests. After all, there was nobody to come. She had no family except in far Seattle (all of whom she was sick of, anyway) and I had told her I had no one. She was extremely curious about me, and I eventually had to make up a story about a merchant father who had disappeared and an opera-singing mother who, on a wild trip back from the East, was lost on a sea voyage.

What besides death could keep Mother from my wedding? Here was the impossible—a bride for the hunchback—and I'm sure, if she could have, she would have canceled her life and spent it embroidering napkins and cloths and sheets for our bed, come and counseled Alice on her dress and hat (Mother never would have allowed that bud-green shade) and all the intricacies of married life that my sweet widow, of course, knew all too well. But she did not come. Because I simply never told her.

The greatest cruelties happen slowly. It was easy at first to keep Mother and Mina from my new life: after all, they had settled now in Oakland, an ocean away. Claiming a bad back from dragging her silver through the fire, Mother decided never to make the trip to San Francisco. She said she liked her house in the hills, and could live comfortably on the insurance from our burned and buried South Park. It was more than that, of course. She had loved her old town. She had been born there and seen the gold miners coming down from the hills, the Italians pressing their grapes into Chianti high in North Beach, the maids beating carpets as they sang; she had seen it grow to beauty, and she had seen it fall. So can you blame her if, a witness to death, she did not want to see the bright new life that had taken its place?

By the time I married Alice, Mina had refused to see me. We had told her, back in 1900, the true nature of her Uncle Beebee. She was twelve at the time and had stared at me, fiddling with her bows, not comprehending. "Is he going to die?" she asked, to which Mother replied, "Well, as much as any of us," and then my sweet sister looked at me with tense black eyes and said, "We can't tell anyone, don't tell, please Beebee, don't tell." I knew what she meant. She made me swear it many times over the years. Mina meant that this kind of deformity would reflect badly on the family, especially on her. She cried for her old Beebee. But the creature had to stay in the attic.

What happened, though, was not her fault. Whispering to love-struck admirers, dancing the daring polka at balls in town, no, Mina was not to blame. Nor Mother, staying in her house across the bay, speaking to her spirits. The fault was entirely mine. For I did more than hide my marriage from them. Over a few years, I ceased to return their letters or calls; I made excuses for why I could not join them for holidays or birthdays; I tapered off my visits to brief lunches or walks and then, by the end, to nothing at all. Because I did not want them to break my secret, to destroy the love I had worked so hard to win, I hid my life. I hid myself. I am not the first to do this. Like my father before me, I simply vanished in the snow.

So I was all alone on my wedding day. I came with just my hat, my suit, my heart full of honey. Friendless, orphaned, her Asgar offered himself completely when he slid that ring onto her finger and whispered those little words.

"Well I do too," said Alice. Our witness wept.

The judge pronounced us wed. Birds, sleeping in the spirals of the ruined stairs, flowed out into the sky above us. Alice's hand was cold as February.

"Asgar, are you crying?"

"No, no."

"Oh you are ridiculous. Kiss me."

I was. I did. For there was nobody left in my life but you, dear Alice. I had sent them all away.

What do we abandon to claim our heart's desire? What do we become?

∽

As for the wedding night, well. Prurient reader. My son may be reading this, and he will blush, so I must open a peacock screen across the page. Behind it, imagine what you will: fog air beading a body. Phlox-perfumed memory, a teenage prayer answered at twice that age, the whisper of a beloved name, a false one. An exaltation of swallows. And so on.

∽

Much later, in our older years traveling together in an automobile, Hughie asked me why I never asked *him* to the wedding.

"Are you insane?" I said. "You would have blown the whole thing."

"Max, I would've come in disguise. A false beard and a cape. A parasol. Come on, I would have hidden behind a tree."

"There were no trees left."

"Behind a stout woman. I would have watched over you as a witness."

"It's ridiculous."

"Why didn't you tell me?"

"We weren't close then, were we? There were all sorts of things we didn't tell."

"True."

And he drove on past a lake of aquamarine, shadowed by one solitary cloud, the air through the open window making its syllable sound. I pointed out three boys, loud as crows, jumping from a dock; he smiled. Ah, old Hughie.

But back to married life.

∽

It is a wolfish world, but she relieved it. Somehow, on our meager funds, Alice made a rich and lovely life. In those expensive post-earthquake days, she produced feasts of rice in aromatic spices, talked wealthy friends out of their opera tickets, redid our bed-covers from old dress material, and all so effortlessly—as if it were perfectly natural to melt used candles into multicolored tapers. Did you know you can reuse broken earthquake china to tile your kitchen walls? My wife somehow did. She hired a neighbor boy and had my shoddy kitchen all redone in priceless cracked porce-lain some friends were throwing out. She even had a broken teacup set in there with all the fine Limoges—imagine that, a teacup stick-ing out of the wall, handle and everything—and in it she always kept the fresh blossoms that I gave her.

What my wife and I ate for breakfast: Weetabix from the box. What we learned together, laughing in the privacy of our parlor, but never performed: the turkey trot. What she smelled of in the evening when she stepped smiling into the parlor where I waited: Rediviva.

Tell me: What is the proper wine for rapture? What is the proper fork?

Curse me if you want to, Alice, but say I was no miser. In fact, I gave you everything I could—gowns that I had seen you admire, far beyond our means, that I would buy and hang in the closet for you to discover; and of course the books that you would never have bought, all shipped from New York so you did not have to leave the house to find them—all these I gave you, and more. I even slipped a few dollars into your shoes for you to spend as you wished. I wanted more than anything to make you happy, to see that hard-won shock of joy when you pulled a leather book out of an unexpected parcel. My one luxury was the purchase of that smile, that quick laugh. Gothic villains keep their maidens in sew-ers, or high in foreign castles, sipping their blood like cordials. Jealous husbands are different, but still, we know that it is not enough to have them love us. We have to make a life they cannot leave. Too good to leave. Oh Alice, I did it so you would stay.

And isn't that what Sammy has heard me shouting in my sleep? When the summer lightning slits the sky's throat and Buster shivers in the sheets? *Oh stay, Alice, please stay, please stay, oh stay, stay.*

You're thinking that, having carved her name like a whaler into my very bones so that even my skin bore a faint trace of those five letters, having sailed around the world in my mind in search of her, and having found her, captured her, held her, old Max would soon tire of her. We are restless beasts, after all, and even paradise becomes too plain a prison. It did annoy me, now and then, that her housekeeping was not of the best quality. Shoes somehow propagated under settees. The bathroom, still resounding from her tub-singing, was always as wet as a marsh. And her whims were shortsighted; a harmless prank such as wearing the chandelier-drops as earrings was amusing, but somehow they never found their way back to their proper home, and I always had to set things aright in the end. I recall, as well, how trying it was when Alice would become entranced by some idea—for instance that we would have a mountain picnic—and become so firmly set that when these schemes dissolved, from rain or cost or whatever, it would take her hours to recover from her childlike disappointment. But none of this mattered. Not for more than a minute, two minutes, and I forgave her. With kisses that she accepted along her shoulder. With fingers spread beneath her scented hair, touching the landscape of her scalp like something beneath the sea. With words in her ear that made her whisper, "You're a fool." I forgave and forgave her. Of course I never grew tired. You see, I loved her.

You're wondering: Did she notice? That particular quirk of my body, did she sense it in the early mornings? When she accepted all those kisses of mine, through the years, the lips that grew slightly smoother? The hair that brightened just a little, the lines that faded from my eyes? While she gave up bread to take the voluptuous weight from her thighs (little realizing how I loved each dimple), did she notice that my pants had been taken in to fit a shrinking waist? By our sixth year, when she was forty, could she tell that the man who begged for an embrace before she left—the man who could not seem to get enough of her—did it with the desperation of a youth of twenty-seven?

I did my best to hide it. As I once had worked to cover my age with careful dyes at the barber's, now I came up with other tricks, countercurses. I bought a pair of uncorrected glasses, for instance, in old-fashioned ovals that made me just a little middle-aged. No longer interested in fashion as I once had been when nothing fit me, I chose to dress as old men do, in drab or antique styles, as if I had lost touch with a passing world. I even had my trusted barber put a little gray into my temples—yet when I looked in the mirror, it had come out even blonder, and I saw before me a blinking sun-touched boy whom Alice could never love. We took the color down a few shades, approaching the dull and dusty brown of books. Every day of my life, time was tricking me, embellishing my body with new leanness, long muscles, a rose in each cheek, and each day I did my best to burn the evidence. A telltale heart was beating beneath the floorboards of my skin, the heart of the man I'd buried, and I tried to forget—for love teaches us to forget—that one morning I would find her staring at me, a young stranger, the spell worn off at last.

But I was lucky. What she noticed were her own body's changes, and I often heard low sighs from the bedroom. She joked about her wrinkles and her chin, her new gray hairs (which disappeared at the salon), the bruises that took too long to heal, the aches of her back, her feet. She said these things lightly, as if she didn't care, and I told her over and over that she was lovely. You see, I wanted to see her old. Perhaps it was a product of deformity, but it excited me to think of her body moving through time, her breasts full and low, her neck ringed with folds. By our final years, when she could no longer hide the lines around her mouth, I desired her more than ever. Not the girl I'd met at stung-fourteen, but every variation of that girl. How luscious to see my Alice grow broad and then thin again, frail and gray, pleating her face with laughter! This is what my sacrifice was for: to have her ripen until her death within my arms.

⟿

One cool morning, just after we had finished the dreamlike act of love—something I had pictured so often as a youth, and which in those early years was given to me eagerly, daily—my new wife turned to me and said, "You're not enough for me, Asgar. I need another man." She arranged the bedclothes happily around her and then looked back at me, smiling impishly. "Why do you look like that? Did you bruise something? A son, sweet man. I think we need a son."

You, Sammy, it was you she needed. Alice spoke of you so merrily that morning, full of hopeful plans, almost as if you were a treasure buried long ago within her life and here she was, returned to find you. She knew you in every detail—your clever laugh, your school pranks, your underwater face in the morning, your stunned rapture in the midst of a Jules Verne novel, how you can stand on your head, sing, and whistle through your nose, swim farther on the river than any of your friends—and how is it mothers know these things? Are their dreams built into you, cell by cell, even before you are born? Or do they have some mystic clue to you, a pirate map folded in their heads?

In that first year of our marriage, she talked about you brightly, always when we'd just finished our conjugal embrace and I lay back on the bedsheets, dazed and happy. It was still so fresh and pure, the impossibility that my little Alice, whom I had loved since she was in barley-sugar curls and princess hats, could kiss me so hotly, tear at me with her nails as if she might rip me to shreds. Like a druidess, every morning she burned me to ashes. Our house was ever in fog, but I picture the window stuffed with sun, and a long diamond of light across our bodies. As I lay in my private bliss, your mother curled my hair around her finger and told me how soon you would be coming now, how she could feel you impearling in the nacre of her womb.

The second year, it became an occupation: the thought of you, the implication of you, there between us in the bed. "Don't be so shy, Asgar," she used to whisper, crawling towards me with dark cat-eyes. "Just do exactly as I tell you." I did, dutifully; no teacher was ever better. But those jewel-bright impossible mornings of the first year were gone; instead, we had a job before us, like a crew searching for an uncharted island, and she sometimes batted away my tickling fingers, my whispering kisses, intent only on the necessary parts of love.

The third year was a ghost story. She would put down her book sometimes and stare into a corner, as if she could see you there, barely visible, padding through the hallway. She was not sleeping well and would get up at night, go to the kitchen, where I could swear I heard the faint sound of singing. Alice tried to lift her spirits with her photography and went on long outings during the day. She returned from these outings with images of our city in its rebuilding, of the new Chinatown with its broader streets to keep out rats, its pagoda buildings, its lines of children holding on to each other's pigtails. Boys in the park, mothers gathered in white ruffles on a park bench. She developed these in our bathroom, and many of the pictures she tore to pieces. Was she looking for an image of you? And sometimes I came home to find her in a satin dress and paste diamonds; my Alice, dressed to cheer herself up, just as she had in the old days of South Park. I would find her sitting by the window, glittering, laughing, saying, "I'm feeling grand, darling!" But my heart would drop. What longing was hidden there? What secret? I would laugh and pour a drink, hoping tomorrow would be different. For we hate what is half seen.

Our tangle in the bedroom became less frequent, but more intense again: a séance, calling forth the one spirit who would not come. "I think I felt something that time," she'd whisper, worried, "Or no, no maybe not," and she would lie in silence, sheets wrapped up to her chin, nose red from the cold air. I fell into a quiet despair. You see, as with any lover, I was never sure that she was mine entirely. I knew she could vanish in an instant. But with a son, my son, if she somehow (God forbid) ever stopped loving me, she would love you forever, and it would still be enough. You could have saved my life. And yet—I admit I was also a little anxious. For what kind of creature would come from my incubus loins? Half human, half gorgon, with snaky hair and cockatrice eyes? Or, like myth, immortal?

But you are beautiful, Sammy, you are. I sit here writing on our little shared desk, and you are sprawled out like a dead soldier on your bunk, napping, your mouth agape with wonder at your dreams, the sun lighting your right ear so it glows coral-pink. One cheek is raw from rubbing on the sheet. Your left hand hangs at a crazy angle, soft and hopeless, and your lids pulse with the frenzy of your sleeping eyes. My son, you are beautiful, although you came too late.

A brief intrusion; forgive the dust. These scribblings are from the attic. I've finally found the little doorway leading here— Wonderland-sized—and it is indeed a dreamlike kingdom of broken chairs and dead insects and boxed-up memory. I have to pause here to write about the view from this smudgy window; it is sublime. It is of you, Alice, far below me.

You are stooped in yellow in the rows, your skirt tied in two calf-knots as Roman women used to do, your arms half reddened by the sun and air of summer as you pluck and prune with such decision. You move as unhesitatingly as a card dealer, either absolutely sure of what's a weed and what isn't or, perhaps, immune to regret in this one place. You don't sing or talk or clench your face in worry. You are tender with each dahlia and approach it as if it were the loveliest, the only flower in the world, but once you move on it is forgotten. Ah, there's a bee following your every move.

It's hot up here, Alice. It's full of motherly rubbish and lover's loot. I'm thrilled and exhausted from going through all of Sammy's artwork from his early scribblings—mostly cave drawings that look like spidery heads speared on thin stakes—to recent portraiture of our little family that emphasizes his hands, your hairdo, and my chin. I think I love most the race car drawings he has made for me, and the scribbled inventions that he hopes will make him a fortune. These are what a father hoards—secrets his son shared only with him.

But that is not what I have come to find. Like any great museum, you keep your greatest, most controversial treasures stored away forever, but here they are, all leaning in a row like skeletons in a catacomb: your photographs. All the things you made in the years you spent without me, the years before I found you this last time. Yes, here it is: a self-portrait of you floating in a pond. I love it; I am thrilled by its passion; it intimates a private world of storm clouds, floodwaters, scattered petals, and broken glass. What do our lovers see when they close their eyes? What comes to them in daydreams? Only those who love artists will ever know, though it breaks our hearts to find it's never us.

I must keep an eye on you, Alice Ramsey, if I am to look through your things. But now that I've begun spying on you, I hardly know how to stop. I can't sit in this stuffy room and search for some bit of the past because here you are! What I've searched for so long is below me in the garden. You kneel, and your calves spread out between the hairy curled fists of the poppies, your skin bruised just faintly from when I tagged you in a game the other day; I have made my mark. Those legs, falling out of the skirt. And I picture a little girl like this, searching in the dark grass for a pin, her bloomers rising up her thighs like this. The bee is in the air above you, dipping towards your hair, but you don't notice. You lean back and wipe the sweat from your face with the edge of your elbow, a peasant gesture. The bee, the sun, the air circle around you. So lovely in the garden. Old men and little boys will always love you, Alice Ramsey. Beware.

It was in December of 1912, and I had been happily married to Alice for more than four years, when our lives endured a slight alteration. Her mother, the Widow Levy, who had been living in Pasadena since our marriage, took ill. The doctors never learned the true cause, but as I recall she broke out in a rash of telegrams, delivered weekly to our doorstep until Alice took me aside one night and said it was really very serious.

"How serious, darling?"

"Well, I'm going to have to help."

I considered this for a moment. If I'd had a pipe, I would have smoked it. I posed like a husband in a Sears catalog, in a sweater coat, considered how brief is the life of a rose, and said all right then, her mother could come and live with us.

"Ugh, you don't want that," she said, then added, "Besides, Mama can't travel. I'm going to have to stay with her."

In other words, they had to operate; they had to remove Alice from my life—I would rather they'd cut out a lung! My wife left the room to fill her trunk half with old dresses, half with new books and her cameras. She would be gone for three weeks, back for one, down again for three, and so on until her mother got better. Alice came back into the room and saw my face and sorrow shimmered in her eyes; she came and held my ears in her warm hands, kissed the nexus of my brow. "Oh, honey, it'll only be a few months." My heart brightened; was her mother so near the end? "No, Asgar," she told me, studying my eyes. "No, a few months before she's well."

She was wrong; the woman did not get well. And it took five years.

⟡

Her absences destroyed me. Like Demeter, I made my world a winter without her. Clothes piled up, wineglasses stood in a red-stained battalion on the kitchen table, and every night I slept with my arms coiled around a sofa cushion. Sometimes, when I awoke, smiling, joints creaking, whispering good morning to my lover, and found my arms full only of stuffing and fog, I wept real tears.

We talked in letters, which was romantic. I told her about the stupid happenings of our living room, where I had last heard the scuttlings of our local mouse, what hinge or drawer I had fixed, and any change in the view. I read about her mother's pain and sadness, her lost beauty, her selfish nature in full bloom at last. I read that Alice had joined a photographic club and was apprenticing in a local artist's studio. In fact, she sent me a beautiful picture of herself in an orange grove, smiling at the camera with sly love (at her husband, that is, since the photo was made specifically for me), and it was embossed with the silver *VR* of the studio. I kept the photo by my bed, and when I thought of my distant wife, it began to take the place of my own memory.

I became as jealous as Bluebeard. Meeting her at the Oakland station with a bunch of flowers or some ornament for her hair— something that would win a smile and then, unworn, a place in her Chinese box—I would catch her chatting with a man, frequently mustached and indistinct, letting him help her down from the train before she caught my eye and shot him a quick goodbye. He exited behind the scenery, the steam and boxes. Her smile went on like a filament bulb.

"What was his name?" I'd ask once she'd admired my present.

"Who? What? Oh, Asgar."

"I don't want you talking to any men outside your photographic club."

"Asgar, I'm exhausted. Mother's been making me read romance novels to her, it's pretty shocking how boring those things are, and how explicit, really. Every possible act of love, it's in there. You'd never guess it, but my mother is quite a sex fiend . . ."

"His name."

"It's Cyril, and he sells lumber and I love him. Oh, don't be so typical. I'd never leave you for a Cyril. Now get me somewhere where you can kiss me," she'd say, and I'd hurry her into the car, wondering all the while if I was warming my hands over the fire lit by another. Cyril, or Frank, or Bob; oh the images that emerged nightly in the chemical bath of my skull!

But it all faded. When she was with me, for that one week each month, my life took on the heightened colors of a tinted photograph, and even Alice's bad housekeeping, the socks and shoes found under the sofas, the scattered opened envelopes she left everywhere, came to be adored—they were the sign of my continued luck. My life's hope had come true, and I instructed the maid to keep a sock or two lying around even when the mistress was gone, a hairbrush stocked with glossy brown hair, just to prove to myself I was not dreaming.

∾

It was about two years into her mother's illness that our fortunes changed yet again. One week when Alice was in San Francisco,

I came home from work to find her in our little parlor reading.
I made a noise and Alice looked up at me with a lively expression.

"What is it, darling?"

Mischief fluttered across her face and departed. She said nothing and picked a card from the china bowl: Gerald Lassiter, Esq.
Fairmont Hotel. A corner of it had been turned down to reveal
the word *Affaires*. Business of some sort.

"Oh, what's this?"

"Make a guess."

"How on earth am I . . . ?"

She said, "Okay, I'll give you three hints. Top hat. Oiled rain-
coat. Haunted eyes. That's all I'm saying."

"My bastard son."

Her eyes widened in amusement. "Wouldn't that be fun? No,
an old man. Very odd and irritated. Walked with two ivory-tipped
canes."

"I'm assuming it's not a fellow clerk? Nothing as boring as that?"

"No, no, nothing as boring as that. Come on, guess, Asgar!"

"I give up. William Howard Taft."

She sighed. "You're terrible at this. He wouldn't tell me anything. He just asked for the man of the house. He said it concerned you and another."

"Mrs. Taft."

Her eyes came alive again and she leaned forward in her chair.
"Asgar, I think it must be your father!"

I went the very next morning to the Fairmont Hotel and managed to be allowed in, though it was not a place for a poor clerk,
even in what passed as my best suit. I had the concierge call up to
Mr. Gerald Lassiter, Esq., and I waited a long time on a pierce-
carved couch beside an explosion of tulips.

The concierge returned, his buttons sparking in the lobby air. He waved a hand and from behind him emerged a man in a greatcoat, trim gray beard, his left eye clouded, blind, and his nose barnacled with spots. Alice's powerful imagination had doubled the canes; there was only one, with a carved ivory head. I stood up. The cane was handed to the concierge and the man stared at me with a shuddering intake of breath.

"Father?" I ventured.

"What?" he asked.

Deaf, deaf and hobbling, I thought. "I don't know what to say."

"Say?"

Louder: "You are, you are . . ."

"Mr. Tivoli, I am a lawyer," he said with a hissing throat. "I am here as executor and would have been here long before had you not been so goddamned hard to find. I assumed you did not want your wife to know your real identity. Asgar Van Daler indeed. You are a fool and your father is dead."

It was perfectly simple: my father's footsteps through the snow had led straight to the harbor, as we always knew, and not because he had been stolen out to sea. He had simply walked away from his life and never returned.

He had arrived in Alaska a month after he disappeared from San Francisco and there, with the money he had managed to take with him, bought a small supply store and began a little business in the remotest possible region of America. Who knows what pleasure he had sought there in the lonely cold, the sun a mere gray star? Surely some shivering joy. Perhaps the sudden snow had shown him a vision, a reminder of his long-lost homeland in the north. The shop grew into two, and three, and that was when my father began investing in real estate and mining ventures, which brought him even more profit—in copper, not in gold—and so on in a dull and spiraling accumulation of wealth and stature.

"He did marry," the executor informed me. "A half-Indian

woman named Sarah Howard, but she gave him no children and had no family. Of no fiscal importance here. I believe she died in an influenza outbreak near the end of the last century." There was no more to be known of Sarah Howard. I picture her, of course, in buckskins and a bonnet, tending a woodstove and making johnnycakes for scribbling Dad. Except of course they were wealthy: a maid to tend the stove, to serve the drinks. Indian Sarah would be sewing in the parlor. No buckskins, no bonnet. Silk dress and wearing bustles years after they had gone out of style, her black Aleutian hair lit by the never-setting sun. Poor dead Sarah. Of no fiscal importance, but he loved her.

He lived a decade without her, his mines failing a little, his cannery prospering. The houses were slowly repaired and rented, the business turned over to more willing hands. He got gray and weary of the world and died. There is no deathbed scene, no dying phrase. How could there be? My father had already left without a word.

"A satisfactory life, as your inheritance proves."

This was the life he wanted? A cold and happy, far-off life? He left his house and clothes, he left us, in our famous city? It seemed impossible. Raucous, beautiful San Francisco always seemed to me like the favored daughter of a merchant, whom every man adores, gorgeous and perfumed and gay, and yet there will always be a man who finds her charms too shrill. One who prefers a whisperer with a mole and a sable brow, a chilly smile. There is always my father to choose the wrong, wrong life.

Why do they leave us? Why?

⁓

Twelve copper mines in various locations in Alaska and Montana, three sawmills, two steamers, a fishery, a cannery, one dozen pairs of men's shoes, size 10 (my size, too, Dad, until my feet began to shrink), two dozen silk ties and cravats in a Turkish bazaar of hues,

a kinetoscope with slides of China, India, and various bathing
beauties, a collection of grotesque farmyard majolica, cuff links in
jet and lava, a female hand carved from bog oak, a startling and in-
genious variety of electrical items meant to mix, grind, drill, illu-
mine, project, mesmerize, and cure (none of which worked), a gold
pocket watch engraved "for my love Asgar" which I did not remember, a silver ring which I did (bringing back a sudden memory of the mark it left when he removed it, a double welt in pink),
various pieces of rental property, and a check from the estate which
embodied not my father's account (which was all wisely invested)
but the proceeds from the sale of four houses in Fairbanks, one in
Anchorage, furniture, paintings, and other items too lacking in sen-
timent for Father to itemize as mine, including, apparently, a cast-
iron fountain portraying a boy beneath an umbrella.

And that is all I ever got from my father.

That evening, I told Alice and her face became electric.

"What do you mean?"

We were rich, I said, not grossly rich like bankers or railroad
men she'd known, but still beautifully and comfortably rich just as
she had been before, as I had been as a child; the wheel had come
around for us again. I said I loved our life, the wild kitchen with
its rose-filled teacup, the miracles she could make from her modest grocery list, the lace she bought by the yard to retrim old
dresses, our pure and perfect life in this pure and perfect room. I
said we should be careful not to change a life we loved. And yet.
"And yet I'll give you anything, Alice. Any desire in your heart."

My fantasy was that we should take one of the new cruise ships
around the world. No earthquake could tumble us; no war could
reach us. I could make my dream come true; I could buy a gilded
island. Is there not a people, in some desert place, who are prom-

ised this in heaven? The waves themselves would hypnotize her, insominate her, keep her sleeping where I could watch her, gazing at her dreams, my wave-borne Alice under a porthole filled with sun, perhaps forever.

I told her this (or some abridged version) and she listened, leaning against the mantel with her cheap earrings jingling faintly with the movements of her head.

"No. No. That's not what I want."

"Then what? Alice, tell me."

She held the thought in her mouth, like a cupped bird. Her eyes searched the wallpaper, as if something were written there, some message from her future self. When she spoke at last, it was like a direct current: "I want my own business, a photography studio, and space besides for my own work, yes, yes, oh I want . . ."

You wanted freedom. It's what we always wish for, and I should have known it. I'm surprised, looking back, Mrs. Ramsey, that you didn't leave me long before, that I didn't return to the rooms soon after our marriage and find them empty, or full of everything but you and your favorite dress—the red. Why did you stay so long?

"We'll see, Alice."

A laugh, a fountain of joy. "Oh what a chance! Asgar, what a chance!"

"We'll see."

She began to dance and then caught my reflection in the mirror and winked at me. "Asgar, I think we should celebrate," she said with her timeless smile. "Kiss me right here on my neck. Yes." With the scent of her so willingly given to me, the young parts of me began to burn. I heard her whisper: "Asgar, take this damned dress off of me."

Oh I did, with hot and grateful hands I did. I pulled the wings from the moth. And she got her shop.

∿

"You need to touch up your hair color, Max," Hughie mumbled through his new scimitar mustache.

"What?"

"You look like a paperboy. You could be my son."

"My worst nightmare, Hughie."

We sat in Hughie's club, one that I had been invited to join because of my newfound wealth. So once more I found myself alongside Hughie almost every night in a leather chair carbuncled with upholstery tacks, reading a newspaper still warm from the butler's iron. With Alice gone so often, I was grateful for those evenings with Hughie.

"I like you better rich, Max."

"You idiot, you used to say you liked me better poor."

"I did?"

"You did."

He considered this. "Well, that's because I was poor. But the least you can do is buy a decent haircut."

"Hand me my drink."

"Are you enjoying it, at least? I mean, all this sudden wealth? And Alice? Seems like you're the luckiest man alive."

I was. Alice and I, after years in that stuffy apartment, now had a broad-shouldered house on Green with a chilly view of Alcatraz, a modern garage to hold our Oldsmobile, as well as all the new and foolish things that people have when they come back into money, the trinkets and indulgences we missed so much—the clothes and food and miraculous habits—and which are never half as pleasing. Of course, with this new house, I had to find new hiding places for the evidence of my secret, a few letters and the pendant and chain Grandmother made for me. While it had been easy to keep it in its old grave among my shoes, now I was afraid no hiding place would be good enough; servants will go through everything. Eventually, I slipped it with the letters into a locked box in my dresser and told the maid not to dust it.

I didn't worry about Alice, prying as she was; my wife was hardly ever there. When she did come up to see me, I lavished her as best I could, and she enjoyed it, I think, laughing at the ludicrous jewels I brought to her in little velvet boxes, screaming at the new car when I drove it in front of the house for the first time, but she never wore the jewels and she never drove the car. In fact, with money behind her, she dressed in her same eccentric, inexpensive clothes—and sometimes those pants, underneath, when she could get away with it—and concentrated only on her business plan, on that studio of hers, the one I'd sworn to buy her. I longed to travel back in time and pluck that promise from my lips. But how could I have known? My only hint came too late: on the morning when she stepped from the train, kissed me flutteringly, and, like a magician producing a handkerchief, pulled a piece of paper from her coat: the lease she had just signed. She was so happy; that night she practically melted in my arms. The photography business she had dreamed of. A little studio on an up-and-coming corner. Of course it was in Pasadena.

"She's got to be near her mother," I explained to Hughie when he raised an eyebrow. "They're closer than I realized. Like those fig and cypress trees that grow inside each other in Eastern gardens, it's unexpected. And her business partner, he's down there. She apprenticed with him, he was once quite a famous artist and she says, well, she says she's his muse. He's got clients and experience." An old friend of her mother's, old Victor. I liked to think of him with long white mustaches, brows singed off from flash-powder burns.

"You're taking this pretty well, Max."

I said. "It's what she wants. When you love someone, don't you want their dreams to come true? If you can help them? And she has to be down there anyway. I see her when I can. That's enough, isn't it? When you really love someone."

"I guess," he said quietly.

"So things are good, Hughie."

"Are they?"

"Oh yes."

He stared at me with those blue eyes, fringed by albino lashes. Then he shook his head and touched my sleeve. "You've got to tell her, Max," he said. "You'll lose her."

"I don't want to talk about this."

"It's idiotic," he hissed. Other men looked and smiled at the noise of our argument. "Dying your hair, and I hear you've got a cane now. I'm sure you don't think she's stupid. You'll lose her."

I looked at him, at his ridiculous mustache, as sober and stupid as a bad disguise. "Shut up, Hughie," I snapped. "I don't know why you give advice. Everyone knows you're no good at love."

What I meant, I suppose (must we explain what alcohol makes us say?), was that he was no good at marriage. I had gone to his house one afternoon to deliver an invitation and the maid made me wait for Abigail, who arrived in a long brocade gown with a hallucinated look, her blond hair dull as dust. Shouts from her son rang from the upper stories. "He's not here," she said, and gave me her old social smile. "He's attending to our old property, he's staying there while he makes repairs."

"What old property?"

She winced. "The Pumpkin."

My first thought—and hers, I assume—was a mistress housed quite fairy-like in a pumpkin shell. Of course I ran over as soon as I could, only to find nothing more than rooms of Oriental carpets and lamps, bookcases filled with gleaming new books, a new manservant, and Hughie in shirtsleeves. Simple enough: a masculine retreat. Hughie explained quite innocently that he could not get his reading done in the house with his wife's shouting and her headaches, the child and the numerous cats they had collected. I saw he had covered the walls with army portraits that Abigail would never have allowed, men who were strangers to me, smiling with touched-up faces. Then his man brought in a pipe and—as in the old days—we smoked hashish until we were giggling on the floor. I remember thinking in my state that the manservant, Teddy, was as young as I looked, with slick black hair and red cheeks, but with an almost frightened look of youth that I could never reproduce. Teddy propped my head on a pillow and lay a blanket over me without a word. "Thank you, Teddy," I said.

"It's nothing, sir."

Hughie sighed and repeated, "Thank you, Teddy," and fell promptly asleep, snoring, on his sofa. I'd known him with girls, with Alice, in college and in marriage, and here he was, ever the same. Alone again in his bachelor house, with a manservant and mustache, a wife off somewhere putting a child to bed, singing a song he could not hear. No good at love; he knew what I meant.

I have to put down these pages for a moment. The house has been remade for a cocktail party—a quite illegal affair, darling, but I won't tell—and you are in your bedroom, Alice, shouting for someone to zip up your dress. I've got to run. I must get there before Sammy.

Now let us pick up a dropped detail: the invitation I had brought to Hughie's house. It was not just to one of our normal club events, the numerous dull evenings that rich men must attend; this was something unexpected. His invitation had come slipped into my own—I guess the hostess only kept track of me—and I delivered it because I needed him to come along. For memory, for history. To a ball, given by none other than my old maid, Mary.

It will not surprise even my youngest reader, I hope, that before the earthquake, every senator and merchant plunked coins in her mechanical jukebox and sat for a bottle of champagne with the woman, and more than a few had peepholes reserved for them within the scented walls of the "Virgin Room." Madame

Dupont had even opened a male brothel with a secret entrance for female customers, who wore satin masks so they would not be recognized, and a harem of men who supposedly worked as volunteers. All that was over by the teens, of course. Church pressure, legislation, the death of our dearly corrupted government, all brought Madame Dupont to close her houses. She had done well—broker clients had helped her to invest well, and stock tips were easy to hear in her flocked parlors. But it was not the last we heard of her, for she had often told me, a few glasses into the evening, that her dearest dream had never been to be a success. "I want to be a lady," she'd said, adjusting her blond wig. "Damn it, I deserve it. I've worked as hard as any wife for those men. I want to be at a dinner party with a Vanderbilt and have him turn to me and say, 'Madame, it's been a pleasure.'" So that was why, years after her brothel had shut its doors, and long after most had forsworn the vices she represented, after most of us had forgotten her, each important man in San Francisco received an invitation:

> *Mr. & Mrs. ———*
> *A September Ball*
> *March 20, 1914*
> *8 P.M.*
> *at the home of Marie Dupont*

You cannot stop a whore from making money, and money would buy anything in our city, so we found ourselves at an elegant white house sitting between the residences of a railroad baron and a Spanish count. Night-blooming jasmine, juniper, columns arcing in a Teddy Roosevelt grin. I imagined Mary had spent every cent on this house, chosen not for the comfort of her later years, but for this very night. The approach of glimmering gaslight—not electric—the noise of an orchestra coming like a distant waterfall from the open door; all planned, or hoped for at least when she laid down her million. I picture old Mary wandering through the empty rooms, clasping and unclasping her hands, imagining this party when all her sons and fathers and lovers would gather to claim her, this occasion for her best jewels, best jokes, this evening made, like all reunions, of memories best forgotten.

There was an Englishman, and not a Negro maid, to show us inside, but Madame was there all the same, standing at the newel of the stairs and laughing. I could see almost nothing of her except the abnormality of her thinness, her slight hunch that could only be age, and the expensive blond of her wig. The sexes come to resemble each other in childhood and old age, and she stood hands on her hips in the manner of a sergeant. She must have been seventy.

"Mr. Dempsey! I knew you would come," she said, approaching Hughie with an outstretched hand that shook slightly under the weight of her rings. "And you're looking so handsome and well."

"Madame," he said, kissing those rings. So thin, when did she get so thin?

"No Mrs. Dempsey?" she asked, tensing her port-wine lips.

"I'm sorry, no, we don't go out together these days."

She stared hard—the old procuress stare—but it became a sharp dazzle as she looked on me. "But you've found a beautiful young man, I'm charmed." A low laugh of old thrills.

Something of youth comes back with age. Although it was clear at a glance that nothing could restore her body's beauty, my old Mary, wrapped in her straight black gown, a long egret feather set across and away from her brow, held out her hand and flirted as if love affairs were all before her.

Immediately, though, the hand was withdrawn in a golden jangle. "Well fuck!" she yelled, then a pure yawp of joy. "My God, it's Max!"

∽

"Now wasn't there a girl?" she stage-whispered as I helped her into her ballroom. "Some girl you were in love with, poor Max. Have you seen her since you've gotten so young?"

"Her name was Alice," I told her with tenderness. "And Madame, I married her." I think if she could have cried, she would have. But like a colored gourd, she merely rattled with a sigh, for age and hardness had dried up everything inside her.

"And how's Hughie?" she asked. Hughie was off at the bar getting a glass of champagne, nodding at the few gathered men. He looked as uncomfortable as any of us among our fellow whore-mongers.

"He's happy, I think."

"No. His type isn't ever likely to be happy," she said, then turned to me and examined me thoroughly with the eye of a slaveholder. "I have to tell you something, Max, you haven't turned out at all as I expected. When I knew you as a little boy, I mean."

"No?"

"No, when I first saw you, oh, dear, you were the ugliest thing in the world. What could be sadder than a child in an old man's skin? I thought, God, here's something nobody will ever love. That's the truth. I felt so bad for you, God knows why, the rich little creature. I was so happy to see you'd changed. And you keep changing. I can't tell you what it's like to be a woman of my age, and to be so ugly. A gigantic lizard in silk. And now, you see, we've switched places. Tonight some man will look at me as he's drinking my wine and dancing to my band and think, God, here's something nobody will ever love. Serves me right, doesn't it? But I'm legitimate at last. I'm a lady, Max. So don't you tell them I was ever your maid. Don't you tell them I was ever anything but a lady."

"You are a lady."

"You've grown handsome, Max. Are you surprised? Try not to get younger. Stay just like this and your wife will love you forever."

I saw that the old girl was a little drunk. So I told her the simple truth: "I can't."

To that, she just laid the back of her hand against my cheek.

It did not take more than half an hour. More men from the club gathered in the ballroom and library, smoking cigars and raising eyebrows meaningfully at one another. I recognized one old fellow as the man who once had paid Mary to be her maid. The orchestra had lit once more into *Blue Danube* in the ever-hopeful expectation of bandleaders that some couple will be taken by the spirit and start a craze of dancing that will last until the early morning. There were no couples, however. I could hear Madame Dupont in the other room as more guests arrived:

"But your wife, where is she?"

"I'm sorry, Madame, but she couldn't make it this evening."

"Not make it?"

"You have a lovely house."

It happened time after time.

"I'm bored to tears, Max," Hughie moaned to me. "Since when did Madame Dupont's parties get so boring? *Blue Danube,* Jesus I could scream. And these rotten men who I'm sure I'd recognize better with their trousers around their ankles, sipping champagne in her bordello, all dressed up. It's such a bore."

"It's nice for Madame Dupont."

"It's blackmail. I don't owe her any favors. I paid for everything I got."

"Well, I owe her."

"I'm smashed. Hold my drink. I'll be back."

He was gone for a long time, and in a panic that he had abandoned me, I walked outside to see if the car was still here.

I was relieved to see it parked obliquely on the drive; inside Hughie and the driver were quietly arguing. It was cold out, and I suddenly wanted to go home. I walked down the wet grass and tried to listen to the argument, but some other chauffeur began

to crank his engine and I could only watch my friend and his servant, Teddy, mouthing their complaints, the one in a glistening
top hat and the other in a Scotch cap banded with goggles. It was
a kind of silent feature playing before me; even the night fog ren-
dered them colorless as I watched. I wondered how I had been so
careless not to have seen it before.

I pulled back behind a century plant and nearly cut my hand.
Another waltz had started from the ballroom. Hughie was wincing as he listened to the shouting young man, pressing one finger
against his own temple, giving a soft reply, the young man blinking coldly. Gloves crushed in a fist. Harsh words becoming fog in
the air. You, my more sophisticated reader, have known for ages
what I first allowed myself to recognize here. A letter burned and
thrown into a grate. Friends from college, beloved and then suddenly forgotten. A wife left to her house, a home with Teddy. The
hurt in Hughie's eyes—what other heartbreaks had I missed? I
was enraged, watching these men together. I had never guessed.
But people do not keep their secrets because they are so clever or
discreet; love is never discreet. They keep them because we don't
care enough to notice.

It all happened so quickly, I can't remember my true emotions
at the time—repulsion, I assume, shock and disgust—but thinking back on it, I feel only gratitude. I watched the lovers as they
sat silently and, not smiling, took each other's hand by the finger-
tips. Teddy's face was all sorrow and regret, and I suppose he
loved my friend as best he could, and almost enough. A moment
later Hughie whispered something in the young man's ear,
brushed his lips against his cheek, and kissed it. What an unexpected scene, so perverse and sad. And what wonderful luck. I
write this now, after having known Hughie for over fifty years,
and I ask you: what better companion could I have had all my
twisted life, what greater friend for this friendless beast, than old
Hughie—a secret monster just like me?

Back inside the party, when I retreated, the mood had changed. The liquor had lasted, and now the men were gathered into groups, giggling. A few had made it onto the dance floor, waltzing with one another as in the old days in the diggings, when there were no women to be partners and the world was only men. I would say nothing to Hughie, later. What was there to say? That the heart has more chambers than we can see?

Someone came over and saved me, smiling and whispering.

"What's that?" I asked.

He winked at me; he'd known me once, but didn't recognize me. "I said isn't it awful? Isn't it delicious?"

"The drink's not bad."

He grew quickly annoyed. "No, the wives."

"What about them?"

"You're married, young man, you should know. She's shunned."

"Who?"

"Dupont, the old whore. The wives aren't coming."

From the other room, we heard another man making his excuses: "I'm sorry, she couldn't make it this evening." We all turned around—perhaps the entire room turned—as Madame Dupont, with a friendless smile, entered her own ballroom and graciously accepted another glass of champagne. Her body was hunched slightly, and this willful woman seemed to disappear for once beneath the glitter of her jewels and her dress. She had at last understood the terms of this evening. It was like a wish granted by a genie: she had conjured up the most important society men in town, but it all meant nothing. She must have realized that men were not the goal, not the key to society; the acceptance of a woman, after all, is all that matters to another. And the wives would never accept old Mary.

I cannot describe the desperate, animal hate in her eyes. She stood and stared at the crowd of her customers with the gaze of someone wrongfully imprisoned, who has studied the walls for years until, at last, she picked the lock and slipped through and only found, in us, another wall. She had not gotten away with poverty, and hard luck, after all; she had not gotten away with youth, as we had. For look at us: in our celluloid collars and club rings and fat bellies. Each of us had dressed that evening knowing what would happen. Each of us, whom she had entertained in the orange-soda light of her parlor, had tied our ties and shrugged into the mirror, laughing at the awful trick we were going to play on Dupont, the old whore. We had convinced ourselves, I guess, that youth is something to be forgotten. And that, to forget it, one must not simply refuse to remember; one must destroy the woman who made the memories.

"All men tonight, is it?" she asked in a crystal voice.

There came a cheer from the crowd. Old Mary, we were shouting for old Mary, and our cheer meant: *We won't let you change.*

"Drink up, gentlemen."

The conductor looked away from his band for a moment, expecting, perhaps, a gesture from the hostess. One slash of a finger to stop the music and send them home, her boys, her sons, who had betrayed their old mother.

Then she lifted her head, briefly gay again the way she used to be. "Fuck, boys, somebody step up and dance with me!"

A cheer. Somebody did. I put down my drink and left through the laughing crowd.

It was 1917 and Alice was up in San Francisco for a few days. Her visits had become shorter as business picked up down south, and I remember the sensation of opening the closet one morning to realize that most of her dresses were gone. I helped nothing by responding with fearful jealousy. I would accuse her of ignoring her marriage, and then, when her eyes softened into something like the truth, I would grow too bold and name her accomplice. "Lawrence!" I might yell, referring to a young train attendant, and she'd examine me oh so very much amused. Oh, Alice. You were right to think I was absurd, because I never understood that the form my nemesis would take was not that of a blond, celluloid boy. Hell, you could have had me if you wanted; I was becoming more like one each day.

We had gone, that evening, to see a Mozart opera, and it was during a thrilling soprano aria that Alice began to fumble in her seat, warming her hands against each other like Lady Macbeth trying to rinse away a spot of blood. She leaned forward, wincing, and while at first I whispered for her to calm herself, she gave me one of her hands and it was ice. Then I noticed, upon her bare back, a firebird of fever. A dowager behind us coughed. Alice stared at me and whispered for me to save her—or that's what I heard under the coloratura. We waited until the aria was done and then, draping my wife in a shawl and my frock coat, I led her out into a taxi and, from there, home to bed. How tenderly I unwrapped her. My shivering beauty, with the fever glowing from her loins, between her breasts up to her neck, where it seemed to strangle her as she sighed. All through the night I wet her brow and listened to her breath. Watched her eyelids flicker and stare, flicker and stare. I did not sleep, waiting for her secrets. She gave none. By morning, of course, I was sicker than she.

Our deathbeds were in the same room, and all I can remember are warped and colored scenes and moments, unrelated, and revealed to me as an electric storm reveals the edges of a house:

There was the time, past midnight, I assume, when I awoke with an aching throat and looked across to Alice, who lay watching me with sad, adoring eyes. The room, in my memory, is all streaks of lavender and black, with a stripe of color from the upstairs hall, and Alice was pale from her sickness and probably hallucinating. "Go to sleep, Mother," she said, unblinking, and very dutifully I did.

Many hours later: myself trapped in hot sheets, the room bright despite drawn curtains, our maid giving a glass of water to Alice, who sat on the edge of her bed in a white lawn ruffled slip. A stray bit of sunlight caught the water in the glass and the world seemed to explode. I must have made a noise because the next thing I knew they were both looking at me. "Alice, I need to tell you," I said. She looked at me expectantly, holding herself up with the bedpost. The maid had vanished. "Alice, I need to tell you." She looked confused, pale, and scared, and, for a moment, like my grandmother when she rose from her sickbed. The maid returned and I was given a scarlet pill. Painful swallow. The water flashed again and I blacked out.

Late at night: opening my eyes, hoping days had passed and that I would be well again, only to feel my dull brain wriggling like a sea lion in its hot chamber. Immediately I noticed Alice, fully clothed in black and white satin, standing in the doorway, one hand on the knob. Her eyes were different, stern. I knew enough to feign sleep and it was some minutes before I heard her close the door and walk away. Why was my dresser open? The moon came into the room, old lover, and slept in her empty bed.

It was morning when it happened, I think, a mother-of-pearl morning when, feeling no better but somehow able to walk, I made my way to the chamber pot again and, squatting like a king, gave a grateful piss. The room teetered like a boat. I noticed my box of secrets on the bed, lock broken to splinters. I heard her behind me.

"Asgar, explain."

I craned my neck and saw something gold glinting in her hands. The light was painful to me and the position cramped. "What?"

"Where did you get this?"

She dumped it on the floor, where the chain coiled into an S and the numbers flashed against the wood: *1941.*

I thought of Grandmother in her bonnet. I thought of Father holding me naked from the bath. Dead, buried, gone. I thought of a dinner long ago, Alice touching those numbers one by one, laughing at me.

"I've never seen it before."

"It's yours. I found it in your dresser. Tell me why."

I explained that the room was turning and I could not think.

She showed me a torn envelope with some cursive writing. "And I found this." She tossed it on the floor and I saw it was from Hughie to a certain Max Tivoli.

"I can't think," I repeated.

"Asgar, explain."

"Didn't your mother know him? They must be hers."

"They're not."

"Perhaps at Bancroft's, yes now I remember . . ."

"Asgar, you're lying. Explain."

We are not ourselves when we are sick. We function at the most basic level, are ugly, miserable, and all our ordinary charms that seem to come so naturally to us fall away, and more than anything else we resemble either ourselves as children, crying for a drink of water, or our parents on their deathbeds, mumbling a prayer. Too weary to keep up the brittle artifice of our self, we shed it, like the locust, and become, in public, the sad and inconsolable adult that we so often are in private, which is to say: our true self. Illness always made me dazzled and weak, and this is the only reason I have for why—rather than concoct a more logical excuse, for though she suspected something, surely Alice never suspected the real reason—I told her. For the third time, I broke the Rule. Softly, carefully, as if she were a cobra that might strike, in a hoarse voice that did not belong to me, but with a relief and regret that did, stopped only now and then by gusts of nausea and black spots, I told her the thing I swore I never would: the truth.

You sat on the edge of the bed, Alice, and you looked at me in a way you never had before, not in all the years I knew you, as semichildren, as semistrangers, as husband and wife. You looked at me as if I mattered. As if I were a precious vase you had knocked carelessly against, and time had slowed just enough for you to see its hopeless fall towards the stone floor. As if you cared, at last, too late, to save me. "Oh no," you said. I suppose I began to cry—I was hopeless, and ill, and broken in so many ways— but I only remember you, dressed in white, the kiss of your lips on those words—"Oh no"—and your eyes with a small and tortured Max in each one. Then, with your next words, I was skinned alive.

"Oh no. You're simply insane."

My mind began to flash with nausea, and I could not stop you from leaving the room because just then I lost what little I had in my stomach and began to heave, like a dog, dryly onto Hughie's fallen letter. I saw my own name blotched with bile. A nurse came in and took me to the bed, and I could not speak because a pill was thrust between my lips. I saw your pale back moving down the hallway. You carried your face in your hands; they closed the door.

I awoke, terrified to find myself in the middle of a conversation. It was early evening, still light, and the curtains were open. Alice lay on the other bed, fully clothed in violet plissé crepe, net frill at her neckline, gloves on her stomach as if she had spent the day out. Her coat and hat lay on the foot of the bed. Whiskey on the table, two glasses, both nearly empty; apparently I had been drinking. I came to and she was talking:

"I don't want anything that's here."

"No," I said automatically.

"Things don't matter to me, the rugs and china don't matter. I don't want them. That will be an old life to me soon, my life's been in Pasadena for a long time now, Asgar. You've known that. Everything is down there now. I'll take just some books and some little things you gave me."

"Yes."

"The girl can send everything else to Victor. I'll give her the address."

"Of course. Who's Victor?"

She looked at me quite pitilessly. She was not anyone I recognized. I could feel something dark and hard building behind my eyes. She said, "Asgar. Asgar, you have to listen. I know this is hard."

"Max, I'm Max."

"Stop it. Stop with that."

"Alice, I'm Max!"

Her eyes went to the doorway, where a sea-hag nurse stood with a pill. I nodded and fell back against the pillow and the door closed on her. There was a kind of blur around the edge of my vision, a watery swirl as if we lived at the bottom of something. "Who's Victor?" I asked again, quietly.

"Oh you . . . we've gone through this. Victor Ramsey. I told you. Now I'm going to head downstairs in a minute, I don't want you to come down. You're sick, you'll make a scene. Promise me."

"Okay. Is he a doctor?"

"Asgar, are you even listening? I'm leaving for the train. I'm going down to Pasadena for good now. For good." Victor Ramsey, VR, yes, the clouds were parting from my brain and I recognized that old friend of her mother's, the photographer, her business partner. Him? How impossible. But she was talking: "Asgar, please listen. Please listen. You and I are saying goodbye." Then, more kindly, she added: "No, don't cry."

I could not stop it. You'll think I am so simple a creature that I wept because I was denied a thing I wanted, especially this, my life's goal. A child, a madman, wailing. But it isn't true. I wept because I loved her and because, no matter how she had faded to a visitor in our marriage, a cameo performer with few scenes, still I loved every one. To hear that sigh, Alice, from your dressing room as you tried to fit into an old dress. To find another of your favorite books, ruined by a careless drop into the bathtub, pressed under the dictionary to save it from swelling. To discover, coiled behind a chair, one of your snake-shed stockings, a sign that you were still in my world. Your kitchen singing voice. Your laugh. That foolish sound. Oh Alice, I had to save it.

"Alice," I said. "I'm not myself today. There's something I could say right now that would make all the difference, isn't there? You would stay if I said it, Alice. But I'm not thinking well, I'm in a kind of cloud, so you have to think of it. Help me, Alice, what could I say? Let's think. I know it's about ten words, and not big ones. What are they?"

Your hand was on your hat. "We are strangers, Asgar. There's nothing to say."

"There is, there is, Alice. I have to try. Life is very short." I left my bed, almost sweet with sickness, and sat beside you. Did you flinch? I think you were listening for the first time. "Alice, when I'm well, I will take you away from this house and this city and old Max. You're right, I'm not Max, I was in a fever, forgive me, Alice. Or don't forgive me. Or love me, either, forget all that. We'll travel around the world. You are the whole point of my life. Do you hear that? Not quite the words I want, but close. Alice, you will never meet anyone like me, and you know it. Don't you?"

She said it sadly: "Yes, Asgar, I do."

"You see? Alice, you have to stay."

"No. Here's the truth. I don't . . . I don't know who you are anymore."

"Of course you do! It's me, Alice."

She shook her head and I saw little tears forming there.

The darkness was pressing on my eyes. I leaned forward, talking softly now. "You have to stay, I'll die, you have no idea, do you?"

"Asgar, move away . . ."

Something awful was happening, but I was too much in a fever to stop it. I can hear myself whispering, "*Stay, Alice, please stay, oh stay, stay.*" Throb of blackness, bubble of tar—more lost seconds—then I was kissing her. I remember thinking I felt a little love for me there still, some last desire for her young husband, and my fevered brain realized there is no final form to the universe, that we might change it if we cared enough, and I ravished her, in our bed, my face inches from hers, panting *Stay, stay, stay* until my hot tears splashed into her open eyes.

I warned you. I am a monster.

She said nothing afterwards, when she sat on the bed and buttoned her dress, nor when she put on her coat and looked into the mirror. One pinkie fixed her lips. One hand drove a deadly pin through her hat.

I said, "Alice."

She said, "Don't ever try to find me. Don't ever try to see me again."

"Alice."

She simply stood there facing the door. In my nightmares, I work endlessly on a statue of my wife in just that pose, her back to me. I will never get to carve her face. Then, without turning, she walked out the door to meet her new life, and I had lost her forever this time.

Not quite forever, of course. I have twisted fate, for here she is: lying in the sun beside me in her white skirted bathing suit and sighing to a radio. She has just turned over in the lounge chair and there are welts all along the untanned regions of her womanly thighs, the heart-shaped cutout of her back, and I want to touch them all with my hand and take away the pinkness, wipe them from my lovely Alice. She is sweating slightly in the heat. She is thinner in her fifties than she ever was at forty.

"Sammy, hand me my drink," she says, but Sammy is too high in a tree to help her. "Mom," he yells, "look!" His little father looks and smiles; his mother adjusts her sun hat, squinting. The radio sings: *Button up your overcoat! When the wind blows free!*

Alice, you sing: "*Take good care of yourself!*"

I join in, boy soprano: "*You belong to me!*"

Do you know what I did after you left me, Alice? Do you know why it is such a miracle that I sit here beside you with my comic books and gum? Because I wanted to die and, seeking my death, I pretended to be a boy of twenty-two and joined the army. I did, Alice, me, a man in his mid-forties, not knowing his son was growing secretly in his vanished wife. I drilled until my mind was dull. Then, one month later, I got my wish and tasted death. I went to war.

Alice, your glass is here beside me, hoar-frosted gin. "I'll get it," I say, and hand you the cold thing, jingling with ice.

"Thanks, hon."

You take it and leave my fingers wet. A sip and you sigh, wink at me, return to your sun-sleep. Later, I imagine, when the sun has fallen, you will remove the bathing suit before the mirror and admire your new tan line—that salt point of your kissable skin.

"Cold," you say, and hand the glass to me again. I open my chest and place it where my heart should be.

Sammy, I write this by moonlight and firefly-light, far from our home and its eccentric, modern noises, far from Buster (who must be howling), far from the housebound boredom of summer. I write this on the banks of a gurgling river. White witch of a moon. My family is nearby, asleep; my wife and son, mother and brother, and another. Now, my boy-face is weeping and I have to wait for it to stop. There. We have gone camping.

When Alice mentioned the idea a few weeks ago, I was over-joyed. It seemed like another opportunity—perhaps my last—to huddle in the cave-comforts of my family. I imagined building a fire together, singing songs and roasting sausages on long whit-tled sticks, squinting when the smoke blew towards us, laughing, whispering when we thought—we city slickers—we heard the rus-tle of a bear (extinct in this safe state). I thought of a dark night in a tent, giggling as we tried to fall asleep, the three of us. And in the dark, I thought I could almost pretend I was a man again, a father, lying there beside my wife and son, owls hunting silently overhead, toads yodeling, moon lying like a stain upon the tent roof. In the dark, we can almost have the life we long for.

It did not happen this way.

"Rodney's coming," Sammy told me the night before, as we were packing for our trip. Our little-boy underwear bore our names in pen, by Alice's hand. I stroked those three black bleeding letters with my thumb.

"Who?"

He glared with the annoyance he often shows with me. "Rodney. Your doctor, duckbrain."

"He's not!"

"He is. He's driving. This is his whole duck-brained idea and I think it stinks like heck."

I should have noticed a certain affection growing between you, Alice, and my Dr. Harper—you remember the harmless quack who read my bones—but I'd been too distracted with these pages, and with finding as much time as I could with my restless son, to see it. There have been, of course, times when you left the house for hours and we were left in the charge of a neighbor. I now look back and realize you spent these evenings out with Dr. Harper. It was for him you worried over your outfits, dyed your sky-gray hair, practiced a winning smile.

The biggest clue, of course, was that cocktail party you had. I had the luck to help you with that zipper of yours (my hands quaking religiously), and then I watched as you applied those too-dark shadows and lipsticks and became too modern a woman for my tastes. Sammy and I were sent to bed, so the rest I saw only through the bars of the stairway: neighbors arriving in a bouquet of gay noise, then some muttering retired teachers, and then Dr. Harper with his cigar-store-Indian face, who brought a bouquet of roses and a small stuffed bear and kissed you on my favorite cheek. You had forgotten to start the Victrola, and a neighborly man was put to work. Dance music, not to my taste. But I saw him whispering to you beneath the stairs, my Dr. Harper. I saw how you laughed, blinked, touched his tie. Once, long ago, you wanted me like that.

So Dr. Harper arrived early in the morning in an Oldsmobile

packed with outdoor equipment—I gather he's a fan of this sort of thing—and an old-fashioned horn that went ba*wow*zah, ba-*wow*zah. I was put in the back with my son, and the adults sat up front, talking about books and art in voices too soft for me to hear, and I pouted all the sunny miles until we arrived at the camp. Then I announced that I wanted Mother to sleep with Sammy and me.

"Oh Jeez!" said Sammy.

Harper: "I think she might want her own tent, don't you, Alice?"

Alice, you smiled and tugged at your tennis bracelet—were you unconsciously remembering who gave it to you, one hopeful anniversary? "I'd like that," you said.

Harper: "You boys will have fun together, don't you think?"

Sammy: "Not if duckbrain wets the bed."

Oh, be kind to old men.

Harper: "Fellas, let's get your tent up. See those stakes? I need you to count them out for me there, buster, that's right. And Sammy, pull out those rocks."

The day that followed was atrocious. First there was a picnic lunch—withheld until the two "boys" gathered enough dry fire-wood for a wintering homesteader—and then about four hours of fishing. I suppose this was well meant, and peaceful and summer-green, but there was something positively sick about sitting on a riverbank and listening to my pediatrician give fishing advice to my own son. What made it worse, of course, was that Harper was an excellent fisher and I, a city boy and a freak, was as helpless as if I'd really been a boy of twelve. After half an hour, Harper came over to help me.

"How's it going there?"

"The fish and I have made peace."

"What's that?"

"Nothing."

"Now here, try this. You've got it in the shallowest—how about over there? That's good. You're doing great. There's no trick to it. It's only patience, patience."

I looked up at his great kind and rocky face and thought, *I know more about patience than you will ever know.*

He put his large hand on my head and I felt its weight, its warmth. There was a comfort in this that I tried to ignore.

"Why you're a natural," he said quietly. "Your father ever take you fishing?"

"No, Doctor."

"Alice says he was a good man."

"He was."

"I wanted to tell you I'm so sorry about what happened."

I nodded and stared at the river, silver, rolling like a cylinder in its music box.

"I wanted to tell you that Alice, she's very fond of you," he said. Something in his tone reminded me of old Hughie; I wondered if Alice ever noticed this. "She thinks of you as a son, you know. A son just like Sammy."

"She does?" I could not hide the grain of hope in my voice, so like the boyish character I was portraying.

"Alice loves you very much."

My line in the water was making endless loops of light. Alice loves you. Something I have waited half my life to hear, given to me by her next lover.

Later, after charred meatballs cooked in foil and potatoes that were still hard at the center, Harper told us antique ghost stories that raised the downy hair on Sammy's arms, and Alice had us sing some favorite songs of hers—good old *Goober Peas!* at the top of my tiny voice, to show you I knew all the words—and then we stared into the flame-palaces of the fire, and it was time for sleep.

"Good night, sweet boys," Alice said to us, smiling, as she looked into our tent. The glow of the fire was still behind her, and in the crevices of her eyes. She kissed our foreheads with her feathery lips—my eyes fluttered in a fever—then left, zipping the door into a glowing triangle. There was a little silence as we listened to Alice and the doctor laughing around the flames, uncorking something, whispering. The fire barked and growled and grew still.

"What do you think of Harper?" I whispered, desperate.

Sammy, you lay there a little while in the darkness, the light from the moon and fire coming through the trees in long coils of blurry light. I could hear the funny boy-noise of your breathing and the *sick, sick* as you scratched a finger against the canvas of the tent.

"I don't know," you said.

"Think he's a duckbrain?"

"Naw. I don't know. I don't like doctors much."

Sharp taste of hope. I said, "Pshaw, I don't like them at all."

You laughed. "Pshaw! Pshaw!" you said, in high-pitched imitation of me. "Just like an old man. You're the duckbrain."

"No, you are the duckbrain," I said, and hit you with the first-aid kit.

Your bloody-murder shriek of joy.

From outside the tent, my ex-wife's voice: "What's going on in there, boys?"

Later, after a muffled, giggling quiet, I heard your breath begin to jerk its way into sleep, and though the father in me wanted to hear you sleeping, the sound of your breath which is the shadow of your dreams, I had to take this moment. Time was against me; I might never be able to whisper, lips-to-freckled-ear, again.

"Sammy?"

"What?"

"What was your father like?"

"I don't know. I never met him."

"I mean what's your mom say?"

"Well, she talks about Ramsey like he's my real dad, you never met him, he was with us for I think four years or something. I kind of remember him, Mom says he taught me how to swim. I don't know. But we left there when I was little. He's not my real dad, anyway. He was just some man she married."

I was so glad to hear this; it made her betrayal of me so small, if Victor Ramsey was just "some man" instead of the one who ended my marriage. "So who's your real dad?"

"I just know his name. I'm not supposed to talk about him."

"Why not?"

"I don't know. I think maybe she's afraid of him," you said, your sweet voice in the darkness. Then your tone became quick and bright: "Or I think maybe—see, maybe he's got a different name now. Maybe he's someone famous, maybe a movie star or something, I saw *The Iron Mask,* last year it's got Douglas Fairbanks and this scene with swords in a castle, did you see it? I saw that and I think maybe he's my dad. Only he's too famous for people to know. So Mom's trying to be quiet, or maybe because someday he's going to come and find me, you know, take me to Hollywood and give me lots of money. Only they're trying to keep it a little secret. 'Cause of how famous he is."

We sat in the dappled silence of the forest. Finally, I said, "You think so?"

"Oh yeah, I just know my dad's a great guy," you told me hastily. Then you added: "Not like Ramsey."

There was some laughter from outside the tent, the snap of fire.

"Or Harper," I said.

"Yeah, I guess."

"What if your dad came and got you?"

There was no response for a little while. "I don't know."

"What if he did this, went camping with you?"

"Jeez."

I could not see you, but we were so close, that night, that I could smell you under the smoke and charred potato: all milk and green-apple sweat. You were shifting uncomfortably and I wanted to reach across that little space of darkness, take your shoulder, and say, *I'm here, I've come, it's all right*. "Sammy, what if he turned up right now?"

"Shut up," you said loudly. "Duckbrain, you shut up." There was the sound of rough breathing and I knew I had gone too far. I said nothing more, but like any animal caring for its young, I sniffed the thick air. Sammy, I could smell your tears.

I came out here beside the river a little while after I knew you were asleep—after I heard the mumbles and sighs you always make in your dog-dreams. The fire was long dead, faintly glowing under its shroud of ashes, the adults gone, leaving just the evidence of Alice's slippers, an illicit bottle of booze, and mismatched glasses. I saw a deer come down with moon-iced antlers and sip at the water. I heard the splash of an insomniac fish. Then, as I sat staring at the sky and wondering how I could be a father to my son, how I could suck the poison from his snakebit life, I saw another movement in the night that robbed my breath. It was a man, slipping out from the parallelogram of his tent. Dr. Harper in his nightclothes.

A stumble, a curse, then a shuffling movement towards the farther tent, my Alice's. Sammy, you still slept while the doctor unzipped that flimsy door and whispered, when that old girlish laughter rang through the air, when his back straightened with confidence as he stepped inside and closed the tent. You slept through all your mother's indiscretions. But I, the old loving husband, had to listen to every laugh and whisper under that hex of a moon. And I wept.

∽

This is a love story, so I will spare you the bombs and broken skulls. There is nothing to tell of war. At the conscription office, I was convincing as a young man and, because I was not afraid to die, I was even mistaken for brave. I was sent to France with the first troops, and it is proof of a godless world that every young man I met there, every poor ordinary boy, had his life mutilated or lost in those fields while I—devil in the trenches—came out with only the scars that, these days, I try to pass as chicken pox. Mist, and burning eyes, and boys screaming from jawless faces. There is nothing to say of war. When it was over and I was shockingly alive, intact, blood thick as gasoline, I lay in a London ward and received a note from Hughie, who had sad news to tell. In California, thousands were dead from a flu epidemic, among them his son, Bobby, and my own mother.

How do we forgive ourselves? Our parents watch us so carefully when we're children, desperate not to miss a first scream, first step, a first word, never taking their eyes off us. Yet we do not watch them. They near the end in solitude—even those who live beside us die in solitude—and rarely do we catch their own milestones: the last scream before the morphine settles in, last step before they cannot walk, last word before the throat seals.

Still I can feel it, the sudden drop of the heart—that I would crack the world open if I could, that I would sell my bones to have her back—for though she held me as a child, my mother never got to see me as a boy.

My mother's death was the end of my sanity. I went into a private tornado and the army returned me to my country only to imprison me, for two years, in a veterans' asylum called Goldforest House. It was perhaps the coziest place for me on the planet. The inmates there called me "the Old Man" and unhesitatingly believed my life's story, but the doctors did not and cast me back out into the world. My father's fortune allowed me to travel the globe at last, but eventually, bored, I returned once more to my country. I tried to pass myself off as nineteen and went to a Rhode Island college, but I found it brutish and illiterate—I was paddled twice for not wearing my freshman "dink"—and I did not graduate. I found my way back to San Francisco and rented a room in a cheap flophouse where no one would find me or bother me. I grew young and blond, but my heart never healed. A finned beast lying at the bottom of a black lake, waiting to die; the last of its kind. That was how Hughie found me in 1929.

Poor Hughie, picking through the trash and blown-paper streets where I finally landed—Woodward's Gardens—situated, of course, in the Irish neighborhood where my old playland used to stand. Nothing grand or green about it now; just a wasteland of apartment houses and laundry hanging on the line, some supper clubs that didn't serve liquor, one downstairs joint that did, and streetcars full of people heading to the Old Rec Park to watch a game. I had chosen it because, of all the places I could live, I wanted to be in the old wooden pit once again, where Splitnose Jim used to climb a pole for a peanut and scratch his dusty hide for me. Sometimes, in my postwar dreams, it seemed that it was me, and not Jim, who came out of his cave one morning to find a German with a gun.

I heard "Max!" shouted a few times and then an indecipherable conversation behind the door before the crystal sound of keys meant my landlady Mrs. Connor, her chest too scrawny for a heart, had betrayed me.

Feeble scratching, crack of the door. Muttering (paying of a bribe, I assume) and the sound of kicking over bottles—no no, things were not as bad as you imagine. I kept my igloo clean and the only gin of the house slept, warm as a pet, in bed with me, where I lay doing the crossword. That morning, I had drunk it from a coffee cup, which lay on a table; I am a tidy wino. Stomp of boots; in came my best friend.

"Well at least you're not dead," he said, standing skinny and bald in a long tweed coat.

"Hughie, get out."

He came over to me. "I thought all that travel and, well, Turkey, that would kill you for sure, I thought you'd get shot, but, well. Apparently this is where you want to die."

"It is."

"Max, this is stupid."

"Get out. I have a lady coming."

"Do you?"

In fact I did. Don't be jealous, Alice, but there was a likable girl in those days who used to pal around with me, surprisingly clever and well dressed, with celluloid legs and a laugh like a cougar. I would give her an alias here except I'm fairly certain she isn't alive; despite her many charms, she was a part-time hophead and the skin between her toes was tattooed with needle-pricks. Sabina liked to stop by around noon to help me with the crossword, maybe lift me out of bed to dance a little, but usually by two she would be weepy over her parents—I understood she had a wealthy father whose heart she broke—and had to go out and find a fix. I would usually not see her again for days, sometimes a week. I gave her a little money. She was young and never believed my true age. "Ha! Why you're almost a child!" she'd croak, borrowing a cigarette. "I should get arrested, baby!" She didn't love me, though. She was too broken.

I said, "Actually, you'd like her."

He laughed and then threw himself onto the bed beside me. From the window, we could hear a crowd cheering. A Seals game at the Old Rec Park. He said, "Give me some of that gin."

"It's coffee."

"The bottle." I handed it to him; he kicked off his shoes and took a slug.

His remaining hair was ginger and gray, and no longer seemed to belong to his pale face, but here was the lucky thing about Hughie: since he was born with no particular grace, no exceptional features, time could do almost nothing to him. While what we remember of beautiful people is their skin, their eyes—and why we gasp when, at sixty, they have all dried to sand—what I recognized as Hughie was none of these in particular, but simply the way he used them. The explosion of lines on his forehead was much the same whether those lines were permanent now or not, and the thoughtful smacking of his lips sounded just as irritating as it had when we were boys, even though his lips were thinning every day. Age is kind, at least, to the unlovely.

"Where'd you get this stuff?" he asked, handing me the bottle.

"I made it. Potato alcohol from the bootlegger, comes in a tin. A gallon and a half of distilled water, juniper berries, and a secret ingredient. All right, ginger. Let it steep. That's my humble recipe."

"Ugh, it's awful."

"You're right, it's no good. Oh, I have a story to tell you, Hughie."

But he didn't hear me. "You know I'm retired, Max?"

"That's crazy. You're too young."

"I'm not too young. I'm done with it, that's all. Abigail's gone back to her mother's, it was a relief after Bobby's death. I have nothing to hold me anymore. I think I'm going to get a farmhouse maybe north of here. With chickens. I think that sounds nice."

"Chickens? I never heard about this."

"I haven't seen you in years, Max."

"Well."

"Mary's dead," Hughie told me.

"Old Mary?"

"Madame Dupont herself."

"It never occurred to me. Of course she'd be dead."

"Yes, well, she lived to be eighty, they say."

"She always claimed she was sixty-four."

"Good old Mary."

"You know what she said to me?" I told him, then tried to imitate her toadish voice: "'I thought time was not on anybody's side.' That's what she said."

"Not on hers, at least. We've got to get you out of here," he told me.

We could hear people murmuring in the next room, and very suddenly, with the scrape of a chair, it became an argument of round, indecipherable vowels, then just as suddenly faded to the flow of water. Hughie and I chatted for a while about other old things, other changes in the world. Then I said, "I've got a story for you, Hughie. A girl I met in Spain. You'll never believe this."

"What. Tell me."

"I saw her, it was in this little village. This little village and I stayed in an inn. Had a kind of American bar, I guess, and nobody in it but this little girl. Browned, in braids, with a strawberry mouth. I mean little, maybe twelve years old."

"This is recently?"

I was talking quietly, almost whispering. "This is a while ago. Twelve-year-old girl, and she was drinking a shot of something at the bar, and you know what I thought?"

"What?"

"When she looked at me. Kind of cased me out, not like a whore, but like an old woman. And I thought: *She's like me.*"

"Max . . ."

"No really, I thought, It's another one like me. Here in this village. From the way she looked, I can't describe it, like a little speck of hate in her eyes. And I think she knew what I was. I'm sure of it. She must have been sixty or so."

"Did you talk to her?"

"I tried. Would you believe she bought me a drink? But I didn't speak whatever she spoke, not Spanish, and she didn't know English. The bartender treated her funny, with respect but as if he was scared of her. I think they knew about her in that town, I imagined this idea that they'd seen her grow from an old woman into a little girl. That she was the local witch. You know, like me, but a witch. And she just kept staring at me so sad, like: Don't grow old like me, don't grow old like me."

"Max, I don't know."

"Then we'd had a few drinks but of course couldn't talk, and she said something. I think she wanted to come up to my room. And I felt so bad for her, because here I was, I looked like a young man, and there she was in her sixties and who knows the last time some man had loved her, or ever would again. Who'd love the witch in a superstitious Catholic village like that? Is this what's going to happen to me? I felt awful. I felt as if I should save her."

"You didn't, old man, come now . . ."

"Sex, no. I didn't. What if she really was a twelve-year-old whore? I got up and left, it was so sad. Except that look, I can't forget it. You know, Don't grow old like me."

"I'll get you out of here, Max."

"You will?"

"I will."

There was the bumblebee drone of a plane. Two radios competed from open windows—a sorrowful colored woman and an optimistic brass band—then conjoined miraculously with one identical, slightly overlapping advertisement for soap: "*Zog does not scratch, scratch.*" The sun shone on two men in our late fifties sipping gin. It felt very much like the end of our lives. And so it might have been, or at least the end of our story, if it had not been for Hughie.

He said, "Max, I brought this for you."

Out of his pocket came a little envelope; he threw it onto my chest. It was square and white, torn open and slightly soiled at the corners. I noted a nameless address in Massachusetts and a date nearly a year old.

Dear Hughie,

Hello, old friend. You haven't heard from me in a long time. Perhaps you won't even remember me. I've been thinking about people from the past (old folks do this) and how it's rotten I've lost touch with so many. It happens when you move around as much as I have. I heard you were married and had a son; in fact, I saw you and your wife in the park years ago while I was out walking with my husband-to-be. You seemed very happy. Good. I am happy, too. I've had three husbands and can't say much for them, but each love gets you somewhere, doesn't it? From my marriage to Asgar, for instance, I got myself a wonderful son. What a miracle, at my age. Isn't it funny to think of, Hughie, each of us with a son?

I know it sounds odd, but I nearly named him after you. I always wanted a Hughie. But there was another in the family and I wanted to save confusion, so he's Sammy. And I am happy, all on my own after my mother died, after I left my third husband and moved to Massachusetts. Please write to me. I have such grand memories of our time in South Park and the Conservatory of Flowers. It all seems impossibly perfumed with roses, doesn't it? Maybe I'm old and sentimental. Well, we are both old, aren't we? I hope you are still redheaded and smiling. Life is short and friends are few, so write to me.

Sincerely,

Mrs. Victor Ramsey (Alice Levy)

It took only an hour of carefully poured gin and sober argument to talk Hughie into it. After all, hadn't he come to Mrs. Connor's with this very idea? Hadn't he said he would get me out? He lay on the bed while I paced the room, opening curtains and gesturing to a sun that was also shining over miraculous Massachusetts. The Massachusetts of the letter. I spoke of human frailty. I mentioned the passage of time. A son, a secret son named Sammy, and because my body was young and quick and light, I leaped around the room like a faun, explaining that life had very few joys. The country could wait. The chickens could wait. From this very window one could see, calmly parked, a Chrysler the color of blue compacted stars, well cared for, tires in good condition. A home could be made there for a little while. The Nevada sun would bristle on its surface like a prickly pear. I reminded him that the driving age in states between here and Massachusetts was unreasonably low. Consider love, Hughie. Consider lonely old men like us.

The Chrysler was serviced lovingly, its rooms and compartments cleaned until they sparkled, the pipes and tubes legally liquored with its favorite fluids, the undercarriage greased until it dripped a shadow of itself on the concrete, and it was treated like a grand hotel now open for the season. Hughie and I had our hats reblocked according to the latest styles. We brought out of storage my old wicker suitcases. Travel clothes and camping equipment were purchased. The glove compartment was armed in case of highwaymen (a gun: Teddy's army issue, forgotten when he left Hughie at last). A quiet case of booze was placed like a gangster's body in the trunk. We shaved and perfumed ourselves—automobiling was a gentlemanly art back then—and sat in the larded leather of the seats. Fog descended in a dew and evaporated from the engine.

"Ha, Max, this is it!" We were off.

We were very bad travelers, Hughie and I. We often ran out of food or gas or were so charmed by the larch-lit forests of Montana that we put off finding lodging until a dangerously twilit hour, when nothing seemed to move in the darkness except the bugbears of our imagination. We never had enough water. We always had too many cigarettes (although, midway, clerks refused to sell them to me, saying they would "stunt my growth"). We always had too many inquisitive widows, who would appear in cherry-red dresses at drinking fountains, flirting horribly with Hughie and asking him about his darling son, who would smile and pull out that shocking cigarette. Too much coffee, not enough liquor. Too much sleep, not enough photographs (no photographs, in fact). No trace of Alice, or of Sammy.

At first, with masculine optimism, we camped out in fallow fields. It was lovely, and rustic, with the campfire snapping and popping, which I said reminded me of how Hughie cracked his knuckles every hour (on the blessed hour!) as he drove, and which he said reminded him of my loud breathing when I slept. But the dirt was tough to sleep on, and we would awaken early in the morning to a thick and starless darkness that terrified us both. I had yet to join the Cub Scouts and knew nothing of the noises of the forest, and every falling leaf seemed to be a bear or a hunter. And Hughie always awoke stiff and sad; he said he was too old. So we began to use the little traveler's cabins newly built along the road, most of them bare and smelling of insecticide, the shared bed overly soft, but we slept dreamlessly as if at sea.

He told me I had nightmares. I learned this a week into our journey, at the north end of Skull Valley, Utah, after a long day of driving through hot auburn brush and cracked blue skies. He said I shouted as I slept, and cried; he said it always sounded the same, and must have been the war. I can't say. My mind has spared me;

it seems I remember this particular horror only when I am sleeping. He told me I always wept until he held me, stroking my hair, and then I would go limp like the dead.

We found the Massachusetts house but there was no Alice there. A pretty Germanic woman opened the door of the little place (new, white, straight out of an old Sears catalog) and said they had left a while ago. "Funny Mrs. Ramsey," the woman said, smiling, gesturing at the impossibly dark interior, "I guess she put in all these bookshelves." She said she saw her only once, as Mrs. Ramsey was moving out. A boy named Sammy, boxes of books, and framed photographs of nude women. "Pretty crazy gal," the woman told me, taking a drag on her cigarette.

"Do you know where she went?"

She blocked the door with her leg so the cat wouldn't get out. The poor thing undulated back into the house. "Mmm-mmm." That meant no. Nearby, an oriole flew from tree to tree.

As I walked away, under the shadow of overgrown wisteria, I noticed an old wooden toy in the weeds of the front lawn. I picked it up; an unamused wooden duck with wheels, darkened by more than one season in the snow. Left there by local boys? By one particular local boy?

When I got back into the car, I told Hughie I wasn't going to give up. You seemed so close, Sammy, so terribly close. "We're not going home," I insisted, and my friend put his hand on my shoulder, laughing, and asked where was home for us, anyway?

Nobody in nearby towns had ever heard of you or your mother; she had left Ramsey, then she had left Massachusetts, and there was only the rest of the wide world to hide in. And still— still I was convinced I could hear your shout! Or sometimes, when I leaned out the window on a sultry evening, that I could smell your mother's Rediviva on the wind. Like my mother before me, I could swear there were more senses than the ones we knew, and also like her, I fell into the grace of self-deception.

I found you almost every week or so. In Hopkinsville, Ky., on the fourth-grade school roster, when I spotted a Ramsey, S., and ran, with the secretary in limping pursuit, to find only a tow-headed girl in a classroom spelling bee, reciting "O-B-S-E-S-S-H-U-N" with the confidence of the truly dense. Or on the banks of Lake Erie, where I found an Alice Levy in the records of a synagogue, and waited through a perplexing and exotic Hebrew service only to find a gray-haired lady in furs and a wig; she smiled at me and gave me a quarter, sweet girl. An A. Van Daler in Minnesota was no Alice but turned out to be an actual cousin of mine. And so on. City Hall documents, church records, ladies' auxiliary minutes, Scout troop lists, Junior Leagues, and local associations of every kind. So many times I thought I'd found you, of course, just as any true believer will search the Bible and see signs of his particular life. But like the feast of fairies, these pleasures lasted only for the few hours I believed them. Their names were nowhere. I would not find them. America would not reveal its secrets.

I think I would have given up much sooner had not Hughie had a purpose of his own. It was to taste roadside lemonade from Maryland to Missouri and write down on a special pad of paper who had won (Georgia, as expected). Similar contests were announced for diner coffee, meat loaf specials, spaghetti, and a particular favorite of Hughie's called "pandowdy" (only three entries, all of them soggy), as well as more informal competitions for Best Scottish Rites Temple, Most Humorous Barbers, Fattest Policemen, Loudest Swing Sets, and Best Misspelled Cinema Marquee (which went to the Aztec, Greenville, S.C., for THE JAZZ SIGNER, no talkie after all, I guess). I remember the year crammed with these points and scribbles, and with laughter, and I am comforted. I suspect, though, that memory has contracted with the chill of time and mostly the drive was long tiresome stretches of farmland, no longer quaint or fresh, windows rolled up against manure and skunk-scent, radio hissing for days until we reached another station. And it was the radio, Alice, that gave you away in the end.

By Georgia, the thrill of driving had vanished from Hughie's life—policemen had begun to pull me over when I was at the wheel, drawling, "Son, best your daddy teach you to drive somewheres else," so Hughie had all the burden—and while we were getting the Chrysler serviced for an alarming ululation, Hughie shouted out: "Can you attach a radio to that thing?"

"A what?"

"A radio. I can get one in town."

"You mean a cabinet radio?"

The mechanic was young and skinny, friendly, with a falling curl of yellow hair, and looking back, I think we got our beloved radio because Hughie liked to watch his tanned muscles in the Alabama sun. No more than that—nothing obscene or desperate—just an admiration of youth. Hughie and I did go into town, and he chose a gleaming Philco shaped like a small confessional, with those classic mesh panels. Our young man hauled it to the backseat and began, with a smile, to do the wiring. This was no simple job. Strips of antenna were laid across the roof. A long discussion of tubes and batteries and conversions took place, and the poor dashboard had to be drilled, but Hughie patiently watched the shining movement of the boy's arms, and at last he turned a wooden knob and the sounds of the *Happy-Go-Lucky Hour* appeared in the air. My friend tipped him a crisp five dollars and gave a sigh as we drove away.

"A radio, Hughie?"

"Shut up. Turn up the volume."

Well, that was always a problem; the noise of the car and the wind was always louder than the radio, and we had to come close to a stop to hear anything in particular of the news. Music did better, so we tried to find it whenever we could, and since the pickings in the middle of the country were fairly slim—few transmitters, and what few listeners there were used wind-powered radios—we learned to appreciate the ugly, modern clatterings that young people seemed to adore. I know they adored it because when we stopped in small towns, girls in pinafores and boys in Ucanttear knickers would huddle around us, listening, fascinated as Pacific Islanders. One or two sometimes knew an obscene dance to go with it. This was often stopped by elders and we were encouraged to move on. Still, it was nice to be popular, and it would have been a great way to meet women had I not looked a pimply thirteen.

Endless stretches of static nearly drove us home, but every time we grew disgusted with that empty ocean sound, Hughie would tell me to "try it one more time" and some precious local program would appear, first as a phantom, then materializing in full color. For the entire, stunningly dull length of Texas, we grew fond of a particular mystery serial set on an ocean liner ("Bang! Crash! What was that? The telegraph, oh God, the telegraph!"), and almost turned around when, in Deaf Smith County, the whole cast drowned under a wave of crackling sound. Fanny Brice followed us everywhere with her annoying "Baby Snooks," and on mountaintops we could hear the opening words of "The Fat Man": *"He's stepping on the scales now. Weight"*—a pause for the scale to settle—*"three-sixty. Who? The Fat Man!"* "Yowsah yowsah yowsah," the maestro Ben Bernie used to whisper to us, and "Au revoir, pleasant dreams." And advertisements, of course, an interesting insight into the obsessions of the middle class: "If you want your teeth to shine like pearls, buy Dr. Straaska's Toothpaste." I admit it; I bought some. In the Southwest, we became fans of an amusing cooking show where the woman (surely a man in falsetto) would tell listeners, "Now get a pad and pencil, I'm waiting, go get it, this one's a good one," then pause, humming, before she went on to recite the most ludicrous recipe you could imagine. I swear some "specials" in local restaurants must have been made by listening suckers.

I have carried this unlikely love of radio with me. You, Sammy, have taught me your favorite programs and on certain Radio Evenings nights, we sit with Alice in awe of orphan-and-pirate adventures, complete with loud footsteps and slamming doors, utterly fake thunder, and hair-raising silences as harrowing as if the lights had all gone out. I remember when I first got here and the radio was broken. Alice stood up to turn the dials but it would not speak. Sammy, you put on a good face—"Wadder we gonna to do *now?*"—but you were as broken as an Aztec who has learned his god is dead. After my long travels with Hughie, I understand too well.

Still, the best gift of the radio was news. Traveling for so long, we had become accustomed to living outside of time, outside of the world, and petty details like a wasp's nest in our bathroom, or my (apparently annoying) habit of reading aloud from billboards, took on the significance of world events. With the news read to us, though, we were humbled. Gangster massacres. Stockbrokers in a panic. The South Pole crossed by some flyboy. We heard it usually at night, as we paused beneath a black fringe of pine, and listened to the distant news of riots, earthquakes, fires, and death. Some man's soft, rumpled voice. Some father telling us the nation would prosper and stocks would rise again, and still the world was bad. In the dark night with a halfhearted patter of rain over our heads. Some father telling us we were too far from home.

Not long after we acquired the radio, when we passed through Austin, Hughie, very trickily, led me along a twisting route through the suburbs, claiming he wanted to show me a botanical garden with an orchid named after his mother (why would I be interested?) and then abandoned that mission when he suddenly parked the car and made us rush into a restaurant. It was one of those friendly places whose name—for instance, the Swedish House—meant nothing, since they served the same food everywhere. Hughie was very distracted, mooning out the window, and ordered something I can't imagine he wanted—chicken fried steak—which even the waitress found hard to believe. I had a bowl of chili and it was excellent. Hughie was still staring out the window when I finished, and only then did I bother to follow his gaze. There, across the street, framed by an office window and talking on the phone, was a man with dead-black hair and a handsomely broken nose. A moment passed before I realized it was his old love Teddy.

We sat for a while in silence, as people do when they are watching a sunset. Our subject soundlessly talked, laughing and leaning back in his chair. He had gained weight, but otherwise looked the same. My friend glanced at me and smiled.

He said, "Isn't it funny? There's my old servant."

"What a coincidence." It occurred to me to lock the glove compartment when we got into the car, in case Hughie wanted to return the gun to Teddy (so to speak).

"I sent him a letter of reference. So I knew he lived here. I thought maybe we'd stop by, say hello."

"You haven't eaten a bite."

"It's awful. It's chicken fried steak," he said. "On second thought, maybe we won't say hello."

"Hughie. I know all about Teddy."

My friend rested his head in his hand. He looked at me and he seemed so old, so worn and tired. He said, "I know you do, old man."

Poor old friend. Staring at lost love as if, by the mere magnifi-

cation of hope, you can make it burst into flame. My God, the old
queer; he had become exactly like me.

✧

Somewhere in the mountains of America, while we dallied for
weeks in an endless talcum snow, my body betrayed me at last. In
the last few years, I had noticed a definite shift in things; my muscles lost their form, my shoes became too big, and, most astonishing of all, the world began to rise around me. Mirrors, windowsills,
drawer pulls—through the months they ascended without my
noticing until the day when, extending an arm to open a door, I
found my knuckles bloodying themselves an inch or two below
the knob. I was shrinking. I began to knock over water glasses (a
telescoped arm) and trip over the curb (a shortened leg). Hughie
was amused, especially by my new voice, which sounded like an
orchestra tuning up, and though I laughed with him, and though
the cheap cinema tickets were nice, it worried me. It was never
going to be safe in my body again; I would be stumbling until I
died. I was becoming a child.

It was difficult to realize that the young women who had always honked their horns on our journeys, smiling and laughing at
the teenage boy and his father, the girls who stared at me on the
street while Hughie bought me an ice cream cone—they no longer
saw me. I had passed beneath the surface of some lake, and had
become invisible. I grew weaker, smaller, like something falling out
of sight. But the worst, of course, was when my body paused for
a moment in its decline, took a breath, and silently unsexed me.

There was no particular day. It was just somewhere in the dust-
storm of snow that mild winter, among the dozen coffee shops
with tired waitresses, and cowboys, and desperately poor people
staring at Hughie's watch, while the radio and the sky were equally

static, that I stopped being a man. Hairless as a pup, shriveled below into a sleek little snail. I tried to manipulate it into life, and it still worked for a while, but eventually grew forever soft, rubbery, good only for peeing long distances on the side of the road. I felt a terrible shame. I hid it from Hughie, but as we lived together constantly, it was only a matter of time before he saw me, one morning, getting out of the tub, and realized what a eunuch I had become.

Later, in the car, he grew silent. I knew he'd been shocked by my changed body. At last, he asked if we shouldn't maybe find a good town, perhaps the one we were approaching, and just settle down until the end of our days. Billboards called to us—the Howdy Hut, Reinhardt Bakery, A and V Photography—and budded apple branches brushed the windows. As good a town as any.

"We're never going to find them, Max. Not if we lived forever."

"Settle down?"

Telephone poles passed us one by one, each with a gust of sound. We went through downtown, more stores than expected, a crowd at church, a town that any two monsters could live in and be happy, then we passed through to the other side. The road stretched flat and endless, disappearing in a bluish blur before us, which could have been a mountain, but was only a distant thundercloud, raining on a distant town.

"We'll never find them. It's no fun anymore to try. We could turn around," he said softly. This was his idea, to save the shriveled child he'd seen in the bathroom. "You've got money, we could buy a house today. Come on, it's not a bad idea. We could go back to that town, what's it called? Back there, buy a house. Probably a mansion in this part of the country. With a porch and a yard and a dog out back. Don't you want a dog? Aren't you sick of this car? I mean, really. Really, we can just turn around."

I went along with it; it was a pleasant thought. After all, we were no closer to my son than before. "You could open a law practice."

"I could. I'd have to pass the bar, or I could fake it."

"I could go to grammar school."

"A sort of family. We could live here. Really, I mean, really. We could turn around."

I saw the gravity in his eyes. I think, now, that although he had cared, and worried, and laughed with me over the ridiculous state of my body, he had been so close to my life that he had never bothered to imagine it. Just as we do not think of our grandmother as old; she is merely Grandma, forever, until we visit her one day and realize that, despite her smiles and kisses, she is going blind and will die. I had always been merely Max. I noticed him thinking, and glancing over, and what he saw there was not Max anymore—not that old, lumbering bear, the cub of Splitnose Jim—but a fidgeting boy of twelve, picking at a scab, crinkling his sunburned nose in disgust. Hughie had begun to mourn my death.

"Well, Hughie, old friend, perhaps—"

And then a miracle:

"*Come and take your Easter photos,*" came a deep voice from the radio. "*Crisp and clear, always on time. Alice and Victor Photography, Eighth and Main.*"

Hughie said, "Well, let's—"

"Hush!"

"*Memories forever. I'm Victor Ramsey and I guarantee it.*"

The birds all scattered when the Chrysler came to a stop, and they watched warily from the trees as it swerved, too fast, in a rough, squealing semicircle back towards town.

Ramsey's store wasn't hard to find. A quaint two-story brick building with black iron numbers near the top: 1871. Flower boxes sat empty under the windows, and a trumpet vine had taken charge of a pot originally meant for roses, of which one white bloom remained. A brass spittoon, turned into an umbrella stand, signaled a bygone era. A sign said they were closed on Sundays; the floating choir song from the nearby church reminded me of the day.

Hughie wasn't with me; after much arguing, he had agreed to stay in the car, but he kept a wary eye on me on that newly painted porch; he was not sure what I would do. I wasn't sure myself. I could see Ramsey's shape moving deep in the interior, like a beast in dark water, arranging frames or carrying boxes. I could not, however, see *him*.

A second miracle: the door was open.

The place smelled of vinegar and smoke. Large, striking photographs of ocean waves filled one entire wall, and the other was all billowing wheat, but otherwise the pictures on little stands were of weddings, family groups, babies. A broom leaned exhausted against a wall, a counter and cash register filled the far corner, and two doors were open beyond: one to darkness, the other to wavering light. The waver was the movement of a shadow.

All of a sudden, there he was, standing in the room with me. A tall man, and old, a puff of white hair with bulging eyes and an intellectual's tapering nose. How could she have loved him? Tall, with rolled-up shirtsleeves and large, bony hands. Ordinary, utterly ordinary, but can you tell a villain when you meet him? He stared at me. It began to rain once more against the windows, tear-streaked. He seemed more stunned than I expected.

"Sammy?" he stammered.

It took me a moment to realize I looked exactly like my son.

"No, no I'm Tim."

"Well, Tim, I don't give to the Scouts," he said. British accent, unexpected. He smiled and gave a comical salute. "Military training, it's horrible."

"You're Victor Ramsey?"

"Yes."

"Alice and Victor Photography. Your wife?"

"She was. Still has a share in the shop."

"But she no longer lives here. Where did she go?"

He stared at me curiously. "Tim, let me make some guesses about you. I've been reading detective fiction. Let's see, you came from California."

"She had a son."

"I'll tell you, I knew from the license plate. Not very sophisticated, I know."

"Alice and Sammy."

He waved that aside. "Yes yes, Alice and Sammy, but that's not very current stuff, Tim. Are you writing a report for school? I hate to tell you I'm not a very famous man. Not in this town, not since before you were born, those pictures on the wall are all I'm remembered for, but only in New York, not here. Look at them, take your time. You've done your research, though. Well done, it's swell to meet you, is that what teenagers say? I try to be modern. Just swell. Come again, Tim. Goodbye." And before I knew it he had vanished into the other room. I followed him.

"I have a question."

"Could you hand me my little brush?" he asked. I had emerged into a sun-dappled glen—one of his photography sets—a gorgeous illusion of falling leaves, a summer haze in the distant sky, an unmended fence. My enemy stood on a ladder, painting a leaf on a tree. What did I want from Victor Ramsey? To kill him? There was Teddy's gun in the car; no one would have heard the shot—the nearby choir was bellowing "Rock of Ages," heavy on the soprano. Nor, if I had pushed the old ladder and sent Victor Ramsey flailing into his painted glen, would anyone have found his knotted bones for days. I could have murdered Victor Ramsey in a thousand awful ways, but you see the thought never occurred to

me. In that room, an old man and a little boy among the autumn
leaves, we were not rivals. We were both lost husbands, jilted lovers;
we were both members of the same religion, that Sunday. No, I
found I wanted more even than an address: I wanted words from
someone who had also lost his muse.

"Victor Ramsey, did you love her?"

"Who?"

"Alice. Did you love her?"

"No." He worked at the leaf, effortlessly creating it, moving
on to the next. He did not seem to think anything of a boy asking about love; I was discovering that he was unlike any other
old man I'd known. An artist, I guess, also as if he, too, were a
child. "Not the way men seem to love their wives in this town,
now I don't know your mom and dad, but not like that." Closer,
I could see the ugly wings of his nose. "I worshipped her, Tim.
She was like no one you will ever meet. Strong, independent. I
never took her for granted for a moment, or pretended I understood her, and when she wanted to go I let her go, because she
was art and she was music." He made another leaf, another, each
turning precisely in the breeze that he imagined. "You won't understand. I can't express things. Look behind the door, there's a
photograph."

There was. Alice at the age of fifty or so, lying in a pool of floating duckweed like a bathing girl; she was naked. Her arms were
soft and dimpled, her breasts lopsided under the water, the nip-
ples large and pale, and she gazed grinning up at a sky that had,
through some trick of exposure I will never understand, become
a lake-surface pitted with rain. She was not beautiful. Not the way
I had preserved her in my memory, all symmetry and wet lips, fast
asleep. Silt rose around her in tiny particles, and that smile rose
above the water. How mystifying: my Alice, old, but lovely in
some new way, floating happy and free.

Students of art, you may recognize this portrait from its brief and minor fame, or so I'm told. If you do, keep quiet. Let my love live out her life in peace.

"She did that one," Ramsey said. It did not seem to cross his mind that old men should not be showing nude portraits to little boys. "I taught her the basics, but she was really something, she became a new person behind the camera. Most of these are hers."

I looked around and realized there were portraits of her everywhere, leaning against the walls: Alice eating figs with an amused expression, Alice nearly nude behind a clothesline with the sun in her squinting eyes, Alice asleep the way she always looked, Alice older and older in every frame. All the photographs that you grew up with, Sammy. A catalog of the years without me. I kept staring at this woman whom I guess I never really knew.

From behind me, the quiet voice of my fellow man: "She made me younger, year by year."

"Where did she go?" I asked at last.

He mentioned the name of a village, two days' drive from here. I didn't dare ask for an address.

"You met her in California?"

He nodded, closing his eyes as he contemplated the next color he would choose. "In Pasadena. I knew her mother, and invited her to work with me. It was such a gift that she arrived."

"Why?"

"Hmm?"

My voice came out too harsh: "*Why did she go?*"

I meant me, why did she leave me? But Victor didn't hear it that way. He looked at me with no pity for himself or for anyone. "Well, my boy, she didn't love me."

"I see."

"Could you hold the ladder?"

"Sure."

He grinned again, so impossibly innocent. Instantly I was able to picture him with his bride: Alice fussing clumsily with baby

Sammy, old Victor mumbling and smiling as she filled the room with laughter. Tulip tree in the window, macaroni pie in the oven, Rediviva floating in the air. What a lovely life he'd lost. He said, "I have a theory about my wife. Since you seem interested, though I can't think why. Like all women before her, she couldn't change except by marrying. She wanted to change all the time, be a new woman, so she kept marrying, first Calhoun, he let her be brilliant, and then Van Daler, he let her be beautiful, and gave her a child. I . . . well. I taught her the skills with which she could leave me. I wouldn't be surprised if she's married again, who knows what she'll be next? She didn't love me, but I understand. I do. Sentimental girl. There was only one, I think, she ever really loved." And I knew from his expression that it wasn't him or me.

Forgive this last interruption, Sammy, but I have heard bad news. Just yesterday, my wife and son and I visited a friend of Dr. Harper's who lives by a lake. A fat man, happy and generous; also a psychoanalyst, which terrified me. But he gave me no more than one probing glance—that of a botanist identifying a pleasant, common flower—before making us all play a baffling new kind of board game. Both Alice and I lost instantly and she announced we were going for a walk. Lucky me you've always been such a bad sport, Alice. Outside, night birds sang in the moist air, and it was after we walked and listened that she told me.

We stopped by the lake (no moon, but a bright phosphorescence in the clouds) and sat in the shimmering darkness, the lampless darkness she'd said she loved as a girl, the darkness of olden times. There was a distant splash; she said maybe some monster lived in the water. I said I was cold, but luckily she had a sweater with her (good mother), so she had me lift my arms in surrender while she lowered the pullover onto my body. It smelled of my son. We threw some rocks—I was a terrible throw with these shrinking hands—and she laughed, and I tried to laugh, but I was a nervous child in love with an older woman he could never have. At last she told me that Harper had asked her to marry him and she had accepted and that you, Sammy, already knew.

I stared at her like a rabbit in a garden.

"What do you think?"

I said, "Marry Harper?"

"Yes, Dr. Harper. He makes me happy. He says he'll take us all on a trip around the world, imagine that! Any place you ever dreamed of going? I've dreamed of so many."

Alice, you wore your hair down like a girl, and I felt it made a mockery of the girl you used to be, someone who needed no sunburned doctor to take her on trips. Did I invent that girl? Or had she hidden herself decades ago, and lived now only in my memory?

I asked her if her other husbands had made her happy.

"Of course they did."

I am insane; my mind was burning and I could not control it. I have not yet found your diary, Alice, if you have one, so I am forced to ask these things out loud. "Then why'd you leave? Sammy's father, why'd you leave him? Didn't you love him?"

For a moment the old intelligence, cruel and exciting, arose in her like a magic sign, and I thought she was going to say something one should never say to a child. My heart shuddered, terrified that she'd seen through me, and my skin shrank on my bones. Then, like a swan shaking its feathers into the water, she smoothed away her memory and looked at my pure, childish face.

She said, "That was all a long time ago."

"I'm sure you'll be happy together."

A chuckle. "Thanks."

With a whisper of love that surprised her, I fell into her lap.

If Harper ever finds these pages, I'm sure he'll show them to his psychoanalyst friend, and, oh, what a thrill for the old boy! I can hear his pencil chattering away. Let me imagine the notes: "Subject attempts intercourse with mother"—oh, not with my miniaturized equipment, Doctor, but I'm sure you mean something symbolic. Though is it exactly Oedipal if I married the mother before becoming the son? Is there some other myth with a better correlation? No, I am too twisted a knot. There is no untying me, Doctor. To release me, you must cut me in two.

❧

We had the address through a trick at the library, and with the help of a map posted near City Hall, the old Chrysler was humming homeward within an hour.

"What are you thinking, old man?" Hughie asked me.

We had turned the radio off and the only sounds were lingering birds and the rumble of a motorcycle on some adjacent, invisible street. "That I just want to see my son."

"Just him?"

"And her."

"And then what?"

"I don't know."

A green strip of land appeared beside us: Lincoln Park, where you play your baseball, Sammy. Hughie drove on slowly—too slowly for the car behind, which passed us, radio blaring. He said in that voice I hated: "I know you. We've come too far. You're not just going to peek through a window and come back into the car, are you?"

"I thought we'd knock on the door."

He laughed. "That's stupid. She may recognize me."

"I know. That's all right. Say you're passing through town. And I'm your son."

His hand smoothed over his scalp, an old gesture, searching for hair that had been gone now for years, then lay once again on the gearshift. With the smell of rubbing metal, he shifted into the right gear. Then I told him.

I told him what I had planned in Ramsey's chemical-smelling studio. No, we were not just going to knock on the door. Or take a mental picture. I told him my final dream; a poem, really, a work of art. What I wanted from this place, and from Alice, and Sammy. And him. It was a great thing to ask of someone, too great a thing, I guess. But I took his silence for agreement, because he had said it himself: we had come too far.

"Are you going to tell?" he asked at last.

"No. I think now I won't ever tell her."

"I mean Sammy."

"He wouldn't believe me."

"Will he believe you're just a little boy?"

"Everyone else does."

"Well, what do you want me to say your name is?"

I looked out at the road and saw a baby staring at me from its pram, as wary as a woman in an opera box.

"Hughie, of course. Little Hughie. After my father."

He laughed.

But there we were, 11402 Stonewood, and Hughie parked noisily before the car went silent, revealing a quiet barking from behind the house. A plain house, yellow and black, decorative window on the door and the slightly askew woodwork of an added second story, done on the cheap. Church spire above the trees. A side fence opened, and out slipped the cagey dog itself, and there was old Buster, golden as a cake, woofing from a corner of the lawn. Then he paused, turning his head to the doorway. His owner stood there, chewing gum like a maniac. A little boy who looked like me.

∽

"Did your mother make this pie?"

Hughie sat in the glow of the kitchen lamp, smiling and holding out a forkful of apple pie. I could not eat mine; I had already had to visit the bathroom to empty my stomach and sigh into the mirror. Now I could only stare at the boy who blinked at us and tossed a baseball from one hand to the other. He shrugged.

"Well it's very good," Hughie said.

"I guess."

"And you're very kind to let us wait here for your mother."

Another shrug and Sammy stared into the backyard, where Buster made stupid loops around the old hemlock tree, terrorizing a squirrel. A moth was trapped behind the back screen door and nobody, nobody would set it free.

"You're in school now, Sammy?"

Pause, as if this were a trick. "I'm at Benjamin Harrison. I'm in fifth grade. I've got Mrs. McFall and she's been sick so we didn't have any homework for a week last week."

"Do you like her?"

"She's all right. Next year I'll have Mrs. Stevens and I hear she's a . . ." You stopped there before you said some crude word, then you looked at me and smiled. My brain filled with black stars.

Victor Ramsey had prepared me for your looks—not a spitting image of your diminutive father, but alike enough, with enormous ears and blond hair in a cowlicked swirl—but you mangled your dad's face beyond any recognition. It was never still: you elongated it in boredom, or crunched it up in thought; your restless eyes rolled and narrowed and snapped shut as if what Hughie said might put you to sleep; and your lips, God, smack, smack, smacking with the gum you chewed like a betel nut. One elbow was freshly scraped and oozing a little yellow fruit-juice; the other was bruised and blue. You bit your nails even as we sat there. You leaped out of your chair from time to time to yell out the window at Buster, who was doing nothing particularly interesting, but who I suppose was the best friend of your life (and whom I never truly replaced). You were polite to a point (inviting us in when you heard we were old friends) but bossed us around, making us sit in particular chairs and telling us, "Don't eat all the pie 'cause I'm saving it for later." There was no sign, in all of this, that you loved a girl named Rachel. Or that you sat alone in your room and prayed for your mother. That you then imagined awful deaths of teachers and schoolmates, or that these dreams made you fear the devil. That you were like me, a little, in the end. I saw none of it then; I only saw a champion baseballer, a cowboy fan, a runt who thought that everything he said was so brand new and brilliant that he smiled at his own words. A perfect, maddening little boy.

"We're studying Asia," you said.

"Sounds good."

Your face collapsed in disgust at the entire continent. "The swell place has about a million swell little people on it, and about a hundred swell little nations, all of them exactly the same and can't say their names even, except there's China, you know, whose main export is tea. No, silk. No, rice. One of those. And Japan. Would you like to hear my haiku?"

"Yes."

He arranged his head very sternly beneath the light and recited this masterpiece:

> *A little sandwich*
> *Sweetly singing to itself*
> *"Tunafish salad."*

He added, "That's because I was pretty much *starving* when I wrote it. I got an A, though. I get all A's."

Hughie said, "Now you're twelve years old, right?"

"Uh-huh."

"Well that's the same age as little Hughie here! Isn't it? Isn't it, son?" My old friend looked at me so strangely—almost angrily, or as if he were going to cry—and I recognized, crazily, my dead mother's face: *Be what they think you are.*

"Yes, Dad." I said in my sad, hiccupy little voice. "I am twelve."

"You got a gun?" Sammy asked me, and I wondered what kind of child my old wife had raised.

But Sammy didn't wait for an answer. "My mom won't let me have one. She doesn't know anything about it, she never had one, my dad would let me have one, I'm sure of it. Danny Shane down the street's got a BB with a double pump but it busts up sometimes and his dad screams at him like heck, and Billy Easton's got a Daisy." All of a sudden, with remarkable joy, he shouted the advertising line: "It's a Daisy!" Buster ran to the screen door barking and Sammy teased him until he jogged away.

"I knew your mother when she was a little girl," Hughie said, eating more pie. Too much cinnamon, melting in the air.

"It's a Daisy!" my son yelled again.

"You look just like her. Do people say that?" A shrug. "You have her mouth. She was pretty and outspoken and she drove her mother crazy. You never knew your grandmother, did you? She was a wonderful woman. Always funny and kind, imaginative. A . . . a friend of mine said she and your mother used to dress up in old clothes and sit in front of the fire playing chess. Imagine your mother, in crinolines and a Civil War hat! A witty girl. And sharp. She wasn't like other kids. I admired her."

My son laughed. "She told me when she was a girl, she saw a cougar on the street, it had eaten someone's parrot."

"I don't know that story."

"Did you know my father?"

Hughie looked down at the table. "I'm not sure. What's his name?"

I felt nauseated again.

"Van Daler," Sammy said. "That's Danish."

"Is it? Van Daler." Hughie sneaked a look at me. It seemed impossible, but she had told him. Alice, you kind soul, you had kept me alive for our son. "Van Daler," Hughie said again. "No. No, I don't think I knew him."

"Ah well."

"What did your mother tell you about him?"

"Nothing."

"I've got a gun," I said at last.

"You do?" my son asked, thrilled.

"Yes. I do."

"Can I see it?"

Then someone else entered the conversation. Someone in the other room, shouting from the open front door, and all three of us turned to the empty hallway. A throaty laugh, a miracle, a strangled imitation of old memory, the third time I had first heard her voice: "Hey Sammy, I'm home, you're not going to believe what I saw . . ."

She stepped into the room. Black stars, black stars. So many years, so many miles. I began to breathe eccentrically and could focus only on the threaded brown of her irises, how they bled a little into the white. Was it really you? Mid-fifties, eyebrows plucked to commas, hair in an unlikely bun. Wide, oh, still lovely face, and yes, of course it was you. My little paper girl, crumpled in a pocket for half a century, unfolded now before me in the kitchen. Those eyes, starkly wide with hope and shock. They were not looking at me.

"Hi, Alice," Hughie said, smile across his plain, old face.

Her hand went to her heart. We are each the love of someone's life.

We stayed for dinner and, in the low conversation of old people that followed, it was decided that we would stay the night.

"Hotel? Absolutely not," Alice said, shaking her head and frowning.

"Well but it's ridiculous, Alice. We can't stay here."

"You're an old friend."

"The neighbors . . ."

Alice laughed. "I don't give a damn what the neighbors think!" And then, of all miracles, she turned to me. "Don't listen to your father. My house is yours, little Hughie." A touch on my head, a kind glance down into my eyes; no remembrance, none.

I was bunked in Sammy's room and we were told to look at comics while the adults sat out on the porch to watch the sun fall from the trees. We did not look at comics, of course; we looked at Sammy's meager collection of dirty pictures. He was so proud, and I was properly astounded, and then he laid out before me, in the tenderest tableau you can imagine, all the treasured objects of his life: two dozen ordinary stamps in a book, a perfectly round stone, a tin sarcophagus of King Tut, a mechanical bank in which a clown catapulted a coin into a lion's mouth (demonstrated with my own penny), three rose-colored scallop shells, a baseball, a glove, and a photograph of Clara Bow cut from a magazine. We sat and rearranged and stared at these wonders for about ten minutes. Then my son asked if I wanted to play with his Erector set and the treasures were left, abandoned, while he filled the bed with clanking metal.

I claimed I'd never seen an Erector set, and he gave a frog-faced expression of amazement. I recognized his face and gasped: it was Alice's, as a girl. What a strange little haunting in this strange little room. I wondered, if I waited long enough, might I see a fleeting gesture of my own? But I heard faint voices from the open window. I went over and listened through a veil of climbing ivy. Two voices, quiet ones, floating up from the garden below:

"A four-in-hand coach," said the man.

The woman: "A bit. Two bits."

"Gaslight."

"Of course." She laughed. "And bustles."

"Woodward's Gardens."

It was my old friend and my old love, sitting in the twilight. They were playing a sad game. They were naming what was gone forever. I was overcome by my luck, that I could sneak into my son's life and see his treasures, and the face that wanted so much for me to approve; the luck to be a boy with him! But I also mourned the fact that I couldn't be down below, with the old people, pawing through the attic of the past. Hughie in a velvet suit, Alice in a princess hat, old man Max in a mirror. And all of us as we used to be.

"Do you miss it, Alice?"

I could not hear the rest. I leaned out the window.

Sammy was tugging at my sleeve: "All right, I'm gonna make a boat, see, and you've got to make a boat and we'll race them on the bed, which is the river, see."

I did see. There below me, couched in the yellow blossoms of a forsythia fooled by this warm weather, two old people sat on an iron bench, looking just as I would have looked had time gone right for me.

⁓

When Hughie came into his room, I was waiting.

"How is she?"

Sammy had long since gone to bed and I, too old for early bed-times, had waited until I heard the sighs of his dreams before I slipped out. I had first listened to the murmur of the adults, but unable to make anything out, I had come here to the sewing room, where Hughie was to sleep. Fabric for new curtains lay on the table, and a finished apron.

My friend smiled and took off his coat. We did not turn on the lamp; the moon was in the window. He said, "Hi, Max. I thought you'd be asleep with Sammy."

"He fell asleep hours ago."

"How was it, seeing him?" We were whispering.

I clasped my hands in my pajama-lap as Hughie began to dis-robe. I said, "Strange. Amazing. I don't know. I'll have to get used to it. He has an idea that he's going to be the greatest something in the world, he doesn't know what yet, but he'll be the greatest. He's not what I thought a little boy would be like. Not like I used to be."

"You were never a little boy, Max."

"I'm trying. Tell me about Alice. Is she the same?"

"I don't know. I knew her when she was, was it, was she sixteen?"

"Fourteen."

"God, that was a long time ago."

"Is she the same?"

"I remember her as being, I don't know, talking all the time about what was in her head, asking me questions and then, well, she wouldn't really wait for the answer. She'd be off talking about something else. She's a bit like that. But a little dreamy, stares off at the sky and her mind is traveling, who knows where."

"Yes. She's just the same." So I hadn't destroyed her, after all. "Did you talk about me?"

"I didn't tell her . . ."

"I mean about me as her husband. Or me as her old landlord. What did she say?"

"I talked about you as my son. I said you're a rascal. Self-centered and clever, you are, you know, smarter than any of the other kids. I said you never really fit in, that you like to spend your time with me. We play stupid word games in the kitchen and drink watered-down coffee. I told her about our trip and how you liked to pick the bed closest to the bathroom, in case robbers came in and you had to escape. And that you hate beef jerky. I said I tried to teach you to drive and you broke off the side mirror."

"I told Sammy about that. I said you whipped me good."

"I should have. I said girls in school had crushes on you. That you loved books. I said she would love you."

"Thank you."

Grin. "Well."

Hughie faced away from me as he slipped off his drawers. Nude, old man's body of shivering skin. How many years since he had known his brand of passion? He stepped into cotton pajamas, stumbling. The house was quiet, absolutely quiet, and the sky through the window was bright around the moon and starless. I thought it was time.

I told him what he already knew. That he would have to leave me soon.

Without turning, he said, "I told her you didn't like beets, and she said neither did Sammy."

"Hughie."

"I don't want to talk about it now. I'm so tired."

I said I had been thinking about it, and he should go in the morning.

"Let's not do this now."

"Before they wake up. I already put some money in your bag. It's wrapped up in a sock, don't lose it."

"Not tomorrow, Max. I can't."

"We talked about all this."

"I can't do it."

"You promised me."

He explained how there was a better way. That we could both leave. Right now; we could take our things and get into the Chrysler—it was just across the street, sleeping—and silently start it up, and silently leave this awful place. "We could do what we said, we could find a little town and live there. That's the best thing. Doesn't that sound like the best thing?"

I said he had forgotten one thing. That I was dying.

Staring at me, hands on his hips, pajama top unbuttoned so it showed the wisps of gray in the center of his chest. "Don't be dramatic. You've got almost twelve years."

But I didn't, and he knew it. Those twelve years would not be withering and going gray and falling asleep one night, in that town he imagined, letting my heart stop in the first hour of my seventieth birthday, in 1941. Perhaps he might die that way. But I was under a different curse: my last years would be a nightmare of the body. Shrinking, gaining baby fat, losing my mind and memories, my speech, until I could only crawl across the floor, staring at this father with eyes that begged him to kill me. We both knew I'd have to end it long before all that.

"Oh God, Max," he said, shaking his head. "Listen, listen what happens a year from now? When you're two inches shorter? And what about me?"

"They won't notice."

"That your clothes are shrinking?"

"It won't come to that."

"It's stupid. It's selfish is what it is. It's what you've always been, Max, it's selfish. Think about it, just think about it for a second. Haven't you done enough to her? You have to trick her again? And your son? And do this to me?"

"This isn't about you, Hughie."

"Oh, I—"

"Let me stay here. My wife and son are here."

"You can't be a husband! You can't be a father!"

"Hush. I'll be a son. For a little while."

Or something like that. I don't remember the actual words of that conversation, but I remember how it sounded, his final face, and what the light was like, how the room smelled of dust and oil, so I have colored it in from these, as one restores a damaged work of art.

I said, "You can find that little town and live there. I gave you enough money for a long time."

"I don't want your money."

"It's a lot. You could buy a house and a lot of land. With a dog and a woman who comes in at five each night to cook your dinner." I drew a picture he knew well, of a farm with a long drive through cypress trees, a barn, his goddamned chickens, all of it. I said that, if he wanted, he could get another Teddy. No one cares what rich men do. He could love someone.

He was silent for a moment, and turned to face me.

"Someone," he said, and the way he looked at me made me afraid.

There are things we can say only once, and the words I could see forming on his lips he had already said. Years before, decades before in the parlor of his house where I lay, stupefied by hashish, on the sofa as a fire crackled in the hearth. He had looked at me this way, and faced the fire, and muttered something that the snap of flames had covered. I could pretend I hadn't heard it; pretend we were just the way I wanted, and the fire was too loud, or the throb of blood in my ears; I could imagine he was drunk, and I could forget. But over thirty years had passed, and there were his blue eyes, and he had not forgotten. I saw the words arranging themselves, but there are things that we can say only once. He began to button his top. From the way his hands were shaking, I knew that life had gone terribly wrong for both of us.

"Hughie, hand me the whiskey."

"You're too young."

"I'm not likely to get another drink. Hand it over."

"I won't go, Max," he said, though he looked so tired of arguing.

"You will, I know you will."

"I'm stubborn. You remember, don't you? When we were little? You were, God, you were about a foot taller than me and still I'd wrestle you to the ground. I didn't care. I was half your size and I'd beat you."

"This isn't like that."

"Was there anything as good as that? Those lessons together in the mornings? And my dad would unfold a map upside down and start pointing at it like it was a new continent in the world? And later, you'd lift me up and throw me into the grass. Remember, Max?"

"There was never anything as good."

We talked for another hour or so about old things. The smell of chalk as we erased it from the slate, and frogs we hid in the pantry to frighten Maggie and John Chinaman, and the terror of sneaking into my father's parlor and holding each of the wonderful forbidden objects on his whatnot (and how we chipped the monkey's head in glass and blamed it on the chimney sweep). Jokes that would make no sense to anyone but us. Old childhood secrets. A sled ride in snow among the gravestones. By then, the moon had set and I could hear from his soft voice how drowsy he had become. I said that maybe it was time for bed.

He whispered, "No, no . . ."

"It's time to go."

"Sleep here tonight."

"All right, but I'll leave before morning."

"One last thing."

"It's time to go, Hughie."

His voice intensified, one last time, the last energy he had left for this: "Tell me. You won't come with me? Right now? Or wait a few days, we'll leave then. Or I'll go and you can take a bus. Be with your family, then take a bus, or have them drive you to meet your dad. Tell me you'll do it. Come live with me on the farm. It would make me so happy. You'll come, you will, you'll grow old there. You'll . . . you'll become a little boy, a baby, you're afraid of that, but I'm not afraid. I'll be there. I'll take care of you until you die. I will. Oh Max, come with me."

There were sheep on his pajamas. "No, Hughie."

"No," he repeated, and what he heard was *Never*.

"Goodbye," I said.

Quietly: "I won't say goodbye. I won't leave."

"You'll know what to do. When you wake up, you'll decide."

"Sleep here tonight," he said, not looking at me.

"Oh, Hughie."

"Sleep here." I did. I held him in my little-boy arms for a while until his leg gave one jerk and I heard his breathing slow to a dead tide. His face was knotted as if he were concentrating on his dreams, making them better than life, and his mouth lay open. He began to snore softly. That is how I think of him—and I think of him all the time—mouth open not like a child but like an old man, dreaming of the past. I kissed him and crawled out of the sheets, made my way back to my son's room, and fell asleep in that small bed. I was so tired.

❧

I should write that it is my birthday today, and we have had a picnic. I write now barefoot in the grass. It spreads out for acres, the grass, a dozen shades of green among the gravestones, not very carefully trimmed so that here and there are little meadows with tiny birds chattering and fighting in them, and buzzing bees, and clustered green seeds waving in the wind. It's quite beautiful. The September air is cool despite the bright sun, and many of the trees down by the river have jumped the gun and are already falling to yellow. There are very few people here today; just a couple of old widows replacing dead flowers, and two young women doing rubbings from the facets of an obelisk. And Alice, of course, down at the other end. I can see her red scarf floating in the breeze. Somewhere behind her is Sammy.

There is a blanket spread out on the grass, and scraps from our lunch of egg salad sandwiches, tomato soup, a few peach pits, and an orange cake stuck with thirteen melted candles. The ants are already at work. There is also the wrapping paper from my presents, crumpled balls of sky blue. Sammy was very happy with my Erector set, which Alice said "could fit with the other one," but bored by the collection of books—Irving and Blackmore and Joel Chandler Harris—from another century, and quite out of fashion. "I used to love those when I was a girl," Alice told me. I remember, darling. You sent Sammy off to find a grave from the Civil War, and we were left alone.

"I have another present," you told me. You wore a long dress embroidered in red and a little white cloche, and your camera lay like a pet beside you.

"You do?"

You handed it to me. An ordinary envelope. Inside, a card from the government regarding my change of name. No longer just little Hughie. No longer just the son of your old friend who left me in your care. I was now Hughie Harper. You and the doctor have adopted me, in expectation of your own marriage, in expectation of a final form to life.

"You're part of the family, Hughie," you said, laughing at your little prank.

"That's right," I said.

It is not precisely what I'd hoped for, but it is enough. Now, Sammy, you will get your inheritance, your grandfather's fortune, with no legal troubles at all. And as for my new mother: it is as close as I will ever get, dear Alice, to crawling into your womb to die.

"Chin up," you said, and raised the camera. I smiled; ecstatic flash of light. So there will be a photograph of the creature for the doctors to delight in; perhaps a frontispiece to a study. She lay her camera down again.

"Are you happy?" Alice asked me.

How can anyone answer this, at any moment?

She's left now to join Sammy out among the graves. And here I am, avoiding the next part as long as I can. Ants crawl across the page. You know how it goes, don't you? When you sit at midnight, and ask something terrible of someone? You know what happens in the morning.

When I awoke that first morning, the morning after I'd left Hughie's room, the world was bright and cold. I could hear a radio downstairs, and someone singing along, and I saw that the other bed was empty and that I'd thrown my own bedclothes on the floor. I was all alone. The goldfish swam in their Precambrian tank. Through some extrasensory perception, Buster had figured out I was awake and came leaping into the room, ears flying, to lick my face before I could ward him off. He jumped onto the bed and took hold of a stuffed animal by the neck—a tiger—giving a good fight before dropping it, licking me again, and darting back downstairs. More voices. I should join them. But I waited a moment. This would never come again. The sun through the shades in an early morning blue; it would never come again. Whatever had happened, whatever Hughie decided to do, it was done—and nothing would be the same after this morning. And that sun. I had seen it years before, on another morning, when I awoke to find my world utterly changed, once before, covered in a film of snow. The same silence in my heart. The same light in the air, bright as luck.

Out in the hall, I passed the sewing room, but the door was closed.

I could smell waffles from the stairs, and I stopped again. Waffles, and something else frying; it smelled astounding. The radio was playing "The Best Things in Life Are Free" and I could hear Sammy mock-crooning to it, padding around the slick floor in his little slippers, probably singing to the microphone of a whisk. Buster's nails made tap-dance noises; I imagined he was following Sammy, probably begging for scraps. And Alice in her bathrobe, stirring the eggs—for it must be eggs. The green bathrobe, the one she bought a month before she left me. Her hair in a kerchief. The dreamy eyes of someone who has had just one sip of coffee.

"Hey there, late sleeper!" she said when I came in. Old smile, old Alice. Just the two of them.

"What's for breakfast?" I said.

"Duckbrains," my son told me, then whispered something in Buster's ear.

Just the two of them.

My old wife tapped Sammy with a spoon. Yellow robe, ponytail; no matter. "Eggs and waffles and toast. Duckbrains are extra." She turned to me. "Where's your daddy, little Hughie?"

"I don't know. Still sleeping, I guess."

"Not in his room," she said. "He took his car."

"Maybe he went out for more duckbrains," Sammy offered.

She crouched down and squinted at our son: "Maybe he did! Duckbrains!"

"Ha!" said Sammy.

As I sat down and Alice poured me some orange juice, I tried to remember every detail of the moment. The ribbon sewn into the curtains, and the tea-stain of light across the bottom. The smell of waffles and burned toast; the sound of Alice scraping the black bits into the garbage. Her plain face, and how, in the part of her hair, where I had first kissed her back in another century, gray roots showed beneath the dye. How the radio was slightly off its station, and some news report could be heard like a ghost under the new song it was playing.

Alice's brown eyes brightened. "*Toot, Toot, Tootsie, goodbye!*" she sang, tapping her feet, turning up the radio, then she hit Sammy with the spatula and he joined in. "*Toot, Toot, Tootsie, don't cry!*"

It was going to be this way as long as I wanted. Hughie had made it happen. I was going to be here with my wife and son, singing to the radio, half a year, perhaps, before I was too far gone. Was there any luck like mine, anytime in history? And what if the best happened; what if my curse somehow came undone, reversed itself, and instead of slowly dying, melting into a child's body, I would begin—today, this morning, in this kitchen—to grow forward? There are stranger miracles. Every few weeks, Sammy and I would stand against that kitchen door for measurement, and there it would be: an inch, two inches. Older and bigger like all the other boys, regaining the hands and fingers I used to have—and the handwriting as well, dear Reader—and the eyes, the laugh, all of it. A new chance, a new life. Then there would come a day when I was visiting old Mom—me and Sammy, back for Christmas—a day fifteen years in the future when I would be in my twenties and handsome again, and she would look at me, quite old herself and feeble, and wonder if it was age, or just the prickings of memory, that reminded her of an old husband, old Asgar, as young as he looked the evening she left him.

"*Toot, Toot, Tootsie, goodbye!*"

Where would Hughie be about now? Oh, somewhere past Eppers, fiddling with the dials of the radio to get *Amos 'n' Andy* to come in clear. I guessed he'd stop at some service station and have all the fluids replaced, the fabric cleaned, remove all trace of the time spent on the road with a beastly betrayer, and a messy one. A new chance, a new life. Lean against a water tank and pull out the map—where to now, pal? Could a man live out his years in Missoula, Montana, in a small house near the center of town, and buy his groceries at the Saturday market where he could eye the men lifting cargo onto the railroad cars? Or a city life, in New York, with an apartment high above the park and a doorman who appreciated it when you asked about his kids? Or even, in the last decades of this life, back to San Francisco? Back across a ferry into the fog. A house out on the edge of a cliff, with a view of the Golden Gate, the sounds of foghorns lulling an old man to sleep at night. A country to pick from. A new love, somewhere, hidden. And years to find it.

"I'm so happy you and your dad came," Alice said. "I haven't been so happy in—"

"Let's not wait for him, though," I said. "He's probably on one of his morning walks."

"I'm starving!" Sammy revealed.

"You sure?" she asked.

"Let's eat."

I was home. Finally, home. And the sad, the hopelessly sweet and sad part of it was that, in knowing this, I would always be alone.

It was three hours before the policeman came to the door. By then, Sammy and I had finished the dishes and Alice had us already involved in her project of pulling out all her books to dust the bookshelves. They were spread out on the floor around us, an ocean of pages, adored by my old wife through all the dull, happy, and awful moments of her private life—for books are selfish things, unshareable, and every tome I dusted made me think of time she had not spent with me. I recognized so many of them. Then the doorbell rang and Alice had to step gingerly over her Dickens to answer it. Sammy's weary sighs. A policeman's voice, a wail from my old wife. Yes, yes, at last. I had used up the luck of the world.

A fisherman found the car in Indian Lake, five miles from town, and it was pure chance that he was there that morning and had noticed the fender gleaming in the muddy water. All doors were locked and the money was still in the sock, soggy but intact, and I applaud this county's police department, and its dredging crew, for their small-town honesty. The car had not sunk immediately; apparently, as heavy as it appeared, the Chrysler had drowned as far as its windows and then begun to float. At that point, according to the coroner's report, the driver had taken an old army gun out of the glove compartment (left open) and shot himself once through the mouth. It was probably ten minutes before the rest of the car began to sink, and then, with all that metal and the weight of the unusual radio, it would have gone down quickly. Maybe three minutes, maybe less. Of course, the driver was already dead. No shot had been heard, but then it was early morning and roosters were crowing, and anyway, no one lives near Indian Lake since the factory closed in '24.

You know, Alice, what happened, and Sammy, you remember. The policeman who explained all this in the parlor and how I fell into the sea of books and drowned and your mother stood crumpled against the wall, howling. Something has happened to your father, little boy. To whom? To your father, Hughie Dempsey. You remember how I wept the whole night in the bunk below yours, and Buster whined to hear me; how it must have confused you. To hear a boy whispering those curses, and damning your beloved God, and standing in the stark moonlight like a man escaped from a madhouse.

~

On such occasions, in a small town, there is a newspaper article, a sermon in church, and a funeral. We had all these things. The article was just about what I've just written, with a fisherman interview, a police comment ("We're stunned"), and a little report about me, the son abandoned in the swamp of this death. There was a tone of fright and anger to the article. How dare he do this, to the boy, and here, in this golden town! We cannot understand. We are not like this. The sermon was similar. The funeral was widely attended, swelling with music and curious people, though no one but Alice had ever met the man.

I can't quite remember any of it. I know I developed a twitch in one eye that took a week to go away. I think I ate all the time, and wept at night, and would not change my clothes. Even in my stunned state, even with my goblin's blood starving every bit of me that was human, I tried to do good; I found Hughie's wife out in Nevada and called her. This was in the funeral home, when they had left me alone for a little while with the casket (oak and bronze, lid kindly closed, old friend). I found a phone in a corner of the office, among some musty-smelling silk orchids. "Abigail?" I whispered when a woman answered.

"Yes?"

"This is Max Tivoli. You remember me, a friend of Hughie's. I have some bad news. Hughie's dead."

"Who are you, young man?"

"Abigail, it's Max. Hughie's dead."

The operator came on to tell me that the call was finished. I tried again, but this time nobody answered. I looked at the phone and wondered why I had bothered. I suppose it was her right to take him, but I hadn't wanted her to. Or for Teddy to take him, for that matter. I was glad to keep him forever with me now. I went back into the parlor, where they were all waiting for me, a bouquet of eyes staring at me because, of course, they assumed I was a broken little boy.

Alice made us stay in the house. This was all the Levy that was left in her: to sit shivah for the dead. She never went to synagogue (there was no synagogue, of course), observed no holidays, ate bacon and shrimp when it pleased her, turned on the radio on Saturdays to hear *The Goldbergs*, and as far as I knew did not believe in God, but when it came to death, she was a Jew. A little Levy girl. She had to be. Death makes children of us all; I learned this in the war.

And it did not even make sense, if you thought about it: who was she to Hughie? Not family, of course. Not anyone. They hadn't seen each other properly in forty years; they had exchanged just one letter, one glance in the park. But the town treated her like a widow, and came by with casseroles and stews and roast meats. I was reminded all at once of Mother and me, in Nob Hill, fighting off the ladies in veils. They asked me about my father, and I always said, "He was a good man, and he loved me," and they left in a hurry from the spectacle of Jews in mourning. We wore black; we covered the windows; we rent the fabric over our hearts. We kept kosher. We separated the silver as her mother used to, nearly half a century ago. It was absolute madness, but it was all that Alice had.

I'd never seen her cry before. Not in my whole life. When you squeezed her tender heart, she usually oozed anger, but Alice cried over her Hughie, yes she did. Sitting there in her black silk, staring at the wall, she let the tears trickle as her eyes smoldered in some private fire. Late at night, I heard her moaning. And I could not sleep. After all, I was the one who had given her life this final grief, after all the others.

It took her a long time to ask me. By then, none of my family had been found and I was part of the house, deep in a life I have described to you in these pages. I'd refused to live in the sewing room—"my dad's old room," I called it—and was already semi-permanently bunked with Sammy; I was already enrolled in Mrs. Stevens's class, already Sammy's "duckbrain." It was the night I've described to you: two insomniacs staring at the sky. My Alice in her nightgown, soft and shapeless and old in the night, inviting me downstairs for milk. We sat at the table, with Buster at our feet. She poured little moon-white glasses. Then, in a voice broken by grief, she asked me at last:

"*Why did he do it to us?*"

Old Alice, old irretrievable Alice. But somewhere inside that body: a wife, a woman, a girl, all of them, nesting in there like a Russian doll.

She said, "I'm sorry. I'm sorry I asked that."

"No, it's okay."

"My God, though, I can't sleep. I know you can't either. I hear you walking around at night. Tonight. It's because we can't ever know, isn't it?"

"I suppose not."

"He brought you to me. I'm happy about that. I guess he wanted you to be loved somewhere."

"I guess."

"But it's too much a burden for you. I get so angry with him sometimes!"

"No, please, don't be angry with him."

"I'm sorry. I'm not really. I loved him so much, you see."

"I know why he did it."

Your eyes, those old Darjeeling eyes. I saw them once in wasp-stung pain, and once on a street in San Francisco, full of horror and death. I don't know if I ever saw them in love. I could tell you, darling. I could sit here while the milk makes white shadows in its glass, while darkness mutters behind the window, and wait for a tear to show itself in the creased canthus of your eye. You would weep then, my love. Why did he do it? As simple as this: Because I told him to. Because he loved someone his whole life—he loved me my whole life—and all he wanted was to be near me, and I sent him away. I told him never to come back. And he never did, not ever. Why did he do it? Because he thought no one loved him.

And here you are, the reason for it. The prize I get for murder. You, Alice, and Sammy, for a little while, at least. But no more Hughie now, forever. I cannot live with it, but I have to. We each have an awful bargain in our lives.

"Yes?" you said.

I couldn't tell you the truth. It was too late. So I told you something like the truth, something kind, and what you longed to hear, anyway: "I think it was old love."

You sniffed and looked down into your milk. You heard what you hoped for. You could sleep now, I think.

"Can I kiss you?" I said.

I had done nothing to hide my voice. Your face sharpened; your mouth tensed. Did you know? It didn't matter anymore.

"Mom? Alice?"

"Yes, Hughie?"

"Can I kiss you?"

A pause, eyes searching me in the blank light. "Well, okay."

Forgive me if I held on longer than a good son should. Think of lifelong loves, and a boyish fear of the dark. Think of sad goodbyes.

The very next day, I stole a pen from my teacher. I stole a pile of notebooks. And on that April day, in a sandbox, sniffling, I began to write out all that you have read.

༄

Sometimes I think of the wasp. The one that stung my Alice. Blond and banded like a tiger's eye, living out its life in a hanging hive in South Park. Dead now, of course; squashed forty years ago. But I like to think that, while it lived, it watched sweet Alice through the parlor window. Day after day, it buzzed and murmured in its chamber, observing my girl as she read her bad novels, or did her hair, or sang aloud to the pier glass. It made no honey; it built no comb; it had no earthly purpose except to annoy, and should have been killed months ago, had the landlords been attentive. A worthless bug, but it loved her. It lived to watch her. And in its last days—for life is short for wasps—it closed up its home, stepped out from its lantern porch, dipped twice into the air, and fell at last into her life. It died, of course. A smear of brownish blood. It is a brave and stupid thing, a beautiful thing, to waste one's life for love.

So I have confessed it all. Nothing has been said wrong, but as I try to read it over, I realize that nothing is quite right, either. I have left out a mole on Alice's neck. And a scene of me and my wife in our new Oldsmobile, driving in the spray out by the ocean and laughing. And Hughie out in Kentucky, ringing a farmhouse bell to buy country ham, the clang of it resounding, and him standing there, delighted, surrounded by the echo of the endless hills. But let it be. I've put down as much life as I can bear.

Which leads us, at last, to the end. Here on his grave, scribbling out a few last words. Alice and Sammy are off in the tombstones, and now it is just the grass, and me, and the ants, and the man I murdered. By all rights, he should be buried in Colma beside his family, his son, but I wanted him to be buried here, and here he is, among the suicides and heathens and the clover. I'm sure he wouldn't mind.

I know what I did. Every night I think of him—the first ordinary boy I ever saw, a son to me, a father, an old friend, the one person who loved me my whole life—every night I think of him. And when I do, the nerves are pulled from my body: a weed ripped out by its roots.

You may visit his headstone, if you wish. Far to the left, past the crowd of local Doones and an angel statue, in black granite. Hubert Alfred Dempsey. Navy lieutenant, Spanish-American War. Then his birth and death and the phrase: "A good friend here lies." It does not say that once, when he was a boy, he used to eat paper.

It's time to go. Dr. Harper's prescription pad has gotten me an encouraging supply of pills, all blues and mauves, and while it's still my birthday, and before I sink too badly into the mire of my particular curse, I think I should end things in indigo. Probably tonight, if I finish this. I plan to hide these pages in the attic, in a box that's labeled "Max." I plan to sneak out to the local creek and slip into a tin canoe. There, I'll take my dose of gin and violets. It is my birthday wish to do this.

I can see my wife and son, wandering among the graves of the Civil War dead. How my mother would have loved to lead her grandson there! Grasshoppers are jumping in the tombstone weeds, maple seeds are twittering towards the river, and, most surprising of all, in the bright sky I can see the faint dandelion of the moon. From somewhere I can hear a birdlike sound that I have decided is a group of children, somewhere in the neighborhood, playing a blindfolded game, their crazed voices brought to me only in bits and pieces, softly, on the wind. They will shout and yell like this, carried on the breeze, until they are too old for it, but by then there will be more children, glad and ignorant and wild, and so on, but among them there will never be another one like me.

Sammy is waving to me. He's shouting something I can't hear. I think he's found an old soldier. Bye, Sammy. And Alice, there you are, looking at me in the shade of your hand. Remember this always: there was no moment in my life I didn't love you.

Tomorrow, you will probably be awakened by a phone call. It will be too early in the morning to understand, and you'll grope for your glasses as if they could help you hear, but what the man will say is that they have found a body. Your newest son, lying dead in a boat among the reeds. It will just be light, and you will be frozen for a while as you dress in your haphazard clothes, pull on a sweater, and stumble out to the car. The police will give you coffee at the station, and they will talk softly. It will not make any more sense than it did in the bleary light of morning. You will be given a bag of my belongings. Then you will be shown a body under a sheet. They will remove the sheet. There I will be, as naked as on our wedding night, bloated with water, my skin bruised with blue flowers. Don't be sad. Life is short, and full of sorrows, and I loved it. Who can say why? Don't look at me too long; I will make you think of Hughie, and it will start all over again, the old grief along with this new one. Turn away from me, Alice. Look in the little bag they gave you; there should be a necklace there. 1941. You will understand then. Don't be sad.

One day, you will find these pages. I suspect you will not be cleaning out the attic; I think you'll just be searching for something from your early life to show your new husband. You will move aside the photo albums and there it will be, the box labeled "Max" in my boyish hand. You will pull out the yellow pages, stuck with sand and grass, and some rush will overcome you— sudden hatred, or tenderness, or something for the old man. I expect, someday, you will show them to Sammy and a little mystery will be blotted from his childhood: that odd boy, his brief brother, whom you buried so quickly and never spoke of again. Just as you never spoke of his father. If they fall into the hands of Dr. Harper, as I suspect they will, I'm sure he will dismiss me as a madman, claiming these are not the writings of a little boy but a forgery, certainly by your ex-husband but not by any magical be-ing. Impossible. Perhaps he will publish them in collaboration with Goldforest House, my old asylum, as a study of that delu-sion: everlasting love.

It's time to go.

Grow old and wise, my love. Raise our son to be a good Cub Scout, and a faithful lover; teach him to use his new wealth wisely, start a foundation, and do not let him go to war. Let your hair turn white, and let your hips broaden across the chair, and let your breasts fall on your chest, and let this husband, who loves you, be your last. Do not be alone. It does no good to be alone.

They may not find my body, after all. Water is unpredictable that way. I may drink my poison, kick off from the dock, and never come back to shore. I will lie back on a pillow so I can see the stars. I plan on there being stars; the sky must comply, this once. I expect it to take a full half hour for the drugs to take effect, and if I have measured out my death correctly, and don't simply vomit into the black water, the constellations will brighten and slide above me, and I won't weep, not for all the dead, or because I miss the world. If I am lucky, I will be like the Lady of Shalott in that poem. I will float down the current until it meets the river, slowly, over weeks, for I will just be sleeping, still alive, growing younger every hour, as the river takes me along its swelling cen-ter, a boy, a child, ever younger until I am at last a little baby float-ing under the stars, a shivering baby, dreaming of no particular thing—borne into the dark womb of the sea.

Max Tivoli
1930

A NOTE ON THE TEXT

This work is reprinted almost exactly as it was found in an attic in 1947. Some errors, such as spelling and punctuation, have been corrected, some illegible words (such as in the thunderstorm passage) have been deduced from context, but errors of history, geography, and medicine have been allowed to remain. Printed by permission of the Samuel Harper Foundation.

ACKNOWLEDGMENTS

I am grateful to the Bancroft Library at the University of California, Berkeley, for the memoirs, diaries, and letters I was allowed to search through, as well as to the San Francisco History Center at the San Francisco Public Library. This book would not have been possible without the generosity of the MacDowell and Yaddo colonies and their benefactors. Thanks also to Jonathan Galassi, Carla Cohen, Susan Mitchell, Spenser Lee, and Jessica Craig and to my friends and family and everyone at FSG, Picador, and Burnes & Clegg. Of course to Bill Clegg himself, to whom this is dedicated. Best thanks of all to Frances Coady, who tended Max and transfused him with her very blood. And to David Ross, who never had any doubts.